Hometown Hero

Kellersburg
Book 5

by

Merrillee Whren

Merrillee Whren
http://www.merrilleewhren.com/

Hometown Hero/ Merrillee Whren
ISBN: 978-1-944773-40-3

"The Lord is close to the brokenhearted and saves those who are crushed in spirit."
Psalm 34:18 NIV

CHAPTER ONE

"Hey, sis, guess who's coming to dinner?"

Maisey Norberg turned at the sound of her older brother's voice. "Is that supposed to be some kind of reference to an old movie?"

"No, but only my little sister, the old movie buff, would catch that reference." His short light-brown hair still wet from a shower, Wes strode up the center aisle of the church, then hopped onto the stage, where Maisy was helping with the sound equipment for the praise band. He took her gently by the arm and pulled her to the side. "Mom called me just as I was going out the door."

Maisey frowned as she pulled her hair back and captured it in a scrunchy. "Are you going to make me guess?"

Wes chuckled. "No point. You'd never guess anyway."

"Then quit messing around and tell me." Maisey placed her hands on her hips.

"Zach Dawson and his parents."

The name made Maisey's breath hitch in her throat. She stared at her brother until her heart rate slowed to normal and she could breathe again. Images of Zach with his dark-brown hair and hazel eyes paraded through her mind. She'd had a crush on him since she'd been six years old and he'd been a freshman in high school. "Not possible."

"Yeah. The Dawsons are back in the country and plan to move into their old house again while their new house is under construction. Can you believe it?"

"No." Maisey walked over to the keyboard.

"Believe it. They're going to be here at church this morning, too."

Maisey couldn't wrap her head around the information. Of all the Sundays for Zach to show up—the Sunday she had to sing and play keyboards instead of being in the back on the drums. His celebrity status and disarming smile would have her thinking about him rather than the music. She would have to pretend he wasn't there. "How did this all come about?"

"Mom said she ran into Lara Dawson at the gas station. They've been staying in a hotel until their goods arrive from overseas. Then they'll move into their old home." Wes gave Maisey a knowing look. "Of course, Mom invited them all for dinner, and we'll be expected to be there. We didn't have anything planned to eat at our house anyway."

"So is Zach just visiting for Thanksgiving week?" Maisey played a few chords on the keyboard. "What about Samantha, Zach's sister? Is she here, too?"

"Got me." Wes shrugged. "I think I heard Mom say Samantha's still in Germany. A job and a boyfriend or something."

"What's Zach doing now that he's not playing football?" Maisey walked a fine line between too much interest in Zach and not enough.

Wes shook his head. "Don't know that either. Haven't heard much about Zach since he had that terrible injury in the football game right after Christmas last year."

Maisey tried to block the vision of Zach sandwiched between two monstrous defensive linemen and how his seemingly lifeless body had lain there while medical people rushed onto the field. Even a year later, a sick feeling sat in the pit of her stomach as the images stuck in her mind like a piece of gum on her shoe.

She'd followed his football career along with her parents and most of Kellersburg. High school. College. The pros. She'd watched every game he'd ever played.

And she'd loved him that whole time.

Maisey busied herself by untangling cords and flipping through her sheet music. It wouldn't do to let on to Wes that Zach interested her. "Yeah, he just kind of fell off the radar."

But not Maisey's radar. She hated to admit she cyberstalked him. And now she would share Sunday dinner with the man she'd had a crush on forever. Did Wes even have a clue about her obsession? Hopefully not. Wes had been twelve when Zach went away to college. Slim chance her brother would know about her bad case of puppy love.

Maisey was Zach's superfan, sometimes an overexuberant one. What would he say if he knew she had saved video clips of his most memorable moments on the field or that she had a scrapbook of articles clipped from newspapers and magazines? What would Wes say?

Wes grinned. "Cool that we're having dinner with a celebrity."

"Not cool if you gush over him." She'd remind herself not to do just that.

"Yeah, I suppose, but I have no idea how to act around someone who's famous."

Maisey chuckled. "He used to babysit you. Think of that."

"I barely remember." Wes shook his head. "I just remember him playing football. Mom and Dad would take us to the high school games to watch him play, and we would sit with the Dawsons."

Maisey remembered that, too. She also remembered how her heart almost beat out of her chest when their families spent time together and when Zach smiled at her. Sometimes she'd thought she might melt into a puddle right there in front of him.

And mostly she remembered the day he had rescued her from the class bully.

That day would be forever etched on her mind, the day he'd become not only her crush, but her hero. On a spring afternoon at the end of her second-grade year, as she walked home from school, a boy in her class followed her. She'd ignored him when he called her the teacher's pet. She'd just prayed she would get home before he carried out his threat to steal her backpack.

She had walked faster and faster, hoping to outdistance him, but her short legs were no competition for the biggest kid in class. Tears stung her eyes, but she blinked them away. As she hurried down the sidewalk just a block and a half from her house, she tripped on a crack and sprawled face first on the hard concrete, scraping her hands and knees.

The mean kid snatched the backpack that lay beside her and raced away.

Pain radiated through her body as she sat up. Tears stained her cheeks, and she sniffled. She scrambled to her feet, determined to retrieve the backpack. Blood dripping down her legs, she charged after the horrible boy who was only half a block ahead of her.

She ignored the pain as she raced down the sidewalk. "Stop, stop, you meanie! Give me my backpack!"

Just as the boy reached the end of the block, someone sprinted across the street and grabbed the kid by the arm and jerked him to a stop, then grabbed the backpack. Panting and out of breath, Maisey slowed her pace as she squinted and tried to figure out who had rescued her backpack.

"Don't you ever let me catch you doing that to anyone, especially Maisey. Now get out of here." The words of the raised voice carried all the way down the block.

Maisey's heart jumped into her throat as she recognized Zach Dawson, who lived across the street and three doors down from her house. She watched him approach with her backpack slung over his shoulder. Her heart pounded in her chest, like the thundering herd of unicorns that graced her backpack.

"I believe this is yours." Zach held the pink-and-purple backpack out to her.

Maisey couldn't find her voice. She merely nodded as she took the backpack and held it close, all the time thinking that Zach had touched it. She would never get a new one.

"Whoa. Are you okay? Looks like you took quite

a tumble." He glanced down at her legs where blood still formed little red rivers.

She nodded again, still unable to speak. Why had she chosen a dress today instead of pants? Pants would've given some protection for her knees and hidden her skinny legs from Zach's eyes.

"You don't look okay. Let's get you home." Zach picked her up and cradled her in his arms, as if she weighed next to nothing. "You let me know if that kid ever bothers you again."

Maisey still hadn't found her voice, and she nodded for the third time. Was she dreaming? The pain in her knees told her no.

When Zach reached Maisey's front porch, he rang the bell with his elbow, then turned the doorknob with the hand of the arm he had under her knees. The door swung open. "Mrs. Norberg, it's Zach. Maisey's been hurt."

In seconds her mom, Annette, hurried into the living room. "Maisey, what happened?"

As Zach set Maisey on the couch and sat beside her, he explained about the bully. After he finished, her mother cleaned and bandaged the wounds. The whole time Zach didn't move from his spot, and Maisey had relished every moment. Every day for weeks she remembered how it felt to have him hold her.

A grown-up now, Maisey knew her romantic thoughts were the stuff of puppy love and crushes, but that didn't keep her from thinking about Zach. Today he would grace one of the pews in this church. Could she find her voice to sing with him sitting there? She had to, even though Zach was certainly more famous today than he was all those years ago. She wasn't a starstruck little girl anymore.

"Earth to Maisey."

Maisey looked at her brother and hoped he had no clue what she'd been thinking. "Did you say something?"

"Yeah. I asked if you're ready for your finals."

Maisey sighed, relief washing over her. Wes didn't even think twice about Zach, and neither should she. "I don't want to study too far ahead, or I'll forget everything by the time the tests roll around after Thanksgiving."

"You're smart. You'll remember."

Maisey played a chord on the keyboard as she checked the sound. "I wish I had your confidence."

"Hey, if I can graduate from college, you can, too."

Maisey laughed as she shook her head. "You know you've always been smarter than me."

"Yeah, I am." Wes laughed. "Now what do you want me to do?"

"Check to see if all the connections are good in the sound equipment. The others will be here in a minute, and we'll make a quick run through all the songs." Maisey tried without success to quit thinking about Zach.

"It all looks good to me." Wes's statement brought Maisey's thoughts to a halt.

She looked up and imagined Zach moseying down the aisle, a lopsided grin across his handsome face. Instead, Julianne and Lukas Frye, the couple who led the praise team, came into view. Julianne and her sister, Elise, were part of the Keller family, descendants of the town fathers. They were VIPs in Kellersburg, but not as VIP as Zach Dawson.

Maisey waved them onto the stage, wishing she could strike thoughts of Zach from her mind. "Wes and I have checked all the connections. We're all set."

"Great." Lukas hopped onto the stage. "Elise isn't coming this morning because the baby's sick."

"Oh no. I hope it isn't something serious." Maisey wrinkled her brow.

"No. Just a runny nose and a low-grade fever," Lukas replied.

"Will we be okay with one less female voice on the vocals?" Maisey stepped around the keyboard.

"I wasn't scheduled to sing today, so I'll take Elise's place. Seems like my sister and I are always stepping in for each other. That's what happens when you have little kids." Julianne joined her husband on the stage.

"Do you know the songs?" Maisey asked.

Julianne nodded. "I do, and thankfully, we have a chance to practice everything before the service."

"Let's get started." Lukas plugged in his guitar and strummed it.

Maisey readied her music and thought about how the church music had changed since she'd been in high school. The choir that had sung every Sunday when she was a kid now sang once a month, when they sang the old hymns. She liked the music the praise band did, but like many of the older folks in the congregation, she still liked to sing the hymns that her grandmother loved. Was she out of step with her own generation? Sometimes she thought so.

Maisey joined the others while they practiced the

morning worship songs. As the time for the service drew closer, more thoughts of Zach strummed through her mind, like the guitar chords Lukas played. She hoped Zach would sit in the back and not in the front, where she couldn't help but look at him.

Minutes later Maisey's wish was not realized. Wearing khaki pants and a cream-colored sweater underneath a brown leather jacket, Zach Dawson sauntered down the center aisle with his parents, Lara and Ken. Zach looked almost the same as he had in high school, except his dark hair was cut in a short, neat style rather than the longer unkempt style of his youth.

He stopped along the way as Melanie Keller's boys, Ryan and Andrew, raced over to get Zach's autograph. He smiled at the boys as he signed their church bulletins. That smile made Maisey's pulse pump in double time. She took a deep breath and gathered her emotions. Before Zach joined his parents in the third row, he signed more autographs and shook hands with numerous people—people who had known him while he was growing up in Kellersburg.

Maisey wondered whether her gaze would be drawn to him against her will. She surely didn't want to get caught staring at him. Maybe he was used to that type of thing—women falling all over themselves to get his attention.

She. Did. Not. Want. To be one of those women.

If rumors were to be believed, Zach was quite the ladies' man. He'd had a string of girlfriends throughout his career. According to the tabloids, the latest one had broken up with him just before his injury. Was he still nursing a broken heart almost a year later?

Maisey determined she would either look at her music and the keyboard or stare at the back of the auditorium. She wouldn't let her gaze stray to the pews closest to the platform. That was a promise.

***

Zach focused on one of the big screens on either side of the stage, where a countdown clock indicated less than five minutes until the beginning of the service. He turned to look back down the aisle in search of Phil Waller, the man who had helped save Zach from himself. Phil was a family friend of Zach's former team's owner and had taken an interest in Zach from the beginning of his career. His parents had treaded lightly in their advice, but Phil had come right out and told Zach he needed to get his life on a different track. The older man had been like a grandfather to him, giving him advice and direction.

Just as the clocked ticked down to ten seconds, Phil slipped into the pew. "Sorry for the last-minute entrance. I was talking with the guy in charge of the Christmas-tree lighting, Nathan Keller. Nice guy. He says we're all set for Friday night."

Zach nodded. Nathan, who had graduated by the time Zach had entered high school, was part of the big Keller clan. Nathan's father owned the local bank. Maybe Nathan worked there.

Zach didn't know what had changed in his hometown since he'd left. He had good memories of the place, but it hadn't been on his radar for over ten years. A few months after his high school graduation, his parents had moved to Munich, Germany, when his dad had taken a job there as the international liaison for the medical devices plant in Kellersburg. During Zach's college years, having parents on the other side of the Atlantic had served as a major challenge.

The chatter floating through the auditorium faded as musicians took the stage and played a soft tune. Zach's gaze was drawn to the young woman on the keyboard. A pretty blonde dressed in a bulky red sweater and slim black pants. He didn't need another pretty blonde in his life. The ones he'd dated had only brought him sorrow.

His mother leaned closer. "Do you recognize Maisey Norberg on keyboard?"

Zach knit his eyebrows. "Maisey?"

His mother smiled and nodded as Zach leaned back in the pew and took another look. Maisey, all grown up and prettier than he could have ever imagined. He'd always been attracted to blondes. A weakness that had led him astray too many times. But he didn't need to worry about her, no matter how pretty she was. He would be here a week and then gone.

Sitting between his dad and Phil, Zach tried to concentrate on the words of the hymn displayed on the screen, but his gaze kept finding its way to Maisey. Thankful he'd be gone soon, he quit fighting his attraction. She was nice to look at, and she had a sweet singing voice. For all he knew, she could be married or at the least have a serious boyfriend. He should quit ogling her and sing, but even with the words on the screen, he didn't know the songs.

The differences between the church services he'd

attended here in the past and this one now astonished him. But then, he'd forgotten his roots and the promises he'd made as a high schooler in this building. He'd let fame and fortune lead him away from the faith he had professed here and the God who had showered Zach with blessings, so much more than he deserved.

Zach had anticipated the guilt washing over him as he listened to the songs and read the words. Remorse for the way he'd lived during his pro career inundated him. He'd partied too hard with teammates and disregarded God's instruction about sexual relationships. Was there any redemption for him? Phil said there was. Zach almost believed it. Sometimes.

The song service ended, and the congregation settled in the pews as the band left the stage. Zach let his gaze follow Maisey until she was out of view in the front pew on the opposite side of the auditorium. A good spot for her to help him keep his mind from wandering during the sermon, but maybe he'd rather have her as a distraction. Then the words of the sermon wouldn't puncture his heart.

A middle-aged man in casual dress took the stage, Bible in hand. Zach eased back in his seat, but tension knotted his shoulders. After not attending church for years, he'd been attending with Phil at his home church in Florida in recent months while they'd worked on a project. Zach braced himself for words that would pierce his heart. Every sermon he'd heard as an adult seemed crafted just for him. They reminded him of his sin. Guilt ate at the corners of his heart. When would he shake that feeling?

The pastor prayed, then opened his Bible. "Today

we're going to study a couple of different passages from the Scriptures that talk about God's forgiveness. Let's look at Psalm one hundred and three. We'll start in verse eight and read through verse twelve.

'The Lord is compassionate and gracious,
slow to anger, abounding in love.
He will not always accuse,
nor will he harbor his anger forever;
he does not treat us as our sins deserve
or repay us according to our iniquities.
For as high as the heavens are above the earth,
so great is his love for those who fear him;
as far as the east is from the west,
so far has he removed our transgressions from us.'

"Now we'll look at Jeremiah thirty-one. In verse thirty-four, look at the last sentence. It says,

'For I will forgive their wickedness
and will remember their sins no more.'"

The pastor looked out at the congregation as he flipped through the pages of his Bible. "One more verse from First John one verse nine. 'If we confess our sins, he is faithful and just and will forgive us our sins and purify us from all unrighteousness.'"

Zach let the words roll through his mind. The concept of God's forgiveness was something Zach understood, so if God could forgive, why couldn't Zach forgive himself? The verse from 1 John rattled through Zach's brain again and again. He didn't feel as though he was purified from all unrighteousness. His sin smothered every good thought and weighed him down with guilt he couldn't shake.

Despite the good news of God's forgiveness, Zach's heart ached. Sin littered his path with regret and shame. Jesus had done the undoing. Jesus had taken the blame. Jesus had made the way for freedom from the punishment Zach deserved. The head knowledge didn't help, because the message hadn't penetrated his heart and given him peace. When would that happen? When would he quit torturing himself over his past?

The rest of the sermon was lost on Zach. His mind wandered through the past, piling on more guilt and regret. Thoughts of Jayla Shaw, a former girlfriend, filled his mind. Could he ever forget the haunted expression painting her face the last time they'd spoken? She had moved on with her life. A new boyfriend. A fancy new house. A promising movie career. Her successes mocked him from the front pages of the tabloids.

Nothing he could do could change the past. Phil kept telling Zach to look forward and not back, but the past was like a never-ending film flickering through his thoughts. His failings from the past had a vice grip on his mind. He wanted to remember the good parts, but the bad ones devoured the wholesome ones and left him feeling unworthy of anything good. He prayed the next few weeks, as he launched himself into Phil's project, would help ease his guilt.

Phil elbowed Zach in the ribs. He looked up to realize the pastor was introducing Phil and Zach. This was it. Time to put on the show he didn't feel. How long before the charade of his life would all come crashing down around him?

"Please welcome Phil Waller and Kellersburg's own, celebrated quarterback Zach Dawson." The pastor motioned them to the stage.

Zach manufactured a smile and followed Phil until they stood side by side behind the pulpit. Thankfully, Phil would do most of the talking.

Phil grasped the sides of the pulpit top and looked over at the pastor, then out at the congregation. "Thank you, Pastor Rob, for allowing us a few minutes to talk about this very special project. Possibly over the last year and a half, you've seen ads for The Twelve Dogs of Christmas project."

Pastor Rob nodded. "I love the title."

Phil chuckled. "It fits. I'll give a quick rundown about the documentary being filmed in the next few weeks, which will be shown about this time next year. We spent the early part of this year choosing our recipients for one of the twelve dogs we'll be giving away during December this year. We have picked out twelve special children who wrote an essay about why they wanted a dog. Of course, we got permission from the parents before we combed through the finalists to pick those twelve children. We're in Kellersburg to kick off the celebration by including your town's tree-lighting ceremony in the documentary, since this is Zach's hometown and he's a major player in this film. We invite everyone to take part, but you must sign a release form to be included. The ushers will have forms and more information for you as you leave today. Now I'd like for Zach to say a few words."

Zach stepped behind the pulpit, his heart pounding. He'd much rather be facing down a charging defensive lineman than talking to the congregation of his boyhood. They all thought he was an upstanding person, but he was a fraud.

"Thanks, Phil. I'm excited about this project."

That part was true. "Many of you know me from the years my family lived in Kellersburg. I've been blessed to have a football career that has given me this opportunity to give back. That's why I've joined Phil in this project. We hope you'll be part of the tree-lighting ceremony, and you might even see yourself on TV next year."

As Zach stepped away from the podium, Pastor Rob took over. "Thanks, Phil and Zach. Let's say a prayer for this project."

While Pastor Rob prayed, Zach tried not to think of himself. He'd been doing too much of that this morning. He needed to pray for the families who'd be impacted by the gift of a dog. He prayed it would be a blessing to them.

After the prayer, the pastor escorted Zach and Phil to the back, where they answered questions and passed out flyers. As the folks filed by and greeted Zach, many said how sorry they were about the injury that had ended his career. Despite the pain and lengthy recovery, Zach realized in the end that his injury was the wake-up call he'd needed to get his life back on the right track.

The kindness of the people who greeted him made him remember all the good folks in this small town. He was sorry he'd never made an attempt to visit, even though his parents no longer lived here. He should've been more grateful for the coaches who'd taught him how to play football. If only he'd followed their other lessons as well—lessons on how to lead a good life and be a good person.

As the line finally dwindled, Zach's mom approached. "Remember we're invited to the

Norbergs' for Sunday dinner."

Zach nodded. How many years had it been since he'd heard the expression Sunday dinner? The phrase conjured up visions of pot roast or fried chicken with all the trimmings. He moved closer to his mother. "I have to take Phil to his hotel, then I'll be over."

She laid a hand on his arm. "Nonsense. Phil should come, too."

"You can't just invite another guest."

"Zach, this is Annette and Bryant we're talking about. They'll welcome one more guest with open arms. You should know that."

Yeah. He should know that, but he'd forgotten. His mom and Annette had been closer than sisters when his family had lived across the street and a few doors down. His dad and Bryant had worked together at the medical devices plant.

Their families had spent hours and hours together over the years, enjoying meals, playing games, and sharing a common faith. The Norbergs had been like a second family while he'd been growing up. He'd let that relationship fall by the wayside, too.

"You should check anyway before you issue the invitation." Zach gave his mom a pointed look.

She returned his look with an indulgent smile. "Okay. Just to make you happy."

Not sure what would make him happy, he watched his mom sashay down the aisle toward Annette, who conversed with her husband and his mother, Carol, near the front. Zach's mom hugged Annette, then the two of them talked, nodded, and laughed as they looked his way and waved. He took that as a sign.

"Hey, Phil, my family's going over to our friends'

house for lunch—"

Phil waved his hand at Zach. "That's fine. I can fend for myself while you visit."

"Not necessary. They've invited you to join us, if you'd like."

"That's great. I'd love to. Meeting the locals is on my list of things to do." Phil pointed a finger at Zach. "And one person I want to meet is that young lady who played the keyboard this morning. Do you know her?"

What was that all about? Zach had a bad feeling. "Funny you should mention that. She'll be there. We're eating at the Norbergs, and she's their daughter."

Phil clapped Zach on the back. "This day is turning out better than I ever expected."

Zach wished he could say the same, but something told him whatever Phil was thinking might just be the worst thing for Zach.

CHAPTER TWO

The delightful smell of her mother's pot roast filled the air as Maisey pulled the cobbler apron over her head. She grabbed several plates from the china cabinet and set them on the dining room table. Her pulse pounded at the thought of Zach occupying a place here.

She had rushed over to her parents' house right after church to help out. Her mother had insisted that there was no rush, but Maisey had wanted to get away. She needed time to adjust her thoughts and figure out how to deal with Zach's presence. She'd thought her heart would beat right out of her chest when he'd looked her way during the song service. After that she'd avoided glancing in his direction.

She would muddle through somehow. She couldn't act like some starry-eyed groupie. Would he notice if she did? She finished setting the table and prayed he would sit at the opposite end from her. She looked over her handiwork with a sigh. Everything was in place—a table set for a king. Well, not a king, but a star football player.

As Maisey returned to the kitchen, her parents came through the door from the garage. "Hey, I got the table all set."

"Thanks, dear. How many place settings?"

"Eight. You, Dad, Grams. Me and Wes. Lara,

Ken, and Zach. Eight."

"You'll need to add another place setting. We have one more coming. Mr. Waller, Zach's friend." Annette motioned toward the dining room.

"Are you sure we can cram one more person in? I could always eat in the kitchen."

"Nonsense. We've managed to seat a dozen people around that table. We can certainly do nine."

"Okay, if you say so." Maisey hurried into the dining room and stared at her perfectly appointed table. Adding one more place setting would make things crowded on one side. For sure she would somehow manage to sit at one end on the crowded side, with Zach at the other end.

Maisey squeezed in another place setting. Now to make sure her planned seating arrangement took place. Too bad her mother would laugh if Maisy suggested place cards. There was nothing formal about the Norberg house, so place cards were out of the question.

The doorbell rang, and Maisey's heart jumped into her throat. She put on her game face. *Deep breath. Calm. No sweat. Yeah, right.*

"Maisey, would you get that?"

"Sure." Maisey took another deep breath and headed toward the front door, just as Wes blew in from the kitchen. "Hey, Wes, will you get the door while I help Mom?"

Wes frowned. "I thought I just heard Mom tell you to get the door."

"I can if you want to help in the kitchen."

Wes chuckled. "The door's easier. I'll get it."

"Thanks." Maisey waved as she rushed off. "Hey,

Mom, what can I do to help?"

"I thought you were answering the door."

"Wes is doing that."

"Good." Annette pushed a strand of blond hair behind her ear. "You can stir the mashed potatoes in the slow cooker. Then get the salad out of the fridge and put the dressing on it."

As Maisey stirred the potatoes, conversation and laughter floated into the kitchen from the front hall. The sound of Zach's voice made her heart beat faster. She closed her eyes and took a deep breath. She was getting worked up over nothing. Zach had no idea that she'd had a crush on him since she'd been six years old.

She grabbed the salad and the dressing from the refrigerator and poured on the dressing and mixed it with the greens. Her efforts to not think about him proved futile. Every time he said something, her heart raced. It had a mind of its own. She would be a bundle of nerves by the time they sat at the table.

For fifteen years she'd been building Zach up in her mind, and he surely couldn't live up to the hype she'd created. The real Zach and the crush Zach probably didn't resemble each other in the least. The crush Zach lived in her imagination. He'd dated starlets, singers, models, and tall, good-looking female athletes. He had his pick of beautiful women and would have no interest in the little girl who had lived down the street when he was in high school, even if she was all grown up. She couldn't compete, and she tried to convince herself she didn't want to.

Grown women didn't have crushes. At least that was what she kept telling herself.

"Everything's ready." Annette set the platter of meat on the warming tray as she took off her apron. "Thanks for the help. Let's greet our guests. Sounds like your dad and brother have them entertained."

"Sure." Maisey removed her own apron and loosened her hair from the scrunchy that had held it off her shoulders. This was it, dreams clashing with reality.

Maisey followed her mother toward the living room and stood in the doorway as she summoned a calm she didn't feel. Her mother greeted everyone with a cheery smile.

Phil Waller, an older man with thinning gray hair and sparkling blue eyes, greeted her mom and shook her hand, then looked Maisey's way. "This is the young lady I want to talk to."

He smiled. His tweed suit reminded her of her grandfather who had passed away the year before.

"Me?" Maisey placed a hand over her heart. Now everyone was probably looking at her, especially Zach. She didn't dare look in his direction.

Phil smiled again and waved a hand her way. "You, young lady, have a wonderful singing voice. It made my day to listen to you sing."

Maisey returned his smile. "Thanks."

Annette put an arm around Maisey's shoulders. "She's our songbird. She's been singing since she was a little girl."

"Not only are you a wonderful singer, but I was telling Zach how much you remind me of my granddaughter." Phil motioned toward Zach. "Her smile could light up a room just like yours, but sadly we lost her in a car accident, along with my late wife, a couple of years ago."

"Thank you, Mr. Waller, and I'm so sorry to hear about your wife and granddaughter." Maisey looked Zach's way for a split second. She'd been worried for nothing. Zach talked with Wes and wasn't paying any attention to Phil and her.

Reality.

"Thank you. No need to be formal with me. Call me Phil."

"I'll try to remember to do that. Have you met my grams, Carol Norberg?"

"No, I haven't."

"Then I'll introduce you." Maisey signaled to her grandmother.

Just as Maisey finished introducing Phil and her grandmother, her dad ushered everyone into the dining room. She tried her best to hide in the corner away from the side of the room where Zach stood, still talking with her brother. Her dad picked up a fork and tapped a glass on the table. Conversation stopped, and everyone looked at him.

"Thanks for joining us. It's a joy to visit with old friends." Bryant held out his hands. "Let's join hands and give thanks. After the prayer, you can grab a plate from the table, and Annette will point you toward the food."

After the prayer ended, Maisey snatched a plate from the end of the table closest to the kitchen. Wes and Zach were at the other end and took plates from there. That was a good sign that she wouldn't be anywhere near Zach when they sat down.

Annette insisted their company go first into the kitchen, where the food was set up buffet-style.

Maisey dawdled until she was at the end of the line. She would be the last to sit, and she hoped she would be far, far away from Zach.

That wish came true. She rounded the corner into the dining room and spotted the one empty seat from which she had taken her plate. Phil occupied the next chair, and Zach sat at the other end next to Maisey's grandmother. Her crush was safe from discovery.

Phil patted the back of her chair. "This is working out perfectly, young lady. You get to sit next to me so we can have a good talk."

Maisey smiled. "I'd like that. I want to learn more about your dog show."

Phil's eyes twinkled. If the man had a beard and a pot belly, he'd make a good Santa, with those eyes. "I'm glad to hear you say that. Do you like dogs?"

"I haven't been around dogs much." Maisey slipped onto her chair and set her plate on the table. "My brother, Wes, has been allergic to dogs since he was a little kid, so we never had one."

"That's too bad. Dogs make good companions."

Maisey sighed. "No pets for us unless it was a gold fish. Wes is allergic to cats, too."

"That's double bad. What about you? You could have pets. Maybe you'd like to have a dog, too."

Maisey shook her head. "Can't. I share a house with Wes. And I think he'd nix the whole dog thing."

"And what is your occupation?"

"I'm a CNA, and I'm taking classes to get my nursing degree."

"Excellent." Phil took a forkful of mashed potatoes smothered in gravy and chewed slowly, then looked over at Annette, who sat at the end of the table next to Maisey. "And the food is excellent as well.

"Thank you." Annette smiled. "We're really proud of Maisey. She's working full time and taking classes as well."

"You are a busy young woman." Phil returned his attention to her. "I've found that busy people find ways to get more done."

Maisey shrugged. "I'm not sure that applies to me. I don't see how I can get any busier."

Phil took a bite of the roast beef, then looked at Maisey, his gaze intense. "You should find out."

"My days are full."

"After we finish eating, I'd like to talk to you about that."

Maisey puzzled over his request, and Phil conversed with Grams. Maisey wanted to ask what he meant, but since he didn't go on, she didn't want to be nosy. Maybe he was just making conversation. Worrying about it wouldn't help. His request probably meant nothing. She should eat and not think about it. The only problem now was hearing Zach's voice from the other end of the table. It sent a little zing through her heart.

Maisey, you're a mess. The thought rolled through her mind. Zach would be here for a short time, then gone. The silly schoolgirl crush made no sense at her age. She would get over it as soon as he left town. At least, she hoped.

"Hey, Maisey," Wes called from the other end of the table.

Maisey looked up from her plate. "Yeah?"

"Who was that kid who always bullied you when you were in grade school?"

Careful to avoid eye contact with Zach, Maisey looked over at Wes. "Why?"

"Zach and I were talking about that time he rescued you from that kid when he stole your backpack. Whatever happened to him?"

Maisey's heart caught in her throat. Zach remembered that incident that had been all too clear in her mind this morning. A real surprise. "I don't know what happened to Dennis Porter. I think his family moved when I was in middle school. Anyway, he never bothered me again after Zach warned him away."

Zach chuckled as he leaned forward and looked down the table toward Maisey. "I'm glad he never bothered you again."

Maisey just nodded, unable to find her voice. Zach must think she was ungrateful. She couldn't explain why she was tying herself in knots over a man who remembered her as a kid with skinned knees.

"I remember that." Annette waved a finger in the air. "Zach, you were a hero that day."

Zach shook his head. "Not a hero. Just protecting my young neighbor from a mean kid."

"Well, you were my hero for rescuing my little girl." Annette nodded.

"I'd rescue Maisey any day. She's worth rescuing." Zach smiled Maisey's way.

"Thanks." Maisey hated the way her voice squeaked. Why did Wes have to bring up that incident? Should she be flattered that Zach remembered it? *Quit fooling yourself.*

"Any time I can rescue you, Maisey, you let me know." Zach's hazel eyes radiated sincerity.

Maisey tried not to let those words ignite the flames of her crush. Maybe she should follow the advice she'd given Wes this morning. *Remember he used to babysit you.* "Thanks for the offer, but all the bullies in my life are gone."

"That's good to hear, but if they ever come back, let me know."

"Sure." Maisey laughed, because she was pretty certain that was a joke. His life was filled with beautiful women, and as soon as he left Kellersburg, he wouldn't remember her at all.

Annette clanged her knife against her water glass, and everyone looked her way. "I have dessert." She looked at the end of the table. "I made it just for Zach. I remembered how much he loved my chocolate cake."

Zach's grin filled his face. "My favorite. I've never had chocolate cake as good as yours."

Annette blushed. "It's coming right up. Everyone can go into the living room, and Maisey and I will serve the cake there."

Zach stood. "Let's help Annette clear the table."

Zach's request surprised Maisey. Maybe he wasn't so far removed from his roots as she'd thought. He'd always been polite and helpful. His suggestion didn't help with her campaign to squelch the feelings that could only lead to heartache, but she found too much to like about him. She would so love for him to see her as a grown woman rather than the little girl he'd rescued from the neighborhood bully, but she had to face reality. Zach Dawson had his pick of beautiful women and would have little interest in plain Maisey Norberg.

As everyone helped clear the table and put plates, glasses, and flatware into the dishwasher, Maisey managed to stay in one room while he was in the other. After her dad escorted everyone into the living room, she let out a long sigh. She'd made it. Free from Zach for the moment.

Maisey set the dessert plates on the counter next to the cake.

"I'm here to help."

She whirled at the sound of Zach's voice. "Not necessary. We've got it."

"Yes, necessary. I want to make sure I get a huge piece of that cake." Zach laughed as he wielded the cake server he'd snatched out from under her hand.

"Okay." She eyed him. "We'll serve the others, and you can take the big piece that's left."

Zach laughed as he cut into the cake with a swift motion and placed the pieces on the plates. He held out two of the plates to her, then a couple to her mother. "Here you go."

Annette smiled. "Thanks. You cut cake as well as you throw a football."

Zach returned her smile, but his eyes conveyed sadness. "Unfortunately, my football days are over, but you can call on me any time to cut one of your chocolate cakes."

Maisey scurried into the living room to deliver them. She couldn't get over the look in Zach's eyes. Was he mourning the loss of his football career? What a silly question. Of course he was.

After Maisey finished delivering the cake, she found a spot on the piano bench a good distance from Zach, who sat on a chair near the entry to the living room. Phil occupied the chair nearest the piano, and his blue eyes filled with that twinkle, as if he knew something she didn't.

"Zach was right. Your mother's cake is scrumptious." Phil took another bite.

Maisey nodded. "I've always taken it for granted. I didn't know it was anything special."

Phil waved a finger at her. "Believe me. It's special."

"Maybe I took it for granted because I've always preferred carrot cake, and my mom's carrot cake is definitely special."

"Maybe your mom should open her own bakery."

Maisey laughed as she wrinkled her nose. "My mom prefers to bake for family and friends, not strangers."

"I can see her point." Phil took another bite of cake.

Maisey ventured a glance in Zach's direction. He was busy talking to her mom. What were they talking about? Her mom didn't know a thing about football, even though she'd gone to the local high school games for years. Maybe they were talking about her cake.

"Would you do me a favor?"

Phil's question interrupted Maisey's woolgathering. "What?"

"You have a beautiful voice, and I'd like you to sing a song for us."

Maisey grimaced. "Nobody wants to listen to me sing. They're all engaged in conversation."

"I want to hear you sing."

Maisey wondered what this request was all about.

"What would I sing?"

"I have the perfect song." Phil grinned as he brought a folded paper out of his jacket pocket. "Do you have the music for 'The Twelve Days of Christmas'?"

"Probably, but why do you want me to sing that?"

Phil offered her the paper he had unfolded. "Take a look at this. It's a song I'd like to use in the documentary."

Maisey took the paper and studied it, then looked back at Phil with a frown knitting her brow. "These words to the tune of 'The Twelve Days of Christmas'?"

"Yes, I'd like to hear you sing that."

Maisey nodded. "I'll do it if I have the music."

Phil sat forward in his chair, anticipation written on his face. "Wonderful."

Maisey rummaged through the piano bench and hoped she wouldn't find the music. She didn't want to perform in front of Zach. Her whole obsession with the man was ridiculous, but she couldn't help herself. She didn't know why her schoolgirl crush still lingered, but there it was at the forefront of her thoughts and swirling through her heart.

Her pulse pumped in double time as her gaze fell on *The Giant Book of Christmas Sheet Music*. The song was surely in this. She flipped to the table of contents. As she suspected, the book contained the song.

Maisey handed the book to Phil. "Here you go."

He laughed as he handed it back to her. "You're the one who's going to need this. Not me."

"I can't just say I'm going to sing this song.

Besides, the words aren't with the music."

"I'll remedy that and then make an announcement. Leave it to me." Phil pulled a pen from his jacket pocket as he took the book. His neat handwriting soon filled the correct spots on the music.

How could this possibly go well without a bit of practice? Maisey returned to her spot on the piano bench and looked over the words.

On the first day of Christmas my true love gave to me, a little doggie on a settee.

On the second day of Christmas my true love gave to me, two pounds of Master's.

On the third day of Christmas my true love gave to me, three doggie sweaters.

On the fourth day of Christmas my true love gave to me, four bowls of kibble.

On the fifth day of Christmas my true love gave to me, five rawhide bones.

On the sixth day of Christmas my true love gave to me, six toys a squeaking.

On the seventh day of Christmas my true love gave to me, seven leashes straining.

On the eighth day of Christmas my true love gave to me, eight balls a bouncing

On the ninth day of Christmas my true love gave to me, nine sticks for throwing.

On the tenth day of Christmas my true love gave to me, ten combs for grooming.

On the eleventh day of Christmas my true love gave to me, eleven clippers snipping.

On the twelfth day of Christmas my true love gave to me, twelve collars jingling.

Phil stood and clanged his fork against his plate.

"Hey, everyone, I'd like your attention."

The room grew quiet. Maisey held her breath as she looked at Phil, who glanced around the room. She really didn't want to do this. Her stomach churned. This wasn't like singing with the praise band with guitars, drums, and an electronic keyboard that covered any flaws in her voice. The prospect of just the piano and her made her palms sweat.

Phil motioned toward Maisey. "I've asked Maisey if she would favor us with a song. It's one I want to use in our documentary to give a plug for Master's Dog Food, and I thought it would be fun for you to hear it."

A murmur floated through the room, and Maisey made a point not to look at anyone. She swung around on the bench until she was facing the piano, where she placed the Christmas music book. She smoothed the center of the book to keep the pages open, then lifted the piano lid. Her mind whirled as she stared at the black and white keys. Her fingers touched the cool ivory, and she prayed her voice wouldn't come out in a squeak.

She played an intro to calm her nerves. She would pretend she was singing this for the boys and girls who would be blessed with dogs this Christmas season. She would pretend Zach wasn't in the room. She would pretend that her long-ago crush wasn't alive and well.

***

Zach had tried without success to keep his attraction to Maisey from occupying his thoughts.

After all, she was the little girl he used to babysit—but she wasn't a little girl anymore. He wished he wasn't so aware of that fact. He was also cognizant of the way Maisey appeared to be avoiding him. Maybe she saw him for what he was—a man who had let worldly pleasures lead him away from his faith.

While Zach worked to get his head on straight where Maisey was concerned, he puzzled over the conversation between her and Phil. She looked distressed, and Phil appeared happy. What was he up to? He'd indicated that he wanted to get to know her. Maybe that was what the conversation entailed, but then why did she look so troubled?

As Phil made his announcement, warning signs flashed in Zach's mind. Was Phil trying to recruit Maisey to sing in the documentary? Surely not. She wasn't a professional singer. Although the sudden departure of Zach's female counterpart in the documentary might have Phil reaching for a substitute. No, not realistic. How could he use an untested young woman for that job? But then Phil had taken a chance on Zach.

Maisey's fingers moved across the keyboard as the familiar notes of "The Twelve Days of Christmas" sounded through the room. Then her sweet voice filled the air as she went through every verse. By the end everyone in the room joined in the song.

"On the twelfth day of Christmas my true love gave to me, twelve collars jingling, eleven clippers snipping, ten combs for grooming, nine sticks for throwing, eight balls a bouncing, seven leashes straining, six toys a squeaking, five rawhide bones, four bowls of kibble, three doggie sweaters, two pounds of Master's, and a little doggie on a settee."

As the last note faded, applause and laughter filled the room, and Phil tapped her on the shoulder. "Excellent job. Take a bow."

Maisey jumped up from the piano bench and bowed at the waist. Just as quickly, she returned to the bench. Zach didn't miss her reluctance to look in his direction. She must have a really low opinion of him. Did he want to change that or just let it go? He had once been her hero. Was it insanity to want that again? *Completely*.

"That was so fun!" Annette clapped again. "I can just imagine Maisey singing that song with a cute little dog sitting on the piano bench next to her."

"I'm glad to hear you say that." Phil looked intently at Maisey. "Would you like to sing that song in my documentary?"

Maisey's eyes grew wide as she placed a hand over her heart. "Me? Wouldn't a professional be better?"

"This is a documentary. I want it to be as true to life as possible." Phil nodded. "I'd like you to think about it. Your mother has invited me for Thanksgiving dinner, and that will give you a few days to make your decision."

Astonishment brimmed from Maisey's blue eyes. "I don't know what to say. I need more information before I can even think about making a decision."

"If you give me your email address, I'll send you information." Phil readied his pen.

A knot formed in Zach's stomach. If she took advantage of Phil's offer, that would mean Zach would be working with her. A chance for him to change her opinion of him, but a chance that he would be even more captivated by her sweet charm.

As soon as Phil finished writing, he stood. "Thanks, Annette, for the delicious food, and I'm looking forward to Thanksgiving dinner. I appreciate the invitation. But now I need to get back to the hotel and take care of some business." Phil looked over at Zach. "Zach, would you give me a ride?"

"Sure." Zach sought Annette with his eyes. "Thanks for remembering how much I love your chocolate cake. Like Phil said, everything was delicious."

Annette stepped closer. "Thanks, and you're welcome. It is so good to see you and your parents again. This is such a treat."

"For us, too. This visit brings back good memories of all the times our families spent together." Zach smiled, knowing that was true, even as Maisey had his heart beating a little faster.

Lara joined the group near the door. "Zach, we'll see you later at the hotel. Dad and I are going to help Annette and Bryant clean up, and that'll give us more time to visit."

"Okay. See you later."

"Lara, you don't have to help us clean up, but we're happy to visit longer. We have a lot to catch up on." Annette followed Zach and Phil to the front door. "Zach, would you like to take the leftover cake with you?"

"You know the way to a man's heart." Zach chuckled. "I'd love to do that, if you don't want the rest?"

Annette patted her trim stomach and laughed.

"Chocolate cake won't help me keep my girlish figure. So you can definitely have it. I'll grab it for you."

As Annette hurried to the kitchen, Phil smirked. "I hope you're planning to share."

"I might be persuaded." Zach wondered whether he could use the cake as leverage when he talked to Phil about Maisey. Or maybe he shouldn't bring up her at all. She still hadn't agreed to anything, and he had guessed from her body language that she wasn't excited about Phil's invitation to join the documentary.

Annette returned and held out a plastic container to Zach. "Here you go. Enjoy."

"Thanks. If I wasn't driving, I'd probably eat this on the way to the hotel." Zach laughed again. "See you on Thursday."

"Bring your appetite." Annette waved as Zach stepped out the front door.

As Zach trekked to the car, he couldn't get thoughts of Maisey out of his mind. She was everything he wasn't. Kind, genuine, sweet, generous, and good. Maybe she would rub off on him—the only positive thing about the possibility of working with her.

When they reached the car, Zach held out the plastic container to Phil. "You can hold the cake while I drive if you promise not to eat it."

Phil laughed. "I can't make any promises, but I will hold the cake."

Zach slid behind the steering wheel. "I've got my eye on you."

"You're driving. You need to keep your eyes on

the road."

"Technicalities." Zach started the engine. He enjoyed Phil's company. The man was smart and generous and kind. Just like Maisey. Maybe that was why Phil had made her the offer.

"Well, what do you think about Maisey joining the documentary crew?"

"You like to get right to the point." Zach maneuvered the rental car out of the subdivision and onto the main road.

"You know I do. Do I sense some reluctance on your part?"

"Yes. She's completely untested."

"That's what I like. She's a breath of fresh air. No pretenses." Phil waved a finger in the air. "She's perfect for this project."

"How can you say that when you've just met her? You don't know her."

"But you do."

Zach shook his head. "I knew her when she was a little girl. This is the first time I've seen her since she's grown up. I honestly don't know much about her."

"Then you should get to know her, too."

Zach figured arguing with Phil about Maisey would go nowhere. "And just what do you want me to know about her?"

"I want you to convince her to join this project."

"So you think she'll turn you down?" Zach had sensed her reluctance.

"I don't know, but I can see her with kids and puppies, and on top of that, she can sing."

Zach could see Maisey with kids and puppies, too,

but he wasn't going to say so. "So what if she says no?"

"She won't turn me down, because you're going to get her to say yes."

Zach wished he could do this project without a female cohost. He'd been relieved when Darby Coleman had pulled out because of her mother's poor health. He didn't have anything against Darby, but she'd let him know from the very beginning of their working relationship that she was interested in more.

Still raw from his breakup with Jayla, he didn't want anything to do with another woman. Phil had said much the same thing. Zach didn't need another romantic relationship to complicate his life.

"No response?" Phil said.

"You know I was ready to do this solo."

"And so was I, until I saw Maisey walk onto the stage. I was struck by how much she reminded me of Paige—"

"You can't bring back your granddaughter by hiring her look-alike."

"I'm not trying to do that."

As Zach drove into the hotel parking lot, he glanced at Phil. "Seems that way to me."

"No. Maisey's beautiful voice prompted me to seek her out." Phil eyed Zach as he parked the car and turned off the engine. "I'm going to pray about this, and you should, too."

"I will." Zach wondered whether he should pray that it didn't happen. He should pray that God's will be done, but he wasn't sure God would be listening.

"Good. I'll send Maisey the contract, and we'll leave the rest in God's hands."

Zach looked at Phil over the top of the car as he got out and closed the door. "Does that mean I don't have to convince her to accept?"

"I didn't say that. You still need to use your powers of persuasion with her."

"Isn't that not leaving it in God's hands?" Zach pulled his keycard out of his pocket as they entered the elevator.

Phil chuckled as he shook his head. "We do all we can to persuade her, then leave it in God's hands.

"If you say so." Zach recognized the futility of discussing this with Phil. "I'll see you in the morning for that breakfast meeting with Nathan Keller."

"Good night." Phil entered his room with a wave.

Zach tossed the keycard onto the nearby desk, then plopped onto the bed with his hands behind his head. From the time he'd been a kid, his athletic abilities had been apparent, and people had showered him with praise and accolades. He'd gotten used to the limelight and had let himself believe his ability to throw a ball would gain him everything he'd ever wanted. He had believed a lie.

Now Zach had a chance to make up for his mistakes, but he wasn't sure that was possible. What did God want out of this situation? Phil had told Zach over and over again that God would use him to do good, no matter what he'd done in the past. Then Phil cited all the less-than-stellar people God had used throughout the Bible. Could God do that with Zach?

CHAPTER THREE

Early the next morning, before getting out of bed, Maisey opened her email on her tablet. Phil Waller's name stood out in the list. She took a deep breath as she stared at it. Afraid to open it, she read through the other emails, half of them ads from places where she had previously made online purchases. She answered an email from her friend Caroline Keller, who was getting married in a couple weeks in Florida.

Maisey's heart filled with joy that Caroline and Wyatt had found love. Maisey could hardly contain her excitement about being Caroline's bridesmaid. But thoughts of Wyatt, a rodeo cowboy whose career had come to an end because of an injury, brought to mind Zach and the email she had yet to open. She tapped on the tablet's screen.

Dear Maisey,

It was a pleasure to meet you yesterday and hear you sing. I'm praying and hope you will accept my offer to join our project. You will find a copy of the contract attached to this email. Take your time and read it over. You may want to consult a lawyer to make sure everything is agreeable to you. If you have any questions, please feel free to call me.

The signature line at the end of the email gave her all the pertinent information. Master's Dog Food.

She'd seen commercials for that brand. Now she had met the company owner. Did she want to work for this man? There was one way to find out. Open the attachment.

Maisey perused the document on the screen. There was a lot of legalese, but one thing was clear. If she accepted this job, she would be under contract for most of December. That just wouldn't work. She had tests to take, a wedding to attend, and a job. She would just have to tell Mr. Waller she couldn't do it.

"Hey, Maisey, I've got breakfast ready." Wes's voice floated from the kitchen.

"Coming." Maisey closed out her email and set the tablet on the bedside stand.

As she approached the kitchen, she couldn't mistake the smell of bacon. Whenever it was her brother's turn to make breakfast, she could count on having bacon.

"Pancakes and bacon are warming in the toaster oven. I've already eaten. Got to run." Wes shrugged into his jacket and grabbed his to-go cup of coffee. "See you later."

"Nice talking to you." Maisey waved. "Thanks for breakfast."

While Maisey ate, she wished she'd been able to talk to Wes about the offer. She needed advice. The compensation gave her second thoughts about saying no to the offer. The pay was amazing, more than she'd ever thought about making in a year, much less a month. Could she pass that up? But she had obligations. She definitely would have to discuss this with her parents and have them recommend a lawyer.

Maisey glanced at the clock. She'd done enough

woolgathering. Work called her.

After Maisey arrived at work, she was sure her mind would be occupied with that contract, but the busy morning gave her little time to think about it. That was probably a good thing.

As Maisey delivered the noontime meals to the residents who ate in their rooms, she remembered how cranky Wyatt Bayer had been while he was doing rehab here after his terrible accident. She'd recruited Caroline Keller to deliver his meal, and that was the launch of their romance, although it had gotten off to a rocky start.

Thoughts of Wyatt and Caroline brought Zach to mind and then Phil's offer. She had avoided thinking about it all morning, but now it was front and center. She had one last meal to deliver, then maybe she could somehow put her thoughts on a different track.

After Maisey delivered the last meal, she stepped into the hallway and discovered one of the other CNAs as she hurried down the hall. "Maisey, you have a visitor."

Maisey wrinkled her brow. "A visitor? Where?"

"At the front desk. A very handsome man." The CNA grinned. "You'd better go see him."

"Okay. I'm headed on my break." Maisey didn't want to speculate, but she couldn't help thinking that her visitor was Zach. Is that what she really wished for? He would turn her day upside down.

Maisey rounded the corner and slowed. Zach stood at the counter, talking with the receptionist. He had on the same leather jacket he'd worn to church, but today it was accompanied with blue jeans instead of khaki pants. The chambray shirt and cowboy boots made him look like he'd just stepped out of a commercial for something western. She didn't know what. Certainly not dog food, and that was what this whole documentary was about.

Was Zach here to do Phil's bidding? Maisey suspected as much as she tried to calm her racing heart. "Hi, Zach. I hear you'd like to speak to me."

Zach turned to her with a smile. "I sure do. Can I take you to lunch?"

"I usually eat lunch here or brown bag it. I don't have time to go someplace for lunch." Maisey's heart hammered.

He stepped closer and gazed at her with those hazel eyes, as if he could read her thoughts. "Then I guess we'll have nursing home cuisine. Unless you've brought your brown bag."

"Lunch in the cafeteria."

"How's the food?"

Maisey shrugged. "It's a nursing home. Don't expect much."

Zach chuckled. "I've been warned."

"You have." Maisey gestured down the hallway. "This way to the cafeteria, unless you've changed your mind."

"Never invite a lady to lunch and then rescind the offer. Please lead the way."

Maisey tried to gather her wits as she strode down the hall, her soft-soled shoes barely making a sound on the tile floor, while the heels of his boots clicked against the tile. He obviously had no idea that the lady he'd invited to lunch had a serious crush on him. This was just another business meeting to him.

"So grab a tray and go through the line. The fried

chicken isn't bad."

"Is that what you're having?"

Maisey nodded. "It's definitely better than the pork chops. They're usually dry. Overcooked, in my opinion."

"Then I'll follow your advice."

After they went through the line, Maisey led the way to a table in a far corner by the windows. In the courtyard outside, a few scattered leaves still lay on the grass that had lost most of its green color. The tree limbs rattled in the breeze against a gray sky that suggested snow could be coming.

Maisey slipped into the seat nearest the window as she set her tray on the table. When she looked up, Zach was conversing with an older white-haired gentleman. Maisey wasn't sure of the man's name. Did Zach know the man? She waited for Zach to join her and worried about how she would respond to whatever he said.

"Hey, sorry to keep you waiting." Zach slid his tray onto the table. "That was the father of my high school football coach. He used to have the team over to his house to celebrate our victories."

"What's his name? I think he must be new. I haven't seen him before."

"His name's Richard Becker. My high school coach was Richard Becker Jr., but he went by Rich. Of course, we called him Coach." Zach smiled wryly. "And yes, he's a new resident here for rehab after he broke his leg. I know about that rehab stuff. It's not fun."

"For sure. Lots of people do rehab here." Maisey thought of Wyatt and wondered whether Zach had the same thoughts about the loss of his career as Wyatt had had. Wyatt had been mad at the world and the injury that had stolen his career.

"I'll have to visit him while I'm here. He told me his son moved away several years ago to take a coaching job at a small college in Indiana, so he's here alone."

"Thanks for the information. I like to learn about the residents, and I'll be sure to stop by his room when I get a chance." Maisey considered telling Zach she had prayed for his recovery, but thought better of it. Instead she glanced down at her plate, then at Zach. "Do you mind if I say a prayer of thanks for the food?"

Zach gestured toward her. "Go right ahead."

Maisey bowed her head and said a short prayer, then looked up. She could hardly believe she was sitting here with Zach Dawson, the man of her dreams. Did she ask him what he wanted or let him take the lead? He should start the conversation. The less she said the better. She took a bite of her chicken and chewed slowly. Still he didn't say anything, just glanced around the place.

"So how long have you worked here?"

"About three and a half years." He probably wondered why she hadn't gone to college right out of high school like Wes. Zach probably didn't know about her dad's bad health and how the medical bills had eaten up her college fund.

"I heard your mom say you're studying for your nursing degree."

"Yeah." Should she mention the anonymous donor who had given her money to get her degree? Zach probably didn't care.

"You'll make a good nurse. You care about people."

"Thanks." Heat crept up Maisey's cheeks. "We'd better eat, or our food will get cold."

Zach took a bite of the mashed potatoes, and Maisey lifted the chicken to her mouth. They fell into silence for several minutes. She wished he'd get to the reason for his visit.

Zach set his fork on the edge of his plate. "You might have guessed that Phil sent me here to talk to you about the project."

Maisey's insides curdled. "Yeah, I suspected."

He raised his eyebrows. "Can I change your mind and get you to say yes?"

So this was it. Maisey took a deep breath. "The pay is very tempting, but I have finals to take the first week in December, and I'm in a wedding in Florida in three weeks. I can't blow off either of those things. And besides that, I do have a job here."

"We're not asking you to do that."

Maisey shook her head. "From what I see, I'll be obligated to this project from December first through Christmas Eve." Maisey frowned.

"I'm pretty sure Phil can work around your obligations. Even your job here."

"Why does he want me to do this? I'm not a professional singer or actress. Isn't that what he needs?" Maisey knit her eyebrows.

"We had one of those, and she didn't work out." Zach took a big forkful of the chocolate cake he'd taken for dessert. "Not as good as your mom's."

"I agree." Maisey fiddled with the napkin in her

lap. "How can Phil possibly do anything to work around my responsibilities? Do you think I have what it takes to do this job?"

Zach stopped his fork midair and stared at her, as if weighing his response. "To be honest, I have doubts."

"Then why are you here trying to convince me to do this?"

"Because this is what Phil wants, and I owe him a lot."

"So you don't think I can do the job?" Maisey's heart sank. At least he was honest and didn't try to sugarcoat his answer.

"I didn't say that. I only said I have doubts. You might be the perfect answer. After all, our *professional* didn't work out." Zach made air quotes.

"You still haven't told me why Phil thinks I can do the job."

"You are a talented singer, and you remind Phil of his granddaughter."

Maisey shrugged. "But how does that figure into this job."

Zach shook his head. "It doesn't, as I pointed out to Phil."

"I don't want to do this because I look like his granddaughter."

"That's not why he chose you. He honestly thinks you have talent."

But you don't? Maisey kept the question to herself. No sense in putting Zach on the spot again. "But that brings us right back to the conflicts that'll keep me from fulfilling the contract."

Zach nodded. "Phil can work those things out."

"What makes you so sure?"

"He's an influential man, and he likes to adopt people and help them."

Maisey glanced at her watch as she stood. "I've got to get back to work."

"Okay." Zach stood. "I can take care of your dishes and tray."

"Thanks."

Zach gathered everything from the table. "What should I tell Phil?"

"Tell him I have to talk to my parents and pray about this." Maisey shoved her chair under the table.

"Okay. I would expect that." Zach deposited the things from the table in the appropriate places as Maisey walked beside him. "Thanks for talking with me."

"You're welcome. I guess I'll see you on Thanksgiving."

"Yeah. Then you can give Phil your answer."

Maisey tried to smile. "I don't think my answer will change."

"Maybe your answer will change if Phil works around your conflicts. Maybe that should be included in your prayer." Zach quirked an eyebrow.

Maisey took a deep breath and nodded as they stopped near the front door. "You may be right. Thanks."

"Anytime. See you later." Zach flashed a smile.

Maisey gave a little wave as he gave her one last glance before he went outside. Her heart finally slowed its beat as she walked back to the nurses' station. Nearly a month working side by side with Zach. Could she handle that? Was she using all those conflicts to keep herself from a possible heartbreak? A talk with her parents and her heavenly Father was in order.

***

The next morning thoughts of Maisey filled Zach's mind. Such thoughts were not good. He couldn't get entangled with her, especially if she agreed to do the project. He still had so many regrets about his last relationship. He wasn't ready for a rebound romance. Besides, Maisey was a sweet young woman who deserved someone better than a guy like him, whose life had been filled with decadence. But Phil was determined to get Maisey on board with the project. Zach had given Phil a blow-by-blow account of his meeting with Maisey yesterday. He didn't seem the least bit discouraged with the outcome.

Zach's errand today was finding out where she was taking her nursing courses so Phil could arrange for her to take her finals early. Zach had no doubt the man would be successful in that endeavor. Would that convince Maisey to take the deal?

The wind made a chilly day even chillier as Zach hunched deeper into his coat to ward off the cold. He opened the door to the nursing home and stepped into the warmth. The smell of the noon meal wafted his way.

Zach found his way to the cafeteria and stood in the doorway as he searched for Maisey. His gaze fell on her blond hair as the sunlight from the nearby window made it glow like spun gold. His heart took a leap. He took a deep breath and shook away the feeling. He sensed doom for his foolish heart. What was there in his genetic makeup that attracted him to blondes? He should have learned his lesson by now.

As Zach approached, he recognized Maisey's tablemate, Richard Becker. Maisey laughed at something the older man said, and Richard laughed in return. Zach hoped his presence wouldn't be an intrusion.

"Hey, Maisey."

She turned. A look of surprise and something else he couldn't define filled her eyes. "Hi, Zach. Here for more great food?"

Zach chuckled. "Actually I've already eaten."

"So you didn't want to sample any more nursing home cuisine?" A smile tilted Maisey's mouth.

Zach's mind took him down a path he shouldn't enter. What would it be like to kiss those lips? He banished that question from his mind. "Already had lunch with Mom and Dad at the hotel. I'm just here to get information for Phil. Mind if I join you?"

Maisey motioned toward the empty chair. "Go right ahead."

Zach nodded. "Hi, Richard. Good seeing you again. How's the rehab going?"

Richard placed his fork on his plate. "The physical therapist knows her stuff, but some days I think she's trying to kill me instead of help me."

Zach laughed. "You'll thank her in the end."

"That's what Rich says when I complain to him. They're coming for Thanksgiving, so maybe you'll have a chance to talk."

"That's super." Zach took a pen from his pocket. "Do you mind if I write my number on your napkin?"

"I've got my cell phone right here" Richard produced his phone from the pocket of his blue loose-fitting pants. "You can type it in."

"Even better. I wasn't sure you'd have your phone with you." Zach took the phone and input the number in seconds. "Please have Coach give me a call."

"He'd love to talk with you." Richard nodded as he stood. "I'll let you young people visit while I go back to my room for a little nap. That physical therapy session zapped all my energy."

"You don't have to rush off," Maisey said.

"Thanks, young lady, for visiting with me today. I appreciate it, but I'm tired, so I'll be on my way." Richard turned his attention to Zach. "I'll make sure Rich calls you."

"Thanks. I'll be waiting to hear from him."

As Richard moseyed away, Zach wished he'd kept contact with his former coach. Zach wished a lot of things these days, but he had to remind himself he couldn't go back and redo his life. He had to move forward and make the best of his future. He had to turn things over to God, which he'd failed to do in the past. Zach had to do that with his attraction to Maisey as well.

Besides the horrific breakup with Jayla that warned him away from another relationship, he didn't deserve a woman as sweet as Maisey in his life. He'd only wind up ruining her life like he'd done with so many other women. This time he would shove the attraction to a pretty blonde into a small corner of his mind, slam the door, and lock it. With God's help, Zach would overcome the temptation Maisey presented if they had to work together to fulfill Phil's wish.

Zach glanced at the young woman who was the center of his thoughts. "Now for the reason I'm here. I'm on another errand for Phil. He wants to know where you're taking your classes so he can arrange for you to take your tests early."

"But I haven't studied for them." Her brow wrinkled in the cutest way.

He wanted to reach over and soothe away her concern. He had to purge such thoughts. This project might turn into a project on his self-control. "If it comes to that, I'll help you study."

"You will?" She narrowed her gaze, her blue eyes still filled with an emotion he couldn't read.

"Sure. I'm all for pleasing Phil. After all, that's why I'm here."

"Okay. Yeah, I get it. You'll do whatever you have to in order to make Phil happy, but that doesn't necessarily make *me* happy." She nailed him with those blue eyes.

"What would make you happy?" The question rolled off his tongue as he realized what he had just committed himself to—more time with Maisey.

"I don't know." Misery creased her brow again as she sighed.

Zach's heart skipped a beat. "What can I do to help?"

She shook her head. "You can't help. The decision is mine, and it's so hard to make up my mind."

You can't help. That statement pretty much summed up the last few years of his life. He hadn't helped himself. He hadn't helped those around him. He hadn't helped make anything better in this world.

Could he make up for that now, or would he make one more person miserable?

"Do you mind if I ask what you've done so far to make a decision?"

"Sure." Her expression told him she didn't think much of her decision process. "I talked to my parents, and they said I had to decide for myself. So that didn't help much."

"What else?"

"My dad put me in touch with a lawyer, and she went over the contract with me. She said it's very fair."

"That should help."

"Not really. It just makes me want to do the project when I know I can't."

"Maisey, if you commit to this, Phil will make sure you can live up to all your obligations. That's why he wants to know who to contact so you can take your tests, and I'll help you study." There it was again. A promise he wasn't sure would be wise to keep.

"Ginny Keller, Nathan's mom. She's the dean of students at the local college. I take one in-person class and the rest online."

"Hey, thanks. I'll pass this info along to Phil, and he'll let you know what he finds out." Zach stood. "Now I'll let you get back to work. These folks need to see your smiling face."

Maisey picked up her tray as she stood. "I'll try to remember to smile. Worry doesn't help anyone."

"I'll remember that as well." Zach joined her as she put her tray away.

"Will I see you again tomorrow with more

cajoling?"

"Would you like to see me?" Zach laughed as he let that question slip out of his mouth. Seemed as though Maisey's presence had him saying all kinds of things he shouldn't.

"That all depends on why you want to see me."

He'd walked right into that one. "You would make my life a lot easier if you'd just decide to do the project for Phil."

"This is all about making life easier for you and harder for me." She wrinkled her nose. "Do you think that's fair?"

Another pointed question. "I suppose it isn't, but as my mother always used to say, 'Life isn't fair.'"

Maisey let out a halfhearted laugh. "Yeah, my mom always said that, too. My dad also. Parents love that line."

"Then I guess we have something in common."

"That's probably the only thing."

Maisey's statement shocked Zach. Why did she think they had nothing in common? They'd grown up on the same street, gone to the same local schools, and attended the same church. Should he dispute her claim? Safer to let her statement stand.

"Unless you give me a call, I'm afraid you won't see me tomorrow. Phil and I have business to attend to the next two days. We have to make sure everything is set for the events surrounding the tree lighting." Zach raised his eyebrows. "You'll be there, right?"

Maisey produced what Zach considered a fake smile. "I'm always there unless I have to work."

"Do you have to work?"

"Two days until Thanksgiving." Maisey held up

two fingers. "I don't have to work on Thanksgiving this year, but I do work the following day."

"So that means you won't be there?"

"I'll be there. Thankfully, I'm on the day shift this quarter. I get off at four, and the tree lighting isn't until seven."

"Good. Then I'll see you there."

"And for Thanksgiving dinner."

"Yeah. I can already taste your mom's pumpkin pie loaded with whipped cream."

Maisey chuckled. "I had no idea you were so fond of my mom's baking."

Zach gave her a wry smile. "You probably don't remember *my* mom's cooking. Let's say it can't compare with your mom's."

Maisey raised her eyebrows. "Are you saying your mom isn't a very good cook?"

"I never said those exact words." Zach put a finger to his lips. "Remember that."

A smile crept across Maisey's mouth. "Your secret is safe with me."

"Thanks." Zach wondered whether all his secrets could be safe with her. What would she say if she knew the secret parts of his life? "I'll be on my way. See you on Thanksgiving."

With a wave, Zach hurried from the building, almost as if he was running from those secrets. More troublesome than any of his secrets was the prospect of working with Maisey. Why should he be worried? After all, he used to babysit her. He kept telling himself that, but she wasn't a little girl anymore. She was a grown woman. A beautiful woman. A blonde. Just the kind he always fell for. He wouldn't let a physical attraction cloud his judgment. He promised himself this time would be different.

CHAPTER FOUR

Maisey hugged herself against the cold breeze that rustled the lights in the trees. The rain from yesterday was gone, but the threat of snow still lingered. She looked up at the cloudy sky. The moon shone behind the clouds, giving the sky an iridescent glow. She wouldn't mind if it snowed. The flakes would give an even more festive mood to the tree-lighting gathering.

Sparkling white lights festooned the gazebo in the center of the Kellersburg town square. The trees throughout the square also sported lights. Near the gazebo, the town Christmas tree stood dark, ready for someone to pull the switch and light it up for the town to see. Lights on the stores surrounding the square added to the fairyland feel.

With a pulse-racing excitement, Maisey contemplated meeting Zach tonight. They were actually coworkers now. She had signed her contract to work on the documentary yesterday after the Thanksgiving meal. The whole thing still seemed like a dream. She would spend the next four weeks with Zach Dawson. Even in her wildest dreams she had never imagined such a scenario.

Maisey looked around at the folks who had already staked out their spots to watch the festivities. Wrapped in blankets, they sat on their camp chairs.

The film crew had their cameras set up in several spots around the square. Phil directed people as he pointed here and there. People jumped at his command. He was definitely the boss.

Maisey had met a lot of the crew and the director, who actually took his directions from Phil with a smile. She gathered that they had a good working relationship. Everyone on the team seemed super nice, and she had a good feeling about the project.

Nathan waved as he approached. "Hey, Maisey. Ready for your big debut?"

"Ready as you are."

"We'll knock 'em dead with our rendition of 'All I Want for Christmas Is You.'" Nathan grinned. "Practice sounded really good."

"That was indoors at the church."

"It'll sound the same out here. I've sung outside enough to know."

Maisey took a deep breath. "Yeah, I guess you have the experience. That's why I told Phil you had to sing with me. I'm still a little nervous."

Nathan waved a gloved hand at her. "You'll do fine. Just pretend it's Sunday morning and you're singing in the praise band. Besides, Phil has marked our places with a big X on the floor of the gazebo. Find the X and you'll be good."

Maisey laughed. "Thanks for the advice."

"You're welcome." Nathan pointed toward the northeast corner of the square. "I've got to pick up Melanie from work. The boys are with her. So see you in a few minutes."

"Okay." Maisey wished she were as confident as Nathan. He'd sung for so many things over the years.

She had only done her stint in the church praise band for a few months.

She shouldn't be nervous. The townspeople were here to see the tree lighting. The singing was just a prelude. She knew from past experience that people gathered in groups, and conversations took place over the square while the singers performed. The only time anyone paid attention was when the singers instructed everyone to do the sing-along.

"You look cold."

Zach's voice sent a shiver down Maisey's spine that had nothing to do with the chill. She turned around and tried to smile. His presence always made her heart hammer. "I'm okay."

"You shivered." Zach held out a fleece blanket, its red background covered with Christmas trees. "You should take this."

"But you'll be cold."

Zach shook his head. "I've played football in freezing weather, so I'm used to the cold. How about I get both of us some hot chocolate from that stand over there?"

"That sounds good." Maisey watched him saunter away and wished their circumstances could be different. She had to stifle her feelings for Zach. Business was business and not meant for romance. But if the circumstances were different, he wouldn't give her the time of day. So here she was wishing for the impossible. *Silly Maisey.*

With a smile lighting up his handsome face, Zach returned with two steaming cups of hot chocolate. "This ought to warm you up. Ready to sing?"

Maisey nodded as she took a sip of the hot

chocolate. "Nathan and I practiced our songs, and he says we're ready to wow the crowd."

"I'm sure you will."

Maisey laughed. "Mostly people aren't listening."

"They'll listen to you."

"We'll see."

"Hey, Maisey."

Maisey turned at the sound of a male voice. "Hi, Alex."

"I was hoping I'd get to see you while I was home for Christmas break."

"How's college life?" Maisey wasn't sure what to make of Alex's interest. He hadn't communicated with her in any way after their Valentine's Day date almost a year ago. He'd been away at college in Boston, even summer school, and she'd only had a few passing thoughts about him in all that time.

"Great, but I'm ready to graduate this spring. I've already got a job lined up."

"That's super. Here in town?"

Alex shook his head. "No, in Cincinnati."

"Well, that's not too far away."

"Yeah, that's what I was thinking. It'll give me a chance to see you."

Zach cleared his throat.

Maisey turned to look at him. "Sorry. I should introduce you."

Zach nodded. "That would be nice."

"Alex, this is Zach Dawson. He used to live here in Kellersburg."

"*The* Zach Dawson, quarterback?" Alex's voice sounded full of awe.

Zach held out his hand. "Yeah. I used to play

football for the high school here."

"Wow!" Alex shook Zach's hand. "That was before we lived here. I never thought I'd meet someone famous."

"Fame is short lived." Zach smiled wryly. "I'm last year's news."

"Not in my book. How do you know Maisey?"

"We lived across the street from her family."

Alex looked at Maisey. "You never told me you know Zach Dawson."

Maisey shrugged. "There was never any reason to."

Zach pointed both index fingers at Maisey. "Case in point. Not famous enough for her to mention."

"Yeah, but she's a girl. She doesn't care about football." Alex put an arm around Maisey's shoulders. "Right?"

"Sure." Maisey laughed. She sure wasn't about to tell Alex or Zach how much she followed football, especially one particular quarterback.

"It was good seeing you, Maisey." Alex stepped away. "I've got to find my parents. We have some family shindig after the tree lighting. I hope we can get together sometime while I'm home."

Maisey shook her head. "I'm not sure when that'll be. I'm doing this thing with Zach for a documentary, and I'll be gone most of December."

"Wow! That's cool. What's it for?"

"Dog food."

"Dog food?"

"Have you ever heard of Master's Dog Food?"

Alex nodded. "I've seen commercials on TV for it."

Maisey explained the project and pointed out the camera crews.

"I saw those and wondered what was going on. Now I know. That's cool." Alex gave Maisey a quick hug. "Maybe we can catch up between Christmas and New Year's."

"Sure."

"Hope to see you before I go back to school." Alex turned to Zach. "And it was nice meeting you. Glad you're recovered from your accident."

"Thanks." Zach gave a slight nod.

Alex waved as he trotted away.

"An old boyfriend?" Zach raised his eyebrows as he looked at Maisey.

Maisey gave a halfhearted laugh. "No. Just a friend."

"Just a friend?" Zach narrowed his gaze. "Seemed like more than a friend to me."

Maisey let out a heavy sigh. "In all the time I've known him, we've been on one official date. If he really had a romantic interest in me, he probably would've called or something during all these months he's been away at school. I don't think there's much interest there."

"Maybe he's just shy and you haven't given him any encouragement."

Maisey shook her head. "I don't want to give him encouragement. He's a nice guy, but he doesn't push any of my buttons."

"And what pushes your buttons?" Zach gave her a speculative glance.

Maisey sighed again as she flashed him an annoyed look. "I don't know. When I do, I'll let you know."

"Promise?"

"No. I was joking." Maisey knew one thing. Zach Dawson pushed her buttons, but that was the last thing she would admit to him. "Alex is just a friend. That's it."

Zach held up one hand. "Okay. I've got it. I won't mention him again."

"Thank you." Maisey took a sip of her hot chocolate that wasn't so hot anymore and stared across the square. "I suppose I should find my X in the gazebo."

"Your X? Ex-boyfriend?"

Maisey laughed out loud. "No, silly, the X I'm supposed to stand on when Nathan and I sing."

Zach glanced at his phone. "Not much time before this thing gets started. Do you sing before or after the tree lighting?"

"Before. There are some town announcements from the mayor. Then Nathan and I sing. They light the tree, and everyone sings 'We Wish You a Merry Christmas' and 'Silent Night.'"

"Do I have an X to stand on?" Zach took the last gulp of his hot chocolate, then tossed the cup in a nearby trash barrel.

"If you did, I think Phil would've told you about it, but I'm guessing you're supposed to be up close to the gazebo, because he said you're in the shot when Nathan and I are singing."

"Maybe I'd better clarify things with Phil." Zach searched the crowd. "I thought I knew what was going on. Phil loves to do these things by the seat of his pants, and sometimes that drives me crazy."

Maisey tilted her head. "I never thought of you as an order guy."

"What's an order guy?"

"Someone who has to have everything in its place and someone who doesn't like to do things at the spur of the moment."

"Let's just say I don't like surprises."

"Interesting."

"Why is that interesting?"

Maisey shrugged. "Just is, but I'll keep that in mind while we're working together."

"Good idea." Zach put a hand to her back. "Let's go find that X."

Maisey tried not to think about Zach's touch. It was just a friendly gesture, but it sent little shivers through her body. Maybe she should picture him with his arms around his old girlfriend. She could still see that tabloid photo of them locked in each other's arms on a beach somewhere.

That photo had made her cry. She'd been eighteen and still dreaming of the day he would come back to Kellersburg and find her all grown up. He'd fall madly in love with her, and they would live happily ever after.

Her fairy-tale dreams and childish heart had betrayed her. Three years later, here he was, but there was no mad love or love of any kind. If he had any clue what was on her mind, he would run like he was being chased down the football field by the opposing team. Back to reality, where she belonged.

***

Zach escorted Maisey to the gazebo, the whole time thinking about Alex. Zach didn't want to believe he was jealous of the younger man, but envy had staked its claim on his heart. He couldn't shake the image of Alex hugging Maisey. Zack knew his feelings were trouble. Dealing with them was a difficult challenge, one he had to tackle.

"Hey, there's my X." Maisey sprinted ahead and stood on it.

Zach laughed. "Are you sure that's not Nathan's?"

"Yes, I'm sure." Maisey pointed to her right. "There's Nathan's spot. He's going to stand on that side."

"And where should I stand?"

Maisey looked at the crowd that had already gathered in front of the gazebo. "I think you should stand right there on that crack, next to those chairs. I think someone's sitting in them, so I wouldn't sit there."

"Guess I should've brought a chair."

"No, you have to stand. That's what Phil said." Maisey puckered her brow in that cute frown. "How will people see you if you're sitting?"

"I think the cameras have a way of zooming in."

"Maybe you should ask Phil."

Zach nodded. "Yeah, I was going to talk to him. I'll see if I can find him."

As Zach went down the gazebo steps, Bryant approached him. "Could we talk for a minute?"

"Sure." Zach's curiosity meter soared to high.

"Let's step over here."

"Okay." Zach followed Bryant to an open spot near the gazebo. Bryant's expression filled Zach's gut with trepidation. "What's this about?"

"Maisey." Bryant stared at Zach.

Zach swallowed the lump in his throat before he could speak. "What about Maisey?"

Bryant let out a harsh breath. "I'm not sure how to say this diplomatically, so I'll just say it. Maisey has led a very sheltered life. She's not sophisticated, nor has she traveled widely. I've seen the news items about your relationships with numerous starlets, singers, models, all beautiful women. My Maisey is beautiful, but she isn't one of those kind of women. I fear she may have a crush on you, and she could be very vulnerable to heartbreak. I don't want that to happen."

Zach was all those things Bryant had intimated and worse, but the last thing Zach wanted was to hurt Maisey. If this wasn't a sign from God and an answer to his unspoken prayers, Zach didn't know what was.

Zach looked Bryant in the eye as he held up his hands in a sign of surrender. "Sir, I'm not sure you're correct about Maisey having a crush on me. For the most part, she's been avoiding me, not seeking me out. I honestly don't think she's much interested in me."

Bryant shrugged. "Maybe I've read my daughter wrong, but I'm still going to give you this warning. Don't do anything to hurt her. She's completely innocent when it comes to relationships with guys."

"Sir, I would never do anything to hurt Maisey. She's always been like a little sister to me." *Until now.* "I promise I'll take care of her and never hurt her. I'll watch out for her and make sure this is the best experience of her life." Zach held out his hand to

Bryant.

Bryant shook Zach's hand. "Thanks for that. I know this wasn't exactly an easy thing for you to hear, but I just had to speak up for my little girl."

Zach nodded. "I understand. You can rest easy. I'll take care of her, and Phil is a wonderful mentor. He's helped me in so many ways, and he'll help Maisey, too."

"Thanks. You've made me feel more at ease with sending my daughter off into the unknown." Bryant clapped Zach on the shoulder. "Now let's get a good spot to listen to Maisey and Nathan sing."

With a heavy heart, Zach followed Bryant to a place in front of the gazebo. The conversation with Maisey's dad made it clearer than ever that she was off limits. He had to shut down any temptation to pursue her. He definitely had to make that a matter of prayer. He only hoped God was listening.

Ryan and Andrew, Nathan's stepsons, came running up to Zach. "Hi, Mr. Dawson. Are you going to sit with us during the tree lighting?"

Zach smiled down at the boys. "Are these your chairs?"

"Yeah. We got a front-row seat so we can see Nathan sing." Ryan pointed across the square. "Nathan and our mom are coming."

"So you think it's okay if I sit here with you?"

"Yeah." Andrew grinned from ear to ear. "That would be cool."

"Thanks for inviting me, but I might have to stand because I wouldn't want to take one of your chairs."

"You can have my chair." Andrew pointed at the one with the woolly red-and-white blanket folded across it.

Zach shook his head. "I couldn't do that. It's okay if I stand."

As Nathan and Melanie drew closer, Andrew raced to greet them. "Mom, Nathan, Mr. Dawson is going to sit with us."

"Hi, Zach." Nathan shook Zach's hand. "I hear you're our number one spectator."

Zach frowned. "Who said that?"

"Phil told me you're going to be the focus of the crowd shot while we're singing."

"He did say I'd have a camera on me at some point." Zach made a fake smile. "Guess I'd better practice smiling for the camera."

Nathan chuckled. "I hope our singing will produce a more genuine smile."

Zach chuckled in return. "I'm sure your singing will make me smile."

"Maisey's singing definitely will."

Did Nathan think Zach had something going on with Maisey? "She sings very well."

"You're her number one fan, or at least Phil told me that's what he's hoping for."

Zach's head hurt from thinking about the opposing forces going through his mind. Phil was pushing Maisey and him together, while Maisey's dad was pushing them apart. Maybe things would get better when they started the tour … or maybe they would only get worse.

He would have to spend time with Maisey and not get involved. Little sister. That had to be his mantra. Little sister. That was all she was to him.

How could he keep his wits about him when he

was trying so hard not to let romantic feelings enter his thoughts? Defense. No offense. A good offensive line to protect him from himself.

"You look lost in thought."

Zach turned to find Maisey smiling at him, and his heart did a flip-flop. Being around her every day. Pure torture. Pure joy. He had a tough road ahead to keep from falling for that smile, but he had made a promise to Maisey's dad. And Zach intended to keep the promise, no matter how much trouble it caused him.

His heart settled to a slow gallop. "Thinking about my part in being your biggest fan."

Maisey narrowed her gaze. "My biggest fan?"

"Yeah." Zach pointed at Nathan. "Nathan told me I'm supposed to be your biggest fan. That's my role for the cameras."

"Oh, that makes sense."

Zach caught a flash of emotion in her eyes. Disappointment? Disenchantment? Dejection? He shook the questions away. The crazies had moved into his mind and swept out all rational thought. "I have to play the adoring fan."

"Don't play too hard. I wouldn't want you to strain yourself." She gave him a cheesy grin as she looked at her phone. "It's almost time. I'm getting a little nervous again."

Nathan stepped closer. "Just remember what I told you. We ought to head to the gazebo. I see the band is setting up, and the mayor and Phil have arrived."

Maisey let out a whoosh of air. "Okay."

"I think this is where I'm supposed to say 'break a leg.'"

"For singing? Isn't that just for acting?"

"I believe it applies to both acting and singing?" Zach said wryly.

"Then I should say the same to you." Maisey put a gloved hand to her mouth as her eyes opened wide. "Oh, that was terrible. I forgot that you've actually broken your leg. No wishes for you."

Zach smiled. "As long as you only send smiles my way, I think I'm good."

"So sorry." Maisey grimaced.

Zach patted her on the shoulder. "It's okay. I won't hold it against you."

"Thanks." She turned to Nathan. "Let's go."

"Break a leg," Ryan and Andrew yelled in unison as Nathan and Maisey took the stage in the gazebo.

Maisey turned and blew them a kiss. Zach tried his hardest not to let his mind go there, but the thought of kissing Maisey plowed a furrow in his brain and left a seed there, ready to grow. He was in big, big trouble. Reality. *She blew the kiss to two little boys, not you.*

"Are you ready for the show?" Andrew tapped Zach on the arm.

"I'm ready. Are you?"

Andrew nodded. "I want to see the tree all lit up. We have our tree, and we're going to decorate it tomorrow. Do you have a tree?"

"No. I'm not going to be at my house for Christmas. I'll be here with my parents." Zach realized he'd hardly ever had a Christmas tree since he'd started playing professional football. He wasn't home enough, and many years he spent Christmas with whatever woman he was dating at the time. It was a sad commentary on his life.

"Maybe you can come to our house and help us

decorate our tree." Andrew smiled brightly.

"Andrew, please don't bother Mr. Dawson. He's a very busy man, and I'm sure he doesn't want to help us decorate our tree."

"What do you think?" Andrew looked at Zach for verification of Melanie's statement.

"I'd have to check with Phil and Maisey. They might have something they need me to do." Zach actually thought the idea of helping the boys decorate the tree would be fun. His parents definitely wouldn't have a tree to decorate until their goods arrived.

"Hey, Mom, can Maisey and Phil come with Mr. Dawson? They can all help." Andrew brightened.

Melanie shook her head. "They're welcome to come if they want."

"Hey, boys, you can call me Zach."

"Cool!" Andrew raised his hands in a victory pose.

"Okay, you guys need to settle down and sit in your chairs. Things are about ready to start." Melanie motioned toward the chairs, then looked at Zach. "I wish I'd known you needed a chair."

Zach shook his head. "Really. It's no problem for me to stand. I'll just stand here behind the boys, and maybe they'll get in the shot. Then they'll be in the documentary."

"Wow! We get to be in a movie." Ryan gave Andrew a high five.

"It's starting." Andrew snuggled underneath his blanket.

"That's just to get the crowd to settle and let them know the show will soon start." Zach grasped the back of Andrew's chair.

Zach watched Maisey interact with Nathan, Phil, and the mayor. She had a natural way about her. Zach understood why Phil had hired her. He had an eye for talent that he could groom. Zach was thankful for the opportunity Phil had offered him, even if it now meant having to negotiate the troubled waters of Maisey's presence.

As the band ended the tune, the audience applauded, and the mayor took a microphone as he stepped forward. He greeted the crowd and introduced Phil, who then thanked everyone for coming. He explained the program, and then introduced Nathan and Maisey.

The crowd cheered and clapped. A male voice in the crowd called out, "Maisey, will you marry me?"

Maisey stepped forward and looked over the crowd. "I really can't say yes because I don't know you."

"You can get to know me," the voice called out.

"You'll have to talk to my dad."

The audience laughed and applauded, and the male voice didn't respond.

"I guess that scared him." Maisey grinned, and the audience applauded even louder. "Now that we've gotten the proposals out of the way, let's get on with the show."

As if Zach needed any more reasons to admire Maisey, her ability to think on her feet made her even more likable.

Nathan stepped forward. "We've got a couple of Christmas songs we'd like to sing for you tonight, then we'll get to what you all came for. The tree lighting."

Maisey turned to face Nathan as the band played the intro. She smiled and belted out the beginning chorus of "All I Want For Christmas Is You." Her rendition of the song rivaled any Zach had ever heard. He stood there in awe, eyes fixed on Maisey.

Nathan answered with the following verse until they were trading verses of the song. Their voices rang out over the square, and the crowd clapped to the catchy tune. Zach gripped the back of the chair tighter and wished they'd picked a different song. Was he just a sucker for every pretty blonde that crossed his path, or was there something special about Maisey Norberg that had him wishing the words of the song could come true?

Loud applause, shouts, and whistles accompanied the last note. No one talked during that performance, as Maisey had predicted. Everyone was focused on the singers.

After the applause died down, Nathan introduced the next song. "Now we're going to slow things down and reflect on the reason for the season as we sing 'Do You Hear What I Hear?'"

Again they sang, trading verses until the end, when their voices blended in harmony. The song set the stage for the tree lighting. Applause filled the square as Maisey and Nathan left the stage.

Maisey hurried in Zach's direction, and he braced himself for that feeling of pressure in his chest. As she approached, his pulse raced faster than the chasing Christmas lights that zipped along the outline of one of the nearby businesses.

"How'd we do?" Maisey gazed up at him.

"Great. Phil will be ecstatic about that

performance."

"Thanks." Maisey gave him a shy smile as she slipped in beside him.

Zach wanted to put an arm around her shoulders and pull her close in the worst way. Instead he shoved his hands into his pockets.

The mayor stepped forward and announced the tree lighting and the winner of the drawing to flip the switch. The winner, a middle-aged woman, squealed and waved her arms over her head as she ran to the gazebo.

The mayor shook her hand. "Looks like we have an excited winner. Are you ready to do the honors?"

"I'm ready." The woman took the switch that the mayor handed her.

"Let's do a count down from ten and call out 'lights' after we've said 'one,'" the mayor instructed the crowd.

The countdown echoed across the square. When the crowd yelled "lights," the woman pressed the button on the switch. The multicolored bulbs sprang to life, and everyone cheered.

Zach glanced down at Maisey. The awe on her face made his heart stutter. The lights reflected in her eyes. A lump rose in his throat when she turned to him.

Her eyes sparkled with tears. "I don't know why I cry at the tree lighting every year. It's silly, I know, but it just gets me right in here." She patted her chest.

Zach swallowed the lump in his throat. The tree lighting wasn't getting him right there. Maisey was. "I know what you mean."

"Really? A big, strong football player gets choked

up at Christmas lights?"

Yeah, when I'm with you. "You might be surprised at what gets me choked up."

"Surprise me sometime." She gave him a quirky wink.

Zach thought his heart might beat right out of his chest. "I will."

Before either of them could say anything else, the mayor tapped his microphone. "Nathan is going to lead us in our usual sing-along songs, 'We Wish You a Merry Christmas' and 'Silent Night.' You should've received a glow stick when you entered the square. You can use it during 'Silent Night.'"

Nathan stepped to the microphone again as the band played the intro to the first song. "Let's hear it, folks."

"We Wish You a Merry Christmas" rang across the square as Nathan directed the large group.

Zach leaned closer to Maisey. "Why aren't you singing up there with Nathan?"

"Easier for one person to lead. I said he could do it, since he does it every year."

"That makes sense." With Maisey standing beside him, happiness welled in Zach's heart as he joined in the song.

As the intro for "Silent Night" sounded through the night, Maisey pulled her glow stick out and broke it. The light illuminated her face, giving her an angelic look. The look reminded Zach she was off limits, and all the warm, fuzzy feelings toward her needed to be stuffed into a big bag and shipped to the North Pole, where they could cool.

Zach sang along and forced himself to look at the

tree and not at the woman standing beside him. As the last notes of the song rang out and the mayor bid everyone good night, large snowflakes filled the night air.

"It's snowing!" Andrew jumped up from his chair and danced around as he tried to catch snowflakes on his tongue.

Maisey laughed. "Andrew, you can't catch them if you're moving too much. You have to do it like this."

Zach's heart nearly stopped as Maisey looked heavenward and caught a snowflake on her tongue. Young, innocent, and alluring. She had no idea how alluring.

CHAPTER FIVE

"Maisey, you have a visitor." Wes's voice floated into her room from somewhere in the house.

Maisey stuck her notes into the book she'd been studying for her tests. Who could be here? She didn't have time for a visitor. Her tests were set for Monday and Tuesday of the coming week, and she needed to study. Not visit.

She still had to pack for her trip. She kind of felt like a hamster on one of those little wheels. She was going, going, going and not getting anywhere.

She'd spent this Saturday morning helping her mother decorate the Christmas tree while Wes and her dad had done the outside lights. The afternoon was supposed to be dedicated to study. Now someone was here to ruin her plans.

As she opened her bedroom door, Wes stood on the other side. He grinned. "Loverboy is here."

"Alex?"

Wes laughed. "Not Alex. Zach."

Maisey swatted at her brother and made a face. "So not true. He's not interested in me except that we have to work together."

"I'm not talking about his interest in you. I'm talking about your interest in him." Wes waggled his eyebrows. "I've seen the way you look at him."

"Your imagination."

"I don't think so." Wes gave her a sly grin.

"Well, keep your thoughts to yourself."

"Your secret's safe with me."

"Go away." Maisey swatted at him again.

Wes saluted. "Yes, ma'am. I'll leave you two alone."

Wes disappeared into the kitchen as Maisey walked into the living room. Wearing his familiar leather jacket, blue jeans, and cowboy boots, Zach stood in the middle of the room as he studied the photos on the wall above the worn blue couch.

"Hi, Zach. What can I do for you?"

He turned. "Hey, sorry to barge in on you, but Phil wants us to go over to Nathan's and help them decorate their tree. He's sending over a camera crew to film it."

Maisey tried not to let her dismay show. How could she study if she had to decorate another tree? "Is my presence really necessary?"

"Yes. That's why Phil sent me to drive you over there." Zach rubbed the back of his neck as he nodded. "You won't regret this. Phil has something planned that ties into our dog giveaways. Get used to this. Phil loves to live life on the spur of the moment. Things can change in the blink of an eye. He got wind of Andrew's request last night, and he's charging right ahead with the idea."

Letting out a big sigh, Maisey pressed fingers to her forehead as she gazed at her feet. "I've got those tests to study for."

"I thought we covered all that the other night."

"Not all of it." Maisey tapped the side of her head.

"Besides, I have to review and review. This brain is very forgetful."

"Didn't seem that way to me the other night."

"Believe me. It's a jumbled mess up there."

Zach chuckled. "I think you're exaggerating."

Maisey frowned. "I'm not. My mind is like a sieve. I need to plug the holes with lots and lots of study."

"I'll help you study when we're done, just like I did the other night."

Maisey didn't think that would help. She would be thinking more about Zach than the stuff she was supposed to remember. "That's not necessary. I'll get by. You shouldn't be stuck trying to pound this stuff into my head. I'll get my coat."

Maisey went back to her bedroom and ran a brush through her hair and jammed her stocking cap on her head. She didn't know why she'd bothered to brush her hair. Zach had already seen her with uncombed hair. She pulled on her puffy coat and grabbed the gloves out of the pockets.

When she returned to the living room, Zach was studying the pictures again. "Who took the photos?"

"I did. Those are photos of the Hocking Hills, where we like to go hiking." Maisey pointed to one of the photos. "You used to go there when you lived here, didn't you?"

"Yeah, I remember now. I just didn't recognize it at first. Nice photos!"

"Thanks." Maisey was clueless as to why Zach hadn't recognized Hocking Hills, but then he'd traveled all over the country to places she'd never dreamed of going. He'd played football in Wembley

Stadium in Wembley, London. "I'd better tell Wes where I'm going."

"Sure. I'll wait right here."

"You can go out to the car. You don't have to wait on me."

"Waiting is the polite thing to do."

Maisey nodded. "And I do remember you were always polite."

"I was?" Zach quirked an eyebrow. "You were just a little girl. How do you remember?"

"Because that's what my mom always said. 'That Zach is such a polite young man.'"

Zach smiled wryly. "Glad I impressed your mom."

Maisey raced off toward the kitchen. She poked her head around the doorframe and told Wes about the tree-decorating expedition.

"Have fun." Wes winked.

"I will." Maisey hurried off before Wes could say anything else. He'd already said too much.

"Ready to put your tree-decorating skills to the test?" Zach held open the door for her as they left the house.

"See. You're very polite. You held the door open."

Zach laughed. "That's basic politeness."

"Yeah, but some people are basically impolite these days."

"Good point." Zach pointed a finger in her direction and let the door close behind Maisey.

Maisey matched Zach's stride. He walked with confidence, like he didn't have a care in the world. She would never have guessed that a year ago he lay in pain with a horrific injury on a football field. He'd made a remarkable recovery.

The dusting of snow from the night before had almost disappeared from the warmth of the sun on a cloudless, though chilly, day. Some white patches remained in the shady parts of the yard, but it was a beautiful day for December in Ohio.

On the drive to Nathan and Melanie's place, Maisey gave Zach directions. They didn't say much else, and Maisey wondered what was on his mind. Did he hate getting stuck with her all the time? Maybe not. He had volunteered to help her study again.

When they arrived, Nathan was stringing lights on the outside of the house with the help of Phil, Andrew, and Ryan, who were all wearing ski jackets and stocking caps. The boys ran to greet Zach as soon as he got out of the car.

"Hey, fellas, how's it going?"

"We're almost done with the outside. We've been working on it all morning." Ryan motioned toward the house. "But we can't tell what it looks like until it gets dark."

"I'm sure if you guys worked on this, it'll be awesome." Zach gave each of the boys a high five.

Maisey loved the way he related to the kids. He'd been that way growing up, too. That was part of the politeness her mom had talked about. He never put himself on a pedestal all those years he'd been the star quarterback in high school. He still seemed a down-to-earth guy despite his national fame all these years later. Just one more thing that drew him to her.

"What do you want me to do?" Zach asked.

"You can go inside and help Melanie string the lights on the tree." Phil gestured toward the front door. "We'll be there in a few minutes to help with the ornaments. The film crew is on their way."

"You know I'll be glad to help Melanie if you want to stay out here with the guys."

Zach shook his head. "Why would I want to stay out here with a bunch of guys when I can spend my time with two beautiful women?"

"Nathan might have something to say about that."

Zach gave her a curious look as they walked across the yard. "Are you saying he doesn't think his wife is beautiful?"

"I'm saying he doesn't want you flirting with his wife."

Zach grinned. "Who says I'm flirting with his wife? I just enjoy spending time with good-looking women."

"What about not-so-good-looking women?"

"Now you've put me on the spot." Zach smiled as he shook his head. "Women can be charming no matter how they look."

Maisey didn't know what to make of his banter. Did he really think she was pretty? Melanie was definitely a beautiful woman, with her dark hair and eyes that gave her an exotic look, but Maisey didn't consider herself pretty. She was ordinary, not the kind of woman seen on Zach Dawson's arm over the years.

She might be better off not responding. He could outwit her no matter what she said, but she was never good at taking her own advice. "You certainly know how to manipulate the question."

"How do you think I dealt with those sports reporters?"

"They do ask some pretty dumb questions, don't

they?"

Surprise painted Zach's face. "You've listened to sports press conferences?"

"A few." She wasn't about to admit that she'd listened to any that involved him.

"That's a surprise. I had no idea you had any interest in sports."

"I've watched games with Wes and my dad." Maisey shrugged. "After all, they dragged me to all of your games when I was little. Something had to rub off."

Zach laughed as he went up the front steps. "Don't sound so tortured. We'll have to watch a few games together while we're on the road. I'll teach you the finer points of the game."

"Maybe." She shrugged again. The thought of watching a game with Zach had her heart galloping. "We might be too busy."

"Has Phil talked to you about the schedule?" Zach rang the doorbell.

"No."

"We'll have to do that today sometime." Zach shook his head. "Phil needs to keep you in the loop."

The bell sounded inside the house, and Melanie was at the door in an instant. "Come in. I hear you've been assigned to help me string the lights."

"How did you know?" Zach pulled off his stocking cap and stuffed it into a pocket of his jacket.

"Phil sent me a text." Melanie laughed. "He's quite the organizer."

Zach laughed. "He's organized a whole year of my life."

"During your rehab?" Maisey asked.

"Yeah." Zach gazed at her. "I guess I never told you he was there almost from day one. He's a good friend of my team's owner, and he'd always taken an interest in me. We've known each other for almost my whole professional career."

"Wow! I didn't know that."

"When I was in the darkest time of my life, he pushed me and cajoled me into a better place. He's like a grandfather." Zach turned to Melanie. "That's enough about me. Let's get to work."

"Great!" Melanie pointed to a pile of plastic grocery bags on the couch. "The lights are in those. I know that's not a very efficient way to store them, but it's my method."

Zach grabbed a couple of bags and opened them. "How many strings do you use on the tree?"

"However many it takes." Melanie grinned.

"Do you have a tree topper?" Zach untangled a string of lights.

Melanie nodded. "We put that on last. One of the boys gets to do that. My late husband and I started that tradition with the boys when they were little."

Surprise registered on Zach's face. "I didn't know you were married before."

"Yeah. Tim died suddenly a few years ago. We spent some pretty sad Christmases after that."

"I'm sorry." Zach shook his head. "I didn't know."

"That's okay." Melanie brightened. "Then Nathan came into our lives and made everything better."

"I'm happy for you and the boys." Zach busied himself with the lights, as if he didn't want to talk anymore.

Maisey puzzled over his reaction as she untangled another string of lights, the tree's evergreen scent tickling her nose. The smell of Christmas. "I've got a string that's ready to go on the tree."

"Since I'm the tallest, I get the honors to start the lights." Zach took the string from her, and their fingers brushed. He quickly turned to the tree. "Melanie, you can grab this on the back side and then hand it back to me."

Unraveling another string, Maisey watched Zach and Melanie coordinate to get the lights around the tree. Maisey wondered if Zach had turned away so quickly because he had felt the same jolt of awareness she had when their fingers touched. She shook the crazy thought away. He was only in a hurry to get the lights on the tree. Any other reason was pure fantasy on her part.

Just as Melanie plugged in the lights to see the results of their efforts, Nathan, Phil, the boys, and the film crew trooped into the house.

"We're all done outside." Nathan gave Melanie a kiss on the cheek. "Looks like you've got the lights on. Looks good."

"Thanks to Maisey and Zach." Melanie slipped her arm through Nathan's. "Are you ready to put the ornaments on?"

"Yes," Ryan and Andrew chorused as they scrambled to open the ornament boxes.

"Wait a minute, guys." Melanie stepped up beside them. "You have to take off your coats and hang them up. And you can take our guests' coats and hang them in the coat closet."

"Hey, guys, I want you to meet the camera crew."

Phil gestured toward the two men and one woman who were setting up their cameras and lights. "We have Shirl Pollers, Howie Linz, and Jess Fordham. They'll be traveling with us, and we'll have additional local people we'll use at each stop. But I like the continuity of a core crew going with us."

Maisey marveled at the way Phil had pulled everything together. It warmed her heart that Kellersburg was the beginning of the tour.

Phil waved a hand in the air. "We have to wait a few minutes while the crew gets their cameras and lights set up. And I have to run a quick errand, but I'll be back to see how the tree looks when it's decorated."

After Phil left and the boys had gathered the coats and headed for the hall closet, Melanie waved everyone into the kitchen. "We have a surprise for the boys. Phil has gone to pick it up. We're getting them a puppy."

Zach chuckled. "Leave it to Phil to talk parents into getting their kids a dog. More dog food consumers."

Nathan nodded. "True, but we've been talking about getting them a dog. They've been super good this year, and we said maybe they could get one for Christmas."

Maisey clasped her hands. "That's so great. They'll love a dog."

"I know." Excitement sounded in Melanie's voice. "Phil's getting the dog now, because he thought it would be perfect as a part of the tree decorating."

"Does someone else wish she could have a dog?" Zach gazed at Maisey.

"I'll just be happy to visit Ryan and Andrew's dog." A pup of her own wasn't in the picture.

Before anyone could say anything else, Ryan and Andrew returned and headed straight for the ornament boxes. The adults wandered back into the family room and gathered around the tree. The head of the film crew gave them the go-ahead to start the decorating.

Ryan held up an ornament he'd plucked from a box. "I found the ornament I always put on the tree first."

Zach stepped closer to take a look. "May I see?"

"Sure." Ryan held up the little bell made from a tiny clay pot turned upside down.

"It has your name on it. Did you make this?" Zach asked.

Ryan nodded. "When I was in kindergarten, my dad helped me make it."

"Here's mine." Andrew held up a similar ornament.

"Go for it, boys." Zach pointed to the tree.

Ryan and Andrew sprinted to the tree and found the perfect spot for their ornaments.

"Looks good, guys." Melanie picked two ornaments from a box and held them up. "These are the ornaments I got after each of the boys was born. Their baby pictures."

After Melanie hung her ornaments, Nathan stepped forward with two ornaments he'd taken from a bag. "Since this is our first Christmas as a family, I have two special ornaments to celebrate that occasion." Nathan held them up. "This one has a photo of us at our wedding, and the date. The other one is a photo of the four of us taken this summer at the lake. You guys want to hang these, too?"

Ryan and Andrew held out their hands, and Nathan gave one to each boy. They hung the ornaments in a special place and then gave Nathan a hug. Maisey blinked back tears of happiness for this family. Good things could come out of tragedy.

Zach stepped closer to Maisey. "Do I detect a little mist in those baby blues?"

Maisey blinked faster as she looked up at Zach. "It's so sweet."

"Seems to me you're a real softie."

"Anything wrong with that?"

Zach gazed at her. "No. Tenderhearted is good."

"We'd better get to decorating." Maisey grabbed a couple of ornaments and looked for a spot on the tree. She couldn't get over how Zach had called her tenderhearted. Her heart was tender all right. Tender for him.

With a flurry of activity, the group hung ornaments all over the tree until it could barely hold another one. Christmas music played in the background as Maisey found a spot for the last ornament. The group stood back and admired their handiwork as the cameras rolled.

"We have one last thing to do. Put on the tree topper." Nathan stepped forward as he held the angel. "Whose turn is it to put this on the tree?"

Andrew waved a hand in the air. "Mine!"

Nathan handed Andrew the angel. "Do we need a step ladder, or do you think I'm strong enough to lift you that high?"

"I think you're strong enough."

"I was only kidding." Nathan laughed as he flexed

his muscles. "You've grown so much in the last year that even these muscles can't lift you that high."

"Zach's taller." Andrew pointed in Zach's direction.

Zach shook his head. "Taller, but not stronger. Since my accident, I've become a weakling. You wouldn't want me to knock over the tree trying to hold Andrew up there. I have an idea."

"What?"

"Nathan can put you on his shoulders, and then you'll be able to reach the top of the tree." Zach looked Nathan's way. "What do you think?"

"Good idea." Nathan motioned to Andrew. "Take off your shoes and stand on the kitchen counter. You can get on my shoulders, and we'll make this happen."

After Andrew got on Nathan's shoulders, everyone cheered.

"I can touch the ceiling!" Andrew yelled.

"Let's concentrate on getting the angel on the tree." Concern showed in Melanie's voice.

"We've got this." Nathan walked slowly toward the tree while Andrew held on to the angel. "Are we close enough?"

"Just a little closer," Andrew said.

Nathan stepped nearer the tree. "Now?"

"Good." Andrew reached over and deposited the angel at the top. "It's perfect."

"Yes. Perfect," Melanie said. "Now let's get you down."

Nathan went over to the couch and sat down with care. Andrew hopped off Nathan's shoulders.

"That was fun!" Andrew danced around the room.

"You get to do that next year, Ryan."

Nathan shook his head. "Oh, no! Next year both of you guys will be too big, especially Ryan. He's a year older. We'll use a ladder."

Everyone laughed as they gathered around the tree for a still photo.

Zach stood next to Maisey. "Has anyone told you that you're short?"

With an annoyed look, Maisey looked over her shoulder at him. "I'm not short. You're tall."

"Must be. Phil just told me that the other day." Zach smiled down at her.

Maisey's heart took a little leap, and she looked away. She didn't want him to read anything in her eyes. She didn't know what Wes had seen when he mentioned how she looked at Zach, but she certainly didn't want Zach to see that look.

He leaned closer. "Smile for the camera."

"How can I smile when you keep bugging me?"

"Is someone a little touchy today?"

Maisey held her tongue. She didn't need to say anything that would give her feelings away. Zach's nearness was driving her crazy. She needed to get out of this space. If they didn't finish with the photos soon, she'd have to declare she was claustrophobic in a crowd.

At that moment Phil entered the room. "Hey, everyone. How's the tree decorating coming along?"

"See for yourself." Zach stepped aside and held out a hand toward the tree.

"Looks fantastic." Phil turned toward the camera crew. "Did you get some good takes?"

"We did." The cameraman patted the side of the

camera.

"Great! Now I believe Nathan and Melanie have an announcement to make," Phil said.

Melanie pulled Phil aside and talked with him quietly. Phil nodded.

Melanie stepped back into the center of the room. "Ryan and Andrew, Nathan and I have a big surprise for you, but you have to go to the basement and wait until we get it."

The boys hurried to the basement door. Ryan turned. "How long do we have to stay down there?"

"Until we call you."

Phil looked around the room. "Zach and Maisey, you should keep the boys company."

"Sure." Zach strode across the room to join the youngsters.

Maisey reluctantly followed. She had her suspicions that Phil was trying his hand at matchmaking. He was always throwing Zach and her together.

Zach opened the door to the basement and stood aside as the boys raced down the stairs. Zach waited for Maisey.

As they descended the stairs, Zach leaned forward. "Don't let your enthusiasm show."

"You know I'm worried about getting back to my studies."

"This will be over soon, and I promised to help."

Maisey couldn't refuse his offer of help, or she would seem ungrateful. Her stomach churned. Her brain hurt. Her pulse raced. Would she survive the day, not to mention the evening with Zach as her study partner?

"Maisey, do you know what our surprise is?" Ryan asked.

Maisey nodded. "But I can't tell. Then it wouldn't be a surprise. You'll know very soon."

"Will we like it?" Andrew crossed his arms over his chest as he frowned.

"You're going to love it." Zach ruffled Andrew's hair.

Andrew rubbed his hands together, then pressed his hands to his cheeks. "I can't stand the waiting."

"You and me both. I can hardly wait to see the look on your faces when you see your surprise." Maisey gave them an impish smile.

"Why is it taking so long?" Andrew wrinkled his nose. "Is it something really big?"

"No." Maisey liked the guessing game.

"Something small?" Ryan joined in the questioning.

"What do you consider small?" Maisey asked.

"The size of a baseball or smaller." Ryan made a circle with his hands.

"Bigger than a baseball," Zach answered.

"What could it be?" Andrew paced back and forth.

"Boys, you can come up now." Melanie's voice floated down the stairs. "But no running."

The boys stopped in their tracks at the "no running" command. They took the steps one at a time. Maisey purposely lagged behind Zach, who followed the youngsters. She didn't want Zach leaning up and whispering something in her ear again. She was already wired from the day's activities. She didn't need any more heart-pounding moments, and Zach's nearness made heart pounding a never-ending occurrence.

When they reached the top of the stairs, Ryan and Andrew marched like little soldiers toward the Christmas tree.

Andrew wrinkled his brow as he searched the room. "I don't see a surprise."

"How about this." Nathan came from the kitchen with a brown-and-white puppy in his arms.

"A puppy!" Andrew slapped the sides of his head with both hands and jumped up and down.

Ryan closed the distance between him and Nathan. "Can I hold it?"

Melanie stepped up beside Nathan. "You boys sit down on the floor by the tree, and we'll bring the puppy to you. We don't want to scare him."

"It's a boy?" Andrew scrambled to sit down. Ryan joined him.

"Yes." Nathan carried the pup to where the boys sat. "You guys can figure out a name for him."

The puppy sniffed his way back and forth between Ryan and Andrew. They petted the puppy, and he wiggled from head to the end of his tail with excitement.

"He's as excited to meet us as we are to meet him." Andrew ran a hand down the pup's back.

The puppy licked Andrew's hand, then did the same to Ryan.

Nathan hunkered down with the boys. "Guys, you know having a dog is a big responsibility. This pup is a Jack Russell terrier mix, and those dogs need lots of exercise. That means you will have to take him for a walk and play in the yard with him every day. Do you understand?"

"We do," the boys said in unison.

"It's a good thing we put a fence in the backyard this summer, isn't it?" Ryan asked.

Nathan nodded. "That was part of planning ahead for getting a dog. You have to be careful not to let your dog run off."

"I'll watch out for him. I'll make sure he stays home," Andrew vowed.

"Good." Phil carried a big bag of dog food, along with a canvas bag, into the room. "This is for your new pet, and I've got a few toys in this bag."

"And there's the issue of housebreaking the dog." Melanie eyed her sons. "You have to be diligent in training him. The people who were fostering the dog have already started that, so you boys just have to keep with the program."

The boys nodded as they continued to play with the pup. Phil handed them some of the toys. Maisey itched to get down on the floor and play, too, but she stood there and watched.

"Have you thought of a name?" Maisey asked.

Ryan and Andrew looked up at her as they shook their heads.

Melanie waved her arms in the air. "Let's have everyone write down a name. I'll give each of you a piece of paper. Then the boys can go over the suggestions and pick one. I'll get a notepad and pencils from the kitchen."

Melanie returned and handed each person a piece of paper and a pencil. After Zach got his, he gave Maisey a wry smile and a wink. She wasn't sure what that was for, but maybe he was thinking about all the dogs they would encounter in the next few weeks.

Dogs that needed names. Today was just a taste of what her future would hold. She wrote a name on the paper and handed it to Melanie.

Melanie gave the papers to Ryan and Andrew. "Here's the list. See if there's one you like."

Maisey settled on the couch while the boys went through the papers. Zach sat next to her. He didn't look her way or say a word, but his presence made her heart race like the wagging of the dog's tail. The youngsters whispered together, as if the names were a secret.

"I think they'll pick my name." Zach grinned.

"Maybe they'll pick mine." Maisey laughed. "Or quite possibly they won't pick either one."

The puppy played around the boys while they talked back and forth in quiet voices. Finally, Ryan picked up the pup as both youngsters stood.

Andrew stood next to his brother. "We decided on a name. We picked Rusty because the brown parts of his fur are kind of a rusty color."

"Good choice." Melanie patted the dog on the head. "That was the name I suggested."

Everyone laughed as Melanie gave a victory sign while she raised both arms. Nathan brought out a large kennel filled with goodies for the dog. The boys took out a dog bed, food and water bowls, a leash, dog brush, and more toys.

"Looks like this dog is well supplied." Zach gave each of the boys a high five, then patted the dog on the head. "Thanks for the fun afternoon. Maisey and I have to leave. She has to study for her exams."

"Will we get to see you again?" Ryan asked.

"Sunday at church."

Andrew eyed Zach. "We'll see you when you bring Maisey to the wedding."

Zach looked over at Maisey. She stared at him wide eyed. "Am I taking you to this wedding?"

"It was never discussed." Maisey shrugged as she looked over at Phil. "I just know Phil promised I would be able to be in Caroline and Wyatt's wedding."

Nodding, Phil stepped forward. "For sure Zach will be taking Maisey to the wedding."

"Good." Andrew grinned. "We get to see you at our aunt's wedding. You can dance the chicken dance with Maisey."

"I'm looking forward to that." Zach chuckled. "Now we'd better get going."

"I'll get your coats." Melanie hurried off and returned a moment later.

Zach held out Maisey's coat, and she slipped her arms into the sleeves. There he was again being polite, and her pulse pranced around like the pup playing with his new toy.

"See you all later." Zach put a hand to Maisey's back as he escorted her to the door, then held the door open.

A chorus of goodbyes accompanied their departure. Maisey hurried to the car and opened her own door. What did Zach think about being forced to go to this wedding? After he slid behind the steering wheel, she glanced his way. "You know, you don't have to go to that wedding. Really."

Zach eyed her. "And not do the chicken dance with you? I wouldn't miss it."

"I'm serious."

"So am I." Zach started the car. "Remember what I told you about Phil. He jumps on every idea that appeals to him. You just have to learn to go with whatever he comes up with. Amazingly enough, he hardly ever makes a wrong move. Things I thought would be a disaster have worked out better than even he imagined. He has an instinct for show business as well as dog food."

Maisey wondered if Zach thought hiring her had been a wrong move, but she didn't ask. Her mind buzzed with thoughts of Zach studying with her, going to the wedding with her, and just being with her. His kindness and polite manner didn't do anything to dissuade her from wishing there could be something between them. She would make a mistake in thinking that could happen, no matter how kind he treated her.

CHAPTER SIX

"You don't have to help me study." Maisey opened the front door. "Really."

"Are you still trying to get rid of me?" Zach stayed on the front porch. He wished he could read her better. Did she actually not want to be with him, or did she not want to be a burden? "Because if you want me to go, I will after I go over our itinerary. Phil asked me to do that with you."

"I'm not trying to get rid of you. I just don't want you to feel like you have to do this."

"I wouldn't have volunteered if I didn't want to help you." He gave her a wry smile. "I was kind of looking forward to sharing a pizza with you again."

Maisey shrugged. "Okay. I do want to know what to expect."

"Great." Zach followed her into the house.

"Wes, I'm home."

Wes tromped down the stairs. "How was the tree decorating?"

"Good." Maisey took off her coat and hung it in the nearby closet. "Ryan and Andrew got a puppy."

"Wow! I bet they were excited."

"They were." Zach hung his coat beside Maisey's. He didn't know why seeing their coats side by side made his heart skip a beat. He'd managed to get through most of the afternoon without thinking of her in terms of a romantic interest. Now he had to keep telling himself not to go there.

"Zach's here to help me study, and we're going to order a pizza a little later. You want to join us?"

The hopefulness on Maisey's voice made Zach believe she wanted her brother around. Maybe he should just go over the itinerary, then leave.

"Nope." Wes shook his head. "Got a date with that cute kindergarten teacher."

"Where did you meet a kindergarten teacher?" Maisey asked.

"At church."

Maisey shrugged. "Guess I missed that. Have fun!"

"I intend to. Taking my date to Cincinnati." Wes waggled his eyebrows. "I'll be out of your hair in a few minutes. You two have fun, too."

"Studying isn't fun."

Zach took in the exchange between Maisey and her brother. Zach detected an undercurrent to their conversation. He wondered what that was all about.

As Wes grabbed his coat and left, Zach made himself comfortable on the couch. Maisey disappeared but soon returned with several textbooks, notebooks, and a pen. She set them on the coffee table, then joined him on the couch.

"Are you ready to go over this stuff?" Zach tapped his phone. "I've got all the info right here."

"Can you send that to me?" Maisey asked.

"Sure. Give me a sec." Zach tapped his phone again.

Within seconds Maisey's phone dinged. "Let me open this."

Zach waited while Maisey looked over the attached message. A little furrow developed between her eyebrows as she studied it. A soft spot developed in his heart for this young woman who was about to go on the adventure of a lifetime.

Finally she looked up at him, a questioning look painting her expression. "We're going to every corner of the country."

Zach nodded. "That's what Phil wanted. We have twelve winners spread across the whole United States."

Maisey placed a hand over her heart. "This is amazing. I've hardly been anywhere. Just to Cincinnati, to my relatives in Indiana, and a school trip to Washington, DC, when I was in high school."

"We're going to some great places and some out-of-the way places. We start in Chicago. You'll get to see the lights on the Magnificent Mile." Zach could imagine her eyes lit up with the reflection of those lights.

"I've heard of that. Sounds amazing."

"Then we're off to South Dakota and Montana. Even with all the traveling I've done, I've never been to those two states. So this will be something new for me, too."

"I thought you'd been everywhere."

Zach shook his head. "Hardly. This is a big country with lots of places to visit."

"I hope we don't get snowed in while we're way up north."

"Phil will hire a snowplow if we do." Zach laughed. "Then we're headed to Spokane, Tucson, Dallas, Johnson City, Tennessee. After that we go to

Florida so you can be in that wedding."

"That's the most important thing. I'm really looking forward to that."

"You're not looking forward to the puppies and being with me?" Zach wished he could snatch back the part of the question that involved him. What was he thinking? He wasn't. Something about Maisey made him say the most inane things. He was a grown man with plenty of experience with women, probably too much, but he was acting like a teenage boy with a bad crush.

Her lips parted slightly, Maisey stared at him. "I'm good with the puppies, but I have to admit it's a little intimidating being around you."

"I'm intimidating?"

"I don't know what to think. You're a celebrity, but you're also the guy who used to live across the street and spend time with our family." Maisey made a clapping motion with her hands but didn't have them touch, as if she was pressing together an invisible object. "I can't reconcile the two."

"You don't have to. Just think of me as Zach Dawson, the kid who rescued you from the bully all those years ago." If he could go back in time, Zach would choose the boy across the street. He was sure Maisey would like that version of him better than the one who was a celebrity. The celebrity version had done some things he deeply regretted. He couldn't forget them, even though Phil had told Zach that God had forgotten them.

Maisey smiled. "I'm surprised you remember that."

"How could I forget seeing that mean kid steal

your backpack? And when I saw your skinned knees it made me even angrier with the bully." Zach smiled wryly. "You were a spunky little kid. You chased after him."

Maisey gave a shrug. "That was my favorite backpack. I couldn't let him have it."

"I'm glad I could help." Zach wished he could do all kinds of things for Maisey, but the best thing he could do was protect her from himself. Keep his promise to her dad.

"Me, too." Maisey looked back at her phone. "The rest of the itinerary is Atlanta, Baltimore, Boston, Cincinnati, then back here for Christmas Eve?"

"That's it. A whirlwind tour of towns, dogs, and special people." Zach hoped it would be all Maisey expected. Something wonderful for her. "Did you know that half the dogs are service dogs?"

Maisey shook her head. "Like a guide dog for the blind?"

"That's one of them."

"What are the others?"

"Phil tells me we have a dog for the hearing impaired, one for seizures, one for a diabetic child, a dog that detects allergens, and what they call a mobility dog. That would be one who helps someone in a wheelchair."

"Wow! That's amazing. I had no idea that there were so many different kinds of service dogs."

"I guess that's why they say 'dogs are man's best friend.'"

"Yeah. Dogs can be so special in helping people." Maisey's eyes lit up with excitement.

"The rest of the dogs are for deserving youngsters

who have accomplished something special in their lives. Phil is all about helping people and showcasing good in this world."

Maisey placed a hand on her chest. "That makes me feel like I'm going to be part of something really special."

"You are." Zach could see more clearly every time he interacted with Maisey, why Phil had chosen her. She was something special.

"Question. It says here to pack the necessities." Maisey held up her phone and brought Zach back to the task at hand. "A wardrobe will be provided. I'm not sure what that means."

"We're going to be in all kinds of weather. It'll be cold in the north and mild in the south, so if you packed for every type of weather, you'd have to bring too many suitcases." Zach steepled his hands as he gazed at her. "Phil has made arrangements with local shops to provide us with clothing for our shoots."

"So will they know my size?"

"Phil has that covered. You'll go into the shop before the shoot to get outfitted, but are you one of those women who has to have a dozen pair of shoes?"

Maisey frowned. "No, I'm not."

"Good." Zach scooted closer and pointed to her phone. "You see this list? These are the necessities that you can bring in one suitcase."

Maisey bit her lower lip as she looked over the list. "Good thing my bridesmaid's dress is already in Florida."

"If it wasn't, Phil would make sure it got there. Believe me. He's got a plan for everything." *Except how I feel about Maisey.* The thought popped into

Zach's brain unbidden. He was in so much trouble. They hadn't even started the trip, and he was already fighting off the attraction. But hadn't he been doing that since he'd first laid eyes on her, all grown up and pretty as they came?

"I hope you're right." Maisey let out a big sigh. "I'm getting nervous just thinking about packing."

Zach wanted to give her a pat on the arm or a hug to assure her that everything would be okay, but he didn't dare touch her. She was off limits. Even a brotherly gesture might send him down the wrong path. He rose from the couch and went to the other side of the room. "Ready to start studying?"

Maisey picked up a book from the coffee table. "I guess. I wish I didn't have to study. I wish I was brilliant and could remember everything."

"I think you're brilliant enough." Zach picked up one of the notebooks. "You have your study questions in here?"

"And here." Maisey handed him a stack of notecards. "Fire away."

They spent the next two hours going over the study notes for all of Maisey's tests. Zach gave her encouragement. She remembered a lot from their last study session, and he wanted her to know how smart he thought she was. She was a mix of confidence and insecurity, and he never knew which one would surface. The dichotomy made her even more endearing.

"Okay, time for a break. A pizza break." Zach grabbed his phone. "I'll order, then we can study a little more while we wait for the pizza."

"Sure." Maisey looked at her notecard, as if she

didn't want to give up studying.

Zach made the call. They would eat their pizza, finish studying, and that would be the end of the evening. He was sure she'd do well on her tests and the project, despite his earlier doubts. They would crisscross the country on this adventure, come back to Kellersburg, and go their separate ways. The thought made him sad, but every time he thought about a different ending, the conversation with her father streamed through Zach's mind.

***

The airport buzzed with activity. People scurried here and there pushing or pulling their wheeled luggage with them or stood in line to check in for their flights. Maisey stood behind Zach as he put his information into the kiosk. She watched everything he did so she could imitate it when he finished.

"Your turn." Zach stepped aside.

"Okay." Maisey stepped up to the kiosk.

As she stared at the screen, she told herself the process looked easy enough. Maisey put in her information while Zach waited. Phil and the film crew had already checked in and were waiting at the gate. She and Zach would've been with them, except her parents had insisted on taking them to the airport. Maisey hated feeling like a little kid whose parents had to see her off, but she knew they meant well.

She tried to act like she knew what she was doing, even though it had been over five years since the one and only time she'd flown on an airplane. In a minute the kiosk spit out her boarding pass, and she and Zach took their luggage to the agent waiting at the first-class station. First class. Would this spoil her for all future flying?

Zach helped her put her suitcase on the scale. "You did great! Under the weight limit."

Maisey made a face at him. "Was there any doubt after all the instructions I got?"

Zach laughed as they took their luggage tags and headed to where her parents stood. Maisey hugged her mom and dad.

"Have a wonderful time." Annette hugged Maisey tighter. "Be sure to call us every day and tell us about your adventure."

Maisey stepped out of her mother's embrace. "I can't promise I'll call every day. I don't know what kind of time I'll have."

"You can call right before you go to bed each night."

"Even if it's two in the morning?"

"I hope you're not planning to stay up till two in the morning."

"The time change, Mom."

"Oh yeah. I forgot about that." Annette shook her head. "If it's a reasonable time."

Maisey chuckled. "I'll try to call as often as I can."

Zach gave Annette a quick hug and shook Bryant's hand. "I'll take good care of her like you asked, sir."

"Really, Dad?" Maisey gave her dad an annoyed look. "You asked him to take care of me like I'm twelve instead of twenty-one? I'm a grown up. I can take care of myself."

Zach grimaced. "I probably shouldn't have phrased it that way. Your dad knows you're capable of taking care of yourself, but it's always nice to have someone along for those times when you're not sure about something. It happens to all of us when we're in a strange place."

"Okay. I'm sure a friendly face is a bonus when you're someplace new."

"And Zach is definitely a friend." Her dad's gaze flitted between her and Zach.

"He is." Maisey noticed a subtle message in the look her dad gave Zach. Was her dad still trying to gain Zach as her protector?

"We'd better head to security. You never know how long that will take." Zach motioned toward the line of people.

"Have fun." Annette waved.

"Be good." Bryant saluted.

"Love you!" Maisey waved. "I'll definitely call when we get to Chicago."

"We'll be waiting to hear from you." Annette waved both hands.

Maisey turned and didn't look back. She was sure her mother had tears in her eyes. Maisey looked at Zach as they stood in the line for security. "Sorry about my parents."

Zach smiled. "No problem. They love you and want the best for you."

"I know, but I don't need to be treated like a kid."

"I won't treat you like one."

Maisey widened her gaze. "You'd better not."

Zach's eyes crinkled at the corners. "I'll try very hard."

Did he have to try hard not to think of her as a kid? Did he only remember her as the little girl with the skinned knees? The thought punched a hole in her ego. She wanted him to see her as a woman, not the little girl he used to babysit.

They got through security in a short time, even though the whole thing made her a little nervous. Did TSA agents recognize an infrequent flier? After this trip, she'd be a frequent flier and a seasoned traveler and know the ins and outs of airports across the nation. Her big adventure was about to begin.

When Maisey and Zach arrived at the gate, Phil hurried over to them. "I was about to give you a call to find out what was keeping you."

"Maisey's parents had to say goodbye," Zach said.

Phil gave her an indulgent smile. "I should've remembered what it was like to send your child off. They were probably like me when I took my daughter to college. It wasn't easy leaving her there."

"Speaking of college, I forgot to ask how those exams went." Phil raised his eyebrows.

Maisey shrugged. "I think I did okay. I won't know my grade for a few days."

"I'm sure she did great." Zach grinned. "After all, I helped her study."

"I'm sure that made all the difference." Maisey laughed.

"Of course it did." Zach produced fake annoyance. "You're discounting my excellence as a study partner."

"No. I just don't want you to get a big head."

"Not to worry. Phil will step in to cut it down to size." Zach gave Phil a knowing look.

"That's right." Phil pointed at Zach. "I keep this guy in line."

"He does, and I appreciate it."

Zach's serious expression made Maisey wonder what was behind that exchange. Sometimes she had the feeling that something in Zach's past made him sad. Was it his injury or something else? What would she learn about him on this trip? Would she get to know the real Zach instead of the persona behind a famous football player?

Phil waved a finger in the air. "Now listen up. When we get to the airport, a limo will pick us up and take us to the hotel. After we check in, we have only a few minutes before we're scheduled to get the wardrobe for the shoot the next day."

"Got that?" Zach asked.

Maisey nodded, thinking this was definitely the time when Zach's friendly face would come in handy. Her mind buzzed with the whirlwind pace.

"Great! Our flight is about an hour and a half. We gain an hour, so remember to set your watches back if they don't automatically change like your phone." Phil tapped the watch on his wrist. "We're going to be in a lot of different time zones, so we have to make sure we've got the right time. Now I've got to make a phone call before we board."

"Is it always like this?" Maisey looked at Zach and smacked the side of her hand into the palm of the other. "It's like, chop, chop, chop."

Zach laughed. "You'll get used to Phil and his pace. There's never a dull moment. He loves unscripted, so you better get used to that, too. But you'll grow to love the man. He's one of a kind."

Maisey nodded, thinking that was what she thought about Zach. He was one of a kind, and she didn't have to grow to love him. She already did. At least she was in love with the image of him she had created in her mind over the years. Could he live up to that image?

Besides, was it wise to entertain such thoughts? Probably not. They would only lead to heartbreak. Why would a famous football player have any interest in an ordinary girl from his hometown when he'd dated actresses, models, and tall, gorgeous female athletes?

He wouldn't.

Unscripted. The word burned a hole in her thoughts. These feelings for Zach were certainly unscripted. Maybe she should put her thoughts and plans before the Lord. Maybe? For certain, but she didn't know what to pray for. Guidance? That was a good thing for now. God's plans were the best, but it wasn't always easy to know His plans or follow that path, especially when her heart yearned for something out of her reach.

Maisey let out a heavy sigh. She should be thinking about puppies and sweet children, not the yearnings of her foolish heart.

"That sigh sounded ominous. Is it that bad?"

So glad Zach didn't read minds, Maisey looked wide eyed at him. "Just a little nervous about what lies ahead."

"Specifically?"

Maisey took a deep breath. Specifically couldn't and wouldn't include Zach. "Flying, for one thing."

"I'll hold your hand if you want."

"No, that's okay." Maisey shook her head. "That wouldn't help. You might lose the circulation in your hand if you did that."

Zach chuckled, but his eyes weren't laughing. Had she offended him? Was he looking at himself as the protector her father had asked Zach to be?

"We wouldn't want that to happen."

Before Maisey could respond, the gate agent announced the boarding of first-class passengers.

Zach stood. "That's us. Let's go."

With her large purse slung over her shoulder, Maisey handed the gate agent her boarding pass. She walked into the Jetway with a sense of anticipation and dread. A window seat awaited her, but what else? She sent up a silent prayer. *God, please give me wisdom and guidance to navigate the weeks ahead.*

CHAPTER SEVEN

Cold didn't begin to describe the weather in Chicago. Zach hunched deeper into his jacket, which didn't quite cut the brutal wind. The tip of Maisey's cute little nose was red as she gazed at the lights along the Magnificent Mile. Just as he'd anticipated, the lights shone in her eyes. He loved the joy on her face. The weather was cold, but the Christmas lights were bright.

"You warm enough?" Zach peered at her.

Nodding, Maisey put hands on either side of her head as she tugged her stocking cap farther down. She pulled the knit scarf closer around her neck. "Warm enough, thanks to these new clothes. I'm especially thankful for these fur-lined boots." She stuck a foot out in front of her. "I see Phil's wisdom in getting clothes for each location."

"You'll find the man has thought of every detail." Except how Zach was falling for this sweet young woman, even though he'd warned himself a hundred times not to do it.

Maisey was helping him out in that regard. She showed little interest in him. She was friendly but distant. He should be thankful.

Maisey put a gloved finger in the air. "Except one thing. He didn't order better weather."

Zach laughed. "Phil can manage a lot of things,

but weather isn't one of them. Let's duck into a store to warm up."

"We've barely left the hotel." She gave him a curious stare. "Are you cold already?"

"I thought you were." Zach was tempted to touch the tip of her red nose or rub a thumb across her pink cheeks, but he stuffed his gloved hands into his pockets.

"We'll warm up while we walk over to the Christkindlmarket."

"If you say so."

"I do." She gave him an impish smile. "If we walk fast, we'll warm up quickly, and we'll get there sooner."

Maisey's smile warmed his heart. He wasn't as cold anymore. She was such a change from all the other women he'd dated. Fresh and unspoiled. He didn't want to ruin that.

"Let's get a move on, and we'll stay warm." Maisey charged ahead.

Zach lengthened his stride to catch her. "Are you ready to meet our first winner?"

"Yes. I'm so excited to see his reaction when he gets his guide dog." Maisey put her gloved hands together in a prayerful pose. "I can't imagine what it's liked to be blind. And I loved his letter. It must have been hard to choose all the winners."

Zach let out a soft whistle. "For sure. Phil had us poring over letters and more letters until we had it narrowed down to fifty. Then we had to pick out just twelve from those."

"And that was all filmed?"

Zach nodded. "They even filmed the

disagreements we had over who should be the winners. I'm not sure that will make it into the documentary, but it was captured on film."

"From what I've read about the winners, I think you all made very good choices."

"Yeah, but there were a lot of good ones to choose from. That was the problem."

"Choices. That's what your whole life is. Making choices, and those choices have consequences, so we have to choose wisely."

"Such a profound statement." Zach thought of the wrong choices he'd made. He was trying to make the right choices now. "And how do you choose wisely?"

Maisey's breath formed little clouds as they strode along the sidewalk. "You pray."

"And you get answers?"

"I have to believe you do." A little pucker formed between her eyebrows as she looked at him. "Like the decision to take this job. It wasn't easy, but I had to believe that God guided me to say yes when everything I asked Phil to do came about."

"Are there times when you don't see an answer from God?"

Maisey narrowed her gaze. "You don't seem too sure that God gives answers. Why is that?"

Was this confession time? What would Maisey think if she knew the truth about him? He looked down at the sidewalk until they got to the corner and had to stop for a red light. He looked her way to find expectation in her expression. "Do you want to know the truth?"

"Are you trying to tell me you no longer believe in God?" Maisey's eyes widened.

"No." His heart sank that she would think such a thing, but then he'd lived like he no longer believed in God. Had she seen that? Had she read the tabloids? "I've always believed in God, but I've done things that don't square with that belief."

"We all do that."

"Not on a regular basis." Zach shook his head. "I let fame and fortune lead me in the wrong direction. That's why I'm trying to make up for that now by doing this thing with Phil."

The light changed and they crossed the street, but Maisey didn't respond. Did she think less of him? It shouldn't matter. He was trying to do the right things now—not to impress anyone, but to atone for the wrong he'd done.

When they reached the other side of the street, Maisey stopped at the curb. "You know you can't earn your salvation or God's love. He loves us despite our sin." She waved a hand in the air. "All of this stuff you're doing is good, but it doesn't make up for anything. All you have to do is ask God to forgive you, and it's done. He says if we confess our sins, He will forgive us."

"Yeah, but isn't there repentance in there, too?"

Maisey started walking again. "There is, but you can't look at it as earning your way back into God's grace. Grace is free."

"I knew that at one time, but my life had gotten so far from God that I felt the need to do good things to make up for the rotten stuff I've done."

"I suppose we all fall into that thinking from time to time."

Zach smiled. "Don't try to be nice just because

I've messed up my life."

"I don't know. Your life doesn't seem all that messed up to me."

Zach resisted the urge to put an arm around her shoulders and pull her close. She was just what he needed, but he wasn't what she needed. She should have a guy who hadn't done all the wrong things that he'd done. "Things are on the mend physically and spiritually for me, but I still dream of the crushing blow that splintered my leg. Do you think that was God's way of giving me a wake-up call?"

"You have to find that out for yourself." Maisey shrugged. "I think we have to look at everything that happens in our lives as something God can use. The good and the bad."

"Thanks for reminding me of that. Thanks for the little sermon."

Dismay painted Maisey's face. "I didn't mean to preach at you."

Zach let out a sorry chuckle as he shook his head. "Bad choice of words. You weren't preaching. You just reminded me of things I should remember about God. I appreciate the reminders."

"I just don't want to get on your bad side since we have to work together."

"You're good with me." Better than good. She was a bright spot in the darkness that he was climbing out of. Her goodness made him want to be better than he'd ever been before. "Now let's think about the good stuff like the food we can get at the market."

"Have you been here before?"

"I was here several years ago." He'd been here with one of his many girlfriends. He couldn't remember which one. He didn't want to think about that time. He wanted to think about now and the fresh start he was determined to make. The one he'd been working on since he'd gone to work for Phil.

"Was the food your favorite part?"

"Can't say for sure." He couldn't confess that he'd probably had too many beers to remember clearly. "This will be a new experience that I'll remember. The one thing I do know is the market is very much like the German Christmas markets I went to with my parents when they lived in Germany."

Maisey's hands made a muted sound as she clapped them together. "I want to get my mom and my grams Christmas ornaments."

"I do remember there are plenty of those."

Maisey pointed ahead. "I see the big Chicago Christmas tree. The market is supposed to be right there by the tree."

"It is. We're almost there." Zach had to keep himself from grabbing her hand and running to the market.

When they reached Daley Plaza, they headed for the rows and rows of huts where they could find food, ornaments, and other Christmas gifts. They followed the lines of people through the different huts. Maisey oohed and aahed over the spectacular ornaments and other Christmas items.

"I don't know which ones to choose. They're all so beautiful. And there are chocolates and teas. Maybe I should get some of both." Maisey sighed. "Can you help me?"

"You know your mother and grandmother way better than I do." Zach smiled down at her. "You have to choose. Maybe we should grab something to eat while you think it over."

"All you think about is food."

"Not true." He was thinking about her. Thinking about her way too much.

It was all Phil's fault. He had insisted Zach do the tourist thing with Maisey. If he didn't know better, he'd think the old guy was trying to be a matchmaker. That wasn't the case, because Phil had advised Zach to steer clear of women for a while. That had been good advice.

"Since you're the food guy, what do you recommend?"

"Maybe some bratwurst. Let's see what we can find."

Zach and Maisey wandered through the market looking at the food choices. They finally settled on a dish with brats and sauerkraut. After they finished eating that, they moseyed through more huts. Zach wondered whether Maisey would ever make a decision. He had discovered that she was a deliberate decision maker. Unlike Phil, who could change course in seconds, Maisey thought everything through and weighed every option. Things could get interesting with those opposing dynamics.

"What do you think? Should we get hot chocolate and gingerbread while you mull over your gift choices?"

"More food?"

Zach chuckled. "Yes, because I know you have a sweet tooth."

"And how do you know that?" Maisey placed her hands on her hips as she eyed him.

"Because you've never turned down dessert any time it's been offered, and your grams told me at dinner on Sunday she always gets you a box of your favorite chocolates for Christmas every year."

"Grams does get me those chocolates every year, but I never thought of myself as having a sweet tooth, but maybe you're right." Maisey shrugged.

"There are good chocolates in the market. We should get some for our travels."

Maisey nodded. "Sounds to me like you're the one with the sweet tooth. Cake. Chocolates. Gingerbread."

"Yeah. Let's get that." Zach motioned toward the vendor with the hot chocolate and gingerbread.

Zach let Maisey ahead of him as they stood in line. The temptation to put his arms around her and pull her close against him made him step back. How often was this going to happen to him? He didn't want to know the answer to the question.

As they were handed their hot chocolate, Maisey picked out a heart-shaped gingerbread with German words scrawled across it. "Do you have any idea what this says?"

"I think it means 'you are the best.'" Zach thought the words suited Maisey.

"Do you know that from your time in Germany with your folks?"

"Yeah, they had these gingerbreads all over Germany."

Maisey munched on her gingerbread and took a sip of her hot chocolate, then looked up at him. "I've decided to get my mom the nativity scene ornament and my grams the star ornament."

"Good choices." Zach motioned toward the huts.

"Do you remember where they are?"

Maisey made a face. "Not really, but we can wander through until we find them."

"Lead the way."

They made their way through the huts until Maisey found the items. While she paid for the ornaments, Zach secretly bought her Belgian chocolates and a little angel ornament he'd seen her admire earlier. Maybe it was a mistake to buy something for her, but he couldn't shake his affection for her. So he would quit fighting it.

If he planned to win Maisey's heart, he had to do it in such a way that he would also win the approval of Maisey's dad. That was no easy task, but he was up for the challenge.

***

The following afternoon, Phil looked at Maisey and motioned to the chairs lined up in the room with the light-blue concrete block walls, where the meeting between their winner and his new dog would take place. "Are you ready to do the interview?"

"As ready as I can be." Maisey took a deep breath and tried to smile. Her new deep-pink sweater and winter-white pants made her feel confident despite the butterflies in her stomach. She didn't know if the upcoming meeting or Zach, dressed in a black turtleneck and blazer, created the fluttering in her midsection. She just had to deal with it and not let it interfere with doing a good job.

She didn't want Phil to know this interview idea wasn't something she had expected or wanted to do.

Zach had warned her that Phil did things unexpectedly. On the way to the facility this afternoon, he'd texted her and Zach a list of questions to ask the boy who would receive the dog, as well as his parents and the owner of the facility that had trained the dog.

Phone in hand, Maisey looked at the list again and tried to imagine being an interviewer. She had expected to be a background person during this adventure, except for the song she would sing, but instead she would be front and center with Zach and Phil. She didn't feel ready for the spotlight, but here she was.

While they waited, a casually dressed man with a golden retriever wearing a special harness entered the room.

"What a beautiful dog." Maisey looked at Phil. "Is it okay to pet him?"

"Ask his handler." Phil nodded toward the man who was now talking with Zach.

Maisey approached the two men. "May I pet the dog?"

The man smiled. "You must be Maisey."

"I am." She held her breath and hoped asking to pet the dog wasn't a faux pas.

"I'm happy to meet you. I'm Russ Bolton. We're excited about the interview." Russ looked down at the dog. "This is Brody, and you're welcome to pet him. He's not working now, so it's okay. When guide dogs are working, you shouldn't pet them unless the handler says it's okay."

Maisey hunkered down next to Brody and offered her hand. He sniffed. She petted. He wagged his tail.

She had made a fast friend. "Such a sweet dog."

"He is. He's going to make our young friend a very good guide dog." Phil patted the dog's head. "Let's gather around and say a prayer for our winner and for the success of this first interview session."

The small group gathered around Phil and bowed their heads. Phil's prayer made Maisey realize that this wasn't just about a documentary or dog food or a famous football player. This project highlighted how helping people made the world a better place.

Maisey joined in the final amen. "Show time is getting close."

Phil nodded. "We need to get everyone in place. Zach, our winner is about to arrive. Please take Russ and Brody to the room down the hall."

"Sure." Zach looked over at Russ, then back at Phil. "Will you give them the signal when to come back?"

"Yes, I'll give you the signal. We'll bring the dog back in when we're ready to tell the boy he's getting a guide dog. His parents know, but he doesn't."

As Zach led Russ and Brody away, an excited pressure built in Maisey's chest over the anticipated meeting between the winner and this handsome dog. The dog had a confident bearing, as if he knew he had an important job to do in the future. When Zach returned, he stood next to Maisey, and the excited pressure exploded as her heart raced.

Maisey's mind filled with memories of the night before. Zach had been the perfect guide as they'd strode down the Magnificent Mile and meandered through the shops at the Christmas market. The only downside was having him treat her like a little sister.

Could he ever see her as a grown-up?

She'd been tempted to buy him an ornament at the market, but that was silly thinking. He had everything he needed and more, and what would he think if she bought him something? Besides, he didn't put up a Christmas tree.

Maisey shook away the memories as a couple and a young boy, who looked about ten years old, entered the room. Phil immediately went to greet them, then waved Maisey and Zach over.

"Maisey, I want you to meet Allison and Sean McKnight and their son, Cole."

Maisey shook hands with the parents. "We're excited to have you here."

"Thanks. We're excited too and looking forward to our interview." Allison turned to Cole. "Cole, this is Maisey Norberg, the lady who is going to interview us and tell your story for the documentary."

Cole nodded. "Thank you."

"Cole, I'd like you to meet my interview partner, Zach Dawson."

Maisey thought the boy might recognize Zach's name, but it didn't seem to make an impression. Since Cole couldn't watch football, he probably had no idea he was talking with a famous quarterback. What would it be like not to be able to watch TV or see the world around you? Maisey couldn't imagine. She thanked the Lord for the gift of sight. This experience would not only allow her to see places she had never been, but it would make her appreciate all the blessings she had, especially the ability to see her surroundings.

After everyone was settled in their chairs, Phil

gave the go ahead to the camera crew to start filming. He took the microphone and introduced himself and everyone else. Then he turned the program over to Zach, who started the interview process with Cole. Zach made Cole comfortable and had him talking about his life. Maisey marveled at his skill in bringing the young man out of his shell, even making him laugh. Zach performed like a seasoned interviewer. Maisey only hoped to do half as well. That would be a victory in her book.

After Zach finished talking to Cole, he gave Maisey the stage as she asked Allison and Sean about their hopes for Cole's future. They talked about his school accomplishments despite his blindness, how he had learned Braille and had read as many books in Braille as he could find. They also mentioned how much audio books had helped him.

As Maisey came to her last question, she sent Allison and Sean a knowing look. Phil gave Russ, who was standing in the hallway, the signal to come into the room. Maisey handed Cole a heavy-duty piece of paper. "Cole, I'd like for you to show us how you read Braille. Please read aloud what's written on this paper."

Cole placed both hands on the paper that sat in his lap. "Cole, you are the first winner in the Master's Dog Food giveaway." Wonder shone in Cole's expression, and his fingers stopped moving. "Really? I'm really getting a dog?"

"Yes." Maisey blinked back the tears of joy. She couldn't cry in front of the camera. "Please finish reading."

"Master's Dog Food will give you a lifetime

supply of dog food and the special guide dog training, as well as all the supplies you need to get started with your new guide dog." Cole let the paper fall to the floor as his parents hugged him.

Maisey looked over at Zach and hoped he'd take over so she didn't blubber all over the place. He got the message, almost as if he was completely tuned in to her needs.

Zach stood. "Cole, it's time for you to meet your new partner, Brody."

Russ brought Brody to Cole. Boy and dog met as Russ aided Cole with the harness. After Cole and Brody walked around the room with Russ's help, Cole returned to his seat. Zach interviewed Russ with questions about the guide dog training that Cole would receive at their facilities.

After the interview with Russ, Phil once again took over as he explained how a camera crew would follow Cole to his training. "We want more people to understand what's involved in owning a guide dog."

Handshakes, hugs, and happiness filled the room while the cameras still rolled. Russ removed the harness and let Brody mingle with the group. Cole gave the dog a hug, and Maisey pressed her lips together and blinked like crazy to keep the tears from coming. This was a happy day, and there were more like it to come. She looked heavenward. *Thank You, Lord, for allowing me to be part of this.*

As she ended her silent prayer of thanks, Zach moseyed over to her. "Looks like someone I know might have had a hard time keeping the tears at bay."

Maisey tried to frown, but a smile escaped. "I cry easily, so keeping those sobs from escaping was a huge victory. Happy stuff makes me cry."

"I don't think Phil would care if you shed a tear or two. It's part of the human-interest story here."

Maisey shrugged. "I didn't think the interviewer should cry."

Zach patted her shoulder. "It's okay. You can cry whenever you want."

A lump rose in Maisey's throat, and her heart sank to her stomach. Zach had touched her. She had to get ahold of herself before she melted into a puddle on the floor. Not really, but her weak knees made her think it could happen. Did he have any clue how his touch affected her? She hoped not. That would not be good for the business atmosphere she wanted to have around Zach. If only she could control her heart palpitations as well as she could control her tears.

"Excellent job today, guys!" Phil gave Zach and Maisey high fives. "We got some good stuff today. Great kickoff for this project."

"Thanks." Zach gestured toward the McKnights as Cole played with Brody. "That's one happy boy."

"That's one happy family," Phil added. "Should we grab a bite to eat to celebrate our first success?"

"Zach's always up for food." Maisey looked at him with an impish smile.

Zach gave her a wry grin. "Always. How about Italian?"

"I'm good with whatever," Maisey said.

"Fine with me. I'll get our ride." Phil swiped his phone.

Minutes later they arrived at an Italian restaurant near their hotel. The only Italian food Maisey had ever eaten was spaghetti, and that probably wasn't really

Italian, because the sauce was always from a jar. The only restaurants in Kellersburg that came close to Italian were the pizza places, but she wasn't sure pizza qualified as true Italian either. She didn't plan to let on about her dismal record when it came to Italian cuisine.

"What are you ordering?" Zach looked at her over the top of his menu.

"Oh, I haven't decided yet. There are so many choices." She wouldn't dare order spaghetti, or could she? What if she ordered something she didn't like? "What would you suggest since you're the one who picked this place?"

"Do you like seafood?"

Maisey made a face. "Not that much. I grew up in a family where we ate mostly meat and potatoes."

"Me, too, but my food choices expanded a lot after I graduated from college." Zach eyed her. "How about if I order for you, and I'll order something else. We can share."

Be adventuresome, Maisey. "Sure."

"Good." Zach glanced at Phil. "You want to join in our sharing?"

"Absolutely. That way we can get a sample of several dishes. I like the way you think." Phil set his menu on the table. "Zach can order everything for us."

When the waiter came to take their order, Zach rattled off a variety of dishes, including an appetizer, a pasta dish, a seafood dish, and a veal dish. Maisey hoped she would like at least one thing on the list.

After the waiter left, Phil tapped his water glass with a spoon. "Thanks for a great job today. We have a busy schedule for the next few weeks. Tomorrow is no exception. We have an early flight, so the limo will be picking us up around six thirty. Be down in the lobby at six fifteen."

Maisey nodded. "Will we have a lot of other early mornings?"

"I'm not sure. I haven't memorized the schedule, but you can always look at your itinerary." Phil tapped his phone. "You should find it there."

"Yeah. I wasn't thinking." Maisey wished she hadn't asked the question. Zach probably thought she was a dunderhead, but then she shouldn't care what he thought. But she did. Way too much.

"So we're headed to Rapid City tomorrow. That will be a big change from Chicago." Zach picked up his water glass and took a gulp.

Phil nodded. "Yes, it will. Have either of you been to Mount Rushmore?"

"No, but I've seen plenty of photos of it." Maisey looked over at Zach. "Have you?"

Zach shook his head. "They don't play pro football in Rapid City, so it was never on my travel agenda."

Maisey leaned forward in her chair. "Will we get to see it?"

"You should have time tomorrow after we arrive to do some sightseeing." Phil picked up his phone from the table. "I'll be making the final checks for our meeting tomorrow, so you kids can go off and have fun. I've seen Mount Rushmore several times. It's a magnificent sight. And you should check out the Crazy Horse Memorial as well."

"Thanks for the opportunity to sightsee." Maisey glanced at Phil and wondered about the twinkle in his eyes.

"I want you to use your free time to learn about the places we visit." Phil tapped his phone. "Now I want to introduce you to our winner for tomorrow." He held his phone out so Zach and Maisey could see the photo there. "Our winner's name is Dakota Vance. And here's the drawing she sent us."

"That's amazing. She's quite an artist." Maisey reached for the phone to get a better look.

Zach studied the phone with her. "So she sent you a drawing of the kind of dog she wants. A fluffy gray-and-white dog."

Phil took the phone back and scrolled, then turned the phone so Zach and Maisey could once again see it. "And here's her puppy from the shelter."

"Wow! It's almost an exact match. How did you manage that?" Maisey widened her gaze.

"Prayer and lots of contact with the local animal shelter." Phil laid his phone on the table. "After we chose Dakota as one of the winners, I sent a copy of the drawing to the shelter and asked them to be on the lookout for a dog that could come as close as possible to that picture. Then we prayed. We prayed for all of our winners."

Maisey turned to Zach. "You were in on these prayers?"

Zach nodded. "All of us were, but this is the first I've heard about this puppy."

"That's because the lady at the shelter left a message and this photo this morning, and I haven't had a chance to share until now."

"So before today you didn't have this dog lined up for Dakota?" Maisey raised her eyebrows.

Phil shook his head. "We had chosen another dog we thought would suit."

"Does Dakota have a story we're planning to share?" Maisey asked.

"She does. She was born with a heart defect, tricuspid atresia. She's had several surgeries in her young life. She's now eight and doing as well as can be expected. We will interview her parents. I'll have an interview with her doctors at another time." Phil nodded. "This journey will bring us into contact with all kinds of kids and the people who have helped them."

Maisey nodded in return. "Thanks for asking me to be a part of this. I didn't know what to expect for sure, but just these first few days have been an eye opener."

Phil patted Maisey's arm. "You are very welcome. We're so glad you decided to join us."

The waiter appeared and placed a large plate of something on the table. Maisey wasn't sure what it was, and she didn't know if she'd sound stupid if she asked.

"Let's give thanks for our food." Phil held out his hands.

Maisey took Phil's hand, then looked at Zach, who held out a hand to her. She braced herself for a reaction as she put her hand in Zach's and bowed her head. Her pulse zinged at his touch, and she had a hard time concentrating on Phil's prayer.

If only her childhood fantasies about Zach could come true. She knew him, but did she really? He wasn't the boy whose family had spent hours with her family. He was a grown man with experiences far beyond her scope.

She'd told herself at the beginning of this project that she didn't want to be one of those women who threw themselves at him. If she let her attraction to him prevail, would she become one of those women? Was she brave enough to find out what could be between them?

Prayer. She'd told Zach to pray. She should follow her own advice. Not knowing what to pray for made her hesitant to do so. Their interaction over the coming days could give her an answer. What did God want for her? *Lord, please show me Your will for my life.*

"Amen." Phil gave her hand a squeeze as he ended the prayer.

Maisey dropped Zach's hand like a hot potato. She had no idea what Phil had said in his prayer. She'd been lost in her own thoughts. How bad was that?

"Okay, are you ready to try this calamari?" Zach looked her way.

"Sure." Maisey had no idea what calamari was, but she would try it. She held out the small appetizer plate and let Zach drop a few spoonsful on it.

Maisey waited to try the calamari until Phil and Zach had put a dollop of sauce on their plates. She stared at the sauce. To sauce or not to sauce? How did she know? *Be brave, Maisey.*

"I'll take some of that sauce." Maybe it would cover the taste if she didn't like the calamari. Or it could make it worse.

Maisey stabbed a golden-brown piece of the stuff sitting before her with a fork and dragged the calamari through the sauce. She popped it into her mouth and hoped she wouldn't feel like spitting it out. She chewed. Oh, it was good. Really good. Her culinary experiences were expanding.

"So how's the calamari?" Zach looked her way.

"Very good." Did he suspect that she'd never had it before? Yeah, he probably looked at her as a country bumpkin, unsophisticated compared to the other women he'd had in his life. She was crazy for even entertaining the idea that he might be interested in her.

After they polished off the calamari, the waiter reappeared with the other dishes Zach had ordered. Maisey tried some of them all. She wasn't fond of the seafood dish, but at least she'd tried it. The ravioli was amazing, and the veal parmigiana was so good, she was sorry she had to share.

Maisey finished her food and placed her fork on her plate. "So good. Zach, thanks for ordering the perfect combination of dishes."

"You're welcome." His hazel eyes studied her. "What was your favorite?"

"The veal, then the ravioli. The seafood was okay, but not my favorite." Maisey scrunched up her napkin in her lap.

"I'm glad your least favorite was the seafood because that meant there was more for me." Phil folded his napkin next to his plate. "We'll get the check and be on our way. We have an early start to our day tomorrow."

Maisey stood. "While you're waiting on the check, I'm going to use the restroom."

She hurried across the restaurant toward the ladies' room. After using the facilities, she washed her hands and gazed in the mirror. Her cheeks were flushed, and she couldn't help thinking she looked like one of those girls in the movies who came clueless to the big city. But wasn't that what she was? Why would Zach Dawson even give her a second look?

Back to the hotel, Maisey said good night to Phil and Zach as she went into her room. She got ready for bed and thought about Zach. The debate she constantly had with herself about him made her wish she had the confidence to go after him. No. She didn't want to be one of those women who chased after him. She wanted him to chase after her. Fat chance that would happen.

She plopped onto the bed and lay back as she stared at the ceiling. What would it take for him to see her as someone more than little Maisey Norberg? She closed her eyes against the question she'd asked herself too many times. *Stop! Just stop!*

A knock sounded on the door. Her heart jumped into her throat as she approached the door. Who could this be? She gazed through the peephole. A distorted figure of a man in a suit stood outside her door. Was it safe to answer? She slipped the chain into its slot and opened the door a crack.

"May I help you?"

"I have a delivery for you."

Maisey still wasn't sure it was safe to open the door farther, but she read the name tag on his lapel. Mario "What kind of delivery and from whom?"

The man held up a paper bag. "From Zach Dawson."

"Oh, okay." As she opened the door enough to

take the bag, she hoped the man was being honest.

The man handed her the bag. "You're welcome. Enjoy the rest of your evening."

"Thanks." Maisey was pretty sure she should tip this man, but she had no change in her purse. So she quietly closed the door. Maybe she could leave a tip for Mario at the front desk in the morning.

Maisey carried the bag across the room and sat on the edge of the bed. What could Zach be sending her? She unfolded the top of the bag and looked inside. A folded piece of paper sat on top of a white cardboard container. She plucked the paper out of the bag and opened it.

I took the opportunity to order a dessert for you when you went to the ladies' room. A sweet for the sweet. Enjoy the cannoli. Thanks for making us look good today. Sweet dreams. Zach

Maisey's heart melted. Did Zach really think she was sweet? And what did that mean anyway? In his mind was she the sweet little girl from down the street? Sweet. Maybe that designation didn't mean a thing. It was only a saying, or it could be how he viewed her. Sweet and naïve.

Quit analyzing and enjoy your treat. Maisey pulled the carton from the bag and opened it. Looking decadently delicious, the cannoli lay in the carton. Crisp pastry dough covered in some kind of nuts called to her. She'd never had a cannoli. She lifted it out of the carton and took a bite. The flavor of sweet cheese and chocolate chips filled her mouth. Amazing. If she ate the whole thing, she might get sick from the rich dessert. She would eat more in the morning, or maybe save it for the flight to Rapid City.

Could she get it through security?

As Maisey put the cannoli back into the carton and set it on the nearby desk next to her purse, she glanced at Zach's scrawled handwriting on the note. He'd wished her sweet dreams. What would he say if he knew her dreams were about him?

Thank You, Lord, for the new things I've experienced. Give us safety as we travel, and bless Phil's work. And, Lord, please help me to know what to do with the feelings I have for Zach. Amen.

CHAPTER EIGHT

Blue sky served as a backdrop for the faces of the four US presidents carved into the granite on Mount Rushmore. Sunshine brightened the chilly day, and Maisey's presence warmed Zach's heart. He watched her expression of awe as she took photos with her phone.

"This is amazing. The pictures I've seen don't compare to the real thing." She turned to him, the awe still present in her eyes that matched the sky. "Take a photo of me with them in the background."

"Sure." Zach took her phone and snapped several photos.

She smiled for the camera, and his heart did a little dance. She'd thanked him profusely for the cannoli, but she hadn't said anything about his note. He wasn't used to failing when it came to women, but he should've realized Maisey wasn't just any woman.

He didn't know how to deal with a woman who didn't fall all over herself to impress him. He had tried to impress her, but to no avail. She treated him like an older brother. She'd even shared her leftover cannoli with him on the plane. He hadn't wanted to get involved with her, and she was helping him with that every step of the way.

Why couldn't he take Phil's advice and forget women for a while? He'd intended to do that, until he'd encountered Maisey. She was sweet, funny, and kind, unlike the other women who had come and gone from his life.

Maybe he should talk to Phil. No. That would be a big mistake. Phil didn't need to know what was going through Zach's mind. He had to figure this out for himself.

The thoughts thundered through his mind like a herd of buffaloes while he took the photos. Peace escaped him.

"Thanks." She reached for her phone.

"Not so fast." Zach stepped beside her and held the phone at a distance. "A selfie with the two of us."

Zach looked at the three photos he'd taken. "We look good. Send me these."

"Sure." She took the phone and slipped it into her coat pocket.

"Ready to check out the Crazy Horse Memorial?"

"I want to get a souvenir first."

Zach gestured toward the building. "To the gift shop it is."

He stood around while Maisey perused every aisle and shelf in the place. He was tempted to buy her something, but he'd already bought the stuff from the Christmas market. He hadn't given that to her yet. He couldn't win her heart with gifts, not even a sweet cannoli.

"All set." She bounded up to him with a smile.

"Do I dare ask what you bought?"

She opened her bag and pulled out a couple more Christmas ornaments, one a replica of the carving on the mountain. "The perfect souvenir."

Zach smiled. "If you say so."

"Of course it is." Maisey wrinkled her brow as she replaced the ornament. "No souvenir for you?"

Zach shook his head. "I'm not a souvenir kind of guy."

"They have food."

Zach laughed out loud. "Food does not count as a souvenir, because you eat it and then it's gone, never to be seen again."

"You can save the container."

"I'll pass." He laughed again. "Are you ready to see Crazy Horse?"

"Lead the way."

On the forty-minute drive to the Crazy Horse Memorial, Maisey read on her phone. Zach wanted to ask what she was reading, but he didn't want to sound nosy. It was none of his business.

"This is interesting stuff." She waved her phone. "I don't know how to say this guy's name, Korczak Ziolkowski. I probably murdered the pronunciation, but he's the sculptor that Henry Standing Bear got to do the memorial. Standing Bear insisted that the memorial be done in the Black Hills because it's sacred to the Lakota people. And Standing Bear was a cousin of Crazy Horse. The first blast on the mountain was on June 3, 1948. History is so amazing."

"If you say so. I never cared much for history." Zach gave her a sideways glance but quickly returned his eyes to the tree-lined curving road.

"You should like history. You can learn so much from it."

Zach nodded. "You're probably right, but it's a little late for me to take up the study of history."

"Never too late to read a good history book."

"Can you recommend one?"

"I'm sure we can find one at the bookstore."

"And just exactly what history would you have me study?"

"You could start with the history surrounding the memorial."

"You could get the book and read to me."

"Like your own personal audio book?"

Laughing, Zach shook his head. "Are you trying to make me study just because you had to study?"

"No. You should never quit learning."

"You're right, but I'd like to learn something that interests me, and history isn't that thing."

"What interests you?"

You. He almost said it out loud, but he managed to capture the word before it came out of his mouth. "Good question?"

"That's what they always say when they don't have an answer right away."

Zach held up one finger. "Give me a minute and I'll have an answer for you."

"I'm going to time you." Maisey set the timer on her phone. "One minute from now."

The pressure of being timed made things worse. Nothing would happen if he didn't have an answer in a minute, but his mind froze on one subject. Maisey. Hadn't he decided he would pursue her? But he'd come out of the gate in such a clumsy fashion that he had second thoughts. He had a bad track record with women, and he certainly didn't want Maisey to wind up in his long line of failed relationships, especially with her father's warning.

The timer went off, and Maisey shut off the sound

of the alarm. "So what do you want to study?"

"Speaking of all this studying, did you ever hear back about your tests?"

She flashed him an annoyed look. "You're just trying to get out of answering my question."

"No, I actually want to know how you did on your tests."

"I got two As and one B."

Zach smiled. "Excellent. You can attribute your success to your fabulous study partner."

Shaking her head, Maisey chuckled. "Yes, my study partner was amazing. If it weren't for him, I would've forgotten everything I learned."

"Do I detect sarcasm there?"

"Maybe a little." Maisey held her index finger and thumb about an inch apart, then waved her index finger at him. "No more excuses. What's on your study agenda?"

Zach stared at the road ahead. Would he sound like he was trying to be pious if he said the Bible? He really did need that. What did it say about him that he was a little fearful of saying he wanted to study the Bible, especially to Maisey. She, of all people, would certainly understand.

"I've been thinking about doing a Bible study. I'm not sure where to start, but maybe you have some suggestions."

Maisey let out a low whistle. "I never expected that answer."

"My heathen ways must have preceded me."

"No, I'm the one who never thought of that kind of study." Maisey grabbed her phone. "I'll text Pastor Rob and see if he can give us some suggestions. Then we can study together while we're on the trip."

"Sounds like a plan." Zach didn't know what to make of her suggestion to study together. Was she warming up to him, or was this reform school for wayward football players?

The interior of the car grew silent except for the tapping sound as Maisey typed out her text. Zach contemplated what it meant to study the Bible with her. The beauty and the beast?

"Pastor Rob says he'll get back to me with some suggestions."

"That was a quick response."

"He said his phone was lying on the desk while he was putting the finishing touches on his sermon." Maisey tucked her phone away. "Looks like we've arrived. This should be awesome."

Being with Maisey was awesome. He parked the car and tried to purge that thought from his mind. Wisdom dictated that he forget about pursuing his interest in her. He would only make a mess of things again, she would get hurt, and an angry father would be waiting for him back in Kellersburg.

During the next couple of hours, Zach followed Maisey around while she gazed at the carving on the mountain, toured the museums, and shopped at the gift shop. This time she bought a small piece of Native American pottery and a book about the memorial.

While Zach drove back to Rapid City, Maisey studied the book and graced him with little tidbits of information. Mostly she was quiet though, and that gave Zach time to think. Too much time, and most of that time he was thinking about how he planned not to be pulled in by her charm. He wasn't winning that battle.

By the time they arrived at the historic hotel in downtown Rapid City, Zach had a full-blown headache. Hopefully, an hour in the hotel room would alleviate the pain in his head, but he didn't know what he could do for the one in his heart. Maybe he should pray. He'd thought of that before, but he hadn't acted on it. This was the time.

"Phil sent a text saying to meet him in the lobby at six." Maisey punched the button for her floor as they entered the elevator.

Zach nodded. "That gives us a little over an hour to put ourselves together."

"Thanks for being tour guide again. I enjoyed our afternoon."

"Me, too." *More than you know. Everything except the headache.*

***

After a long day the bed beckoned, but Maisey had to call her parents. So far she'd managed to call them every night before she went to bed. Last night she'd given them every detail about the day with Dakota's family. The church service had been amazing, with many prayers of thanksgiving for Dakota's health.

Maisey had joked with her mom about missing her potato salad at the potluck meal. She told her mom how Zach had mentioned her chocolate cake as he piled his plate with too many desserts. Every time Maisey thought of Zach, her heart hitched.

Her mother had commented about the joy in Maisey's voice as she described the meeting between Dakota and her new pup. The little girl had squealed with delight when Maisey brought out the dog. Joy filled Maisey's heart as she remembered yesterday. The whole experience brought her joy, everything except her unrequited love for Zach.

Was she really in love with Zach or just the idea of Zach that she'd had since she was a kid? Traveling with him had done nothing to dim her feelings or her perceptions of him. Still, she feared she was making him out to be something he wasn't. She couldn't talk to her mother about it because Maisey feared the reaction. She wished she had someone to confide in. Maybe that would help her to sort out her feelings.

Maisey punched the icon on her phone and listened to the ring as she waited for the video call to connect.

"Maisey, how was your day?" Her mother's face appeared on the screen.

"It was great, as always."

"What did you do today?"

"You know it was a travel day. Driving instead of flying because of the snowstorm in Denver that interfered with our connecting flight from Rapid City to Billings. I kind of liked driving instead of flying because we got to see the countryside, although I have to admit that Highway 212 isn't the most scenic road I've ever been on. I do know why they call Montana big-sky country. The sky is huge out here in the wide open spaces." Maisey made a big circle with her arms. "I mean wide open spaces. You drive for miles without seeing another car or a town."

"I'm so glad you're getting to experience different parts of the country." Her mother smiled. "Did you get to do any sightseeing today?"

"I didn't think we'd have any time, but Phil had us stop at the Little Bighorn Battlefield National Monument. It's about sixty miles from Billings. So we stopped on our way."

"What did you see?"

"I imagine you can see more if you come in the summer and are able to hike around. We just drove on this road through the battlefield. It's a lot more wide open spaces with markers where the people died." Maisey shrugged. "Actually, it's kind of a sad place, especially this time of year, when the area is covered in snow."

"So it snowed there, too?"

"A few days ago." Maisey tried to brighten her mood. "I bought Wes a cap as a souvenir."

"Maisey, you shouldn't keep buying us stuff."

"But I like to buy stuff for you."

"I know. You've always been a generous child." Her mother stepped to the side as her father joined in the call.

Her dad smiled into the camera. "How's my girl?"

"Good, Dad. The trip's been amazing."

"Glad to hear it."

Maisey wanted to remind her parents that she wasn't a child anymore, but she refrained. They still thought of her as their little girl. Sadly, Zach also thought of her as a little girl. He kept referring to his remembrances of her as a child. Would that ever change?

"Did you do anything after you got to Billings?"

her dad asked.

"Yeah, we took a drive along the Rimrock. It's kind of a shelf-like ridge that runs along the edge of the city. It looks out over the city and the Yellowstone River. You can even see the mountains in the distance. It's an amazing view."

"Sounds wonderful. I hope you took lots of pictures," her mother interjected.

"I've been taking all kinds of photos. I'll have so many it will take you days to go through them all." Maisey thought of the selfie Zach had taken at Mount Rushmore. Did she want to show that one to her mother? Maisey feared her feelings were obvious in that photo. She didn't know why she didn't want her mother to know how she felt about Zach, but she didn't.

"So what's happening tomorrow?" her dad asked.

"Tomorrow we meet with a family who adopted three siblings, two boys and a girl, a year ago. Now they're going to adopt a puppy. The little girl sent in a picture she had drawn of her forever family. The picture had a little brown-and-white dog in it that she labeled 'Our Adopted Dog.'" Maisey sighed. "Zach told me lots of the contest entries had drawings of the dog the contestant wanted. Phil has worked with the animal shelters to match the dogs to the drawings. So far we have two pretty close matches."

"That's wonderful," her mother said.

"I know, but Phil says it's because they've prayed for each of these contestants and the dogs they get."

"Phil is a very generous man, a remarkable example of helping others. I'm so glad you decided to join his cause." Her dad raised his eyebrow as he looked into the camera. "How are things with Zach?"

That was an odd question. She had thought from the beginning of this adventure that some of her dad's statements indicated his suspicions about her feelings for Zach. Had her dad known all along that his daughter had had a crush on their friends' son? It didn't matter. Maisey intended to keep her feelings to herself.

"Zach's good. Phil keeps telling us we make a good team and he's proud of the job we've done." Maisey let out a heavy sigh. "I hope it keeps going that way. You never know what might happen. You know, like the snowstorm that has us driving instead of flying. We're driving to Spokane, too."

"Wow! That's a long drive," her dad said.

"I like the driving. I get to see the countryside close up, not from thirty-five thousand feet."

"That's true. We'd better let you go. It's late here, and your mother needs her beauty sleep." Her dad chuckled. "We love you. Take care."

"Love you, too, Mom and Dad. Talk to you tomorrow." Maisey ended the call as she recalled how Phil had said Zach needed his "beauty sleep."

Maisey sighed as she set her phone on the bedside stand. Why did everything come back to Zach? She grabbed her pajamas from the bed.

A knock sounded on her door. Was this another delivery? From Zach? She approached the door with caution and looked through the peephole. A distorted image of Zach stared back at her. Why was he here?

"Just a minute." Maisey turned and surveyed the room. She didn't want to let him in if she had underwear hanging out of her suitcase. She threw her pajamas back into the suitcase and closed it.

Maisey opened the door. "Hi. Did you need something?"

"May I come in?"

"Okay." Maisey stepped aside. "How can I help you?"

Zach glanced around the room. "Let's sit on the couch."

"Okay." Following Zach to the couch, Maisey wished she had something more intelligent to say than okay.

Zach stood in front of the light-gray couch that faced the TV mounted on the opposite wall. "Here's the deal. I know Phil said we were going to wing it again tomorrow. Although our meeting with Dakota and her parents went well with that scenario, I wasn't comfortable doing it that way. I need some questions to hang on to. Can we work on some?"

Maisey stared at Zach. She couldn't believe he'd been uncomfortable. He had appeared to be completely at ease during that meeting. She, on the other hand, had been nervous as could be.

Then there was the fact that they were alone in her room. She didn't want to sit on that couch with him. She didn't believe for a moment that Zach would be anything but a gentleman, but the scenario had her thinking things that shouldn't even cross her mind.

"You don't want to do this?" He gave her a puzzled look.

Temptation stood before her in the form of a gorgeous man. Where were these thoughts coming from? She needed an eraser so her mind could be as clean as an unused white board. Zach had done nothing wrong or even hinted at anything that was racing through her mind. He had to leave.

"I'm sorry, Zach. I'm really tired. I was about to go to bed." Terrible choice of words. She had to get ahold of herself. He'd probably laugh if he knew where her mind had gone. She had to get her own thoughts on a righteous path. "My mind just isn't clear." That was a bigger truth than he would ever know.

"Sorry." He shook his head. "I should've known it was too late for a brainstorming session. I don't know anything about adoption, so I was feeling out to sea on the subject."

Maisey placed a hand over her heart as she took a slow breath. Calm. She needed calm. *Lord, please forgive my wayward thoughts.* "I'll talk to you in the morning. You know Wyatt Bayer adopted a little girl, and if he's free tomorrow, I'm sure he'll be glad to talk to you. I'll send him a text, then get back to you in the morning."

"Great. See you at breakfast. I'll just let myself out. Get some sleep." Zach closed the door quietly behind him.

Maisey continued to stand there, her heart still pounding. Even though Zach had absolutely no idea what was going through her mind, the thought of looking him in the eyes tomorrow morning made her cringe with guilt. She would know what thoughts had crawled through her mind. God knew, and that was even worse.

Lust. Lust had taken over her thoughts in a way that had shocked her. She'd never had that temptation or such thoughts before. Not for anyone. Not even in her daydreams of Zach. Why had those images sprung up in her mind now? She'd spent days with him and never had the first inkling to think like that.

Had it been the proximity of the bed in the room? The fact that they'd been alone? Were these the thoughts of other women she knew who liked to hook up with guys because it was fun? No commitments. No expectations. No regrets. That was not where she wanted to be.

Maisey sank to the edge of the bed and put her face in her hands. She would get over this. Zach would never know. This was between her and God. Her Lord understood temptation. He'd been tempted.

She'd already asked for forgiveness, but she now feared those thoughts would pop up again. Zach would be with her every day for another three weeks. She'd better put on the full armor of God because she was going to need it.

CHAPTER NINE

The smell of bacon, pancakes, and syrup wafted Zach's way as he entered the restaurant in search of Phil and Maisey. He wondered how Maisey would greet him this morning. Last night she hadn't seemed like herself. He couldn't put his finger on her behavior, but it wasn't normal for her. Maybe she'd just been tired, as she'd claimed. He hoped things were better this morning.

Zach spied Maisey's blond hair in the booth in the far corner of the restaurant. He quickened his pace. She drew him in like a fisherman reeling in a big catch. He was tired of struggling, but he had to keep up the fight. He'd promised her dad that he'd protect her, and that meant protecting her from himself. A sad, sad situation.

"Good morning. How's everyone?" Zach looked at Maisey. "Did you get a good night's sleep?"

She nodded but didn't meet his gaze. Instead she looked at her phone. "I heard from Wyatt this morning. He said you could call him anytime. I'll text you his number."

"Hey, thanks." Zach glanced at Phil. "Have you ordered?"

"No. We were waiting for you." Phil eyed Zach. "I heard that you want to know more about adoption."

Zach's gaze swung to Maisey. "You told him?"

"I-I didn't know it was supposed to be a secret." Maisey's voice squeaked.

"It wasn't." Zach didn't want Phil to think he was going behind his back.

"I think it's a great idea to get input from someone who has actually gone through an adoption procedure. It'll give you insight for our meeting with the Petersons and their children." Phil nodded. "Thanks for thinking of it."

Zach breathed a silent sigh of relief, and he'd have to apologize to Maisey. His own insecurities were getting in the way. Should he admit that to her? Why not? Because he was trying to impress her. But Maisey was different than any other woman who had ever captured his interest. He had this inexplicable yearning to confide in her, tell her his secrets. That was trouble with a capital *T*.

When breakfast was finally over, Phil excused himself to make sure everything was in order for their afternoon meeting. Zach watched Phil leave, then turned to Maisey. He didn't know what to expect from her this morning. She had turned into someone he didn't recognize.

He'd managed to finally elicit a smile from her near the end of the meal. Normally she chatted and smiled all the time, just not this morning. Maybe she was as worried about today's meeting as he was.

Zach walked beside Maisey as they left the restaurant and went into the hotel lobby. "Hey, you want to be on the call with me when I talk to Wyatt?"

Maisey stopped and looked at him as if he'd grown another head, then lowered her gaze. "I don't know what I'd have to contribute to the conversation."

"Wyatt might like to talk to you. After all, you are going to be in his wedding."

Maisey gave him a reluctant smile. "Okay, but I don't think I'll have much to say."

"No problem."

"Where are you planning to make this call?"

Zach glanced around. "The lobby's quiet. No one here but us. We can do it over there in front of the fireplace, unless you object to the fire."

"No, the fire's cozy." Maisey hurried to the brown suede couch with the wooden arms near the huge stone fireplace and sat down.

When Zach reached the couch, he stood there for a moment and looked down at Maisey. Where should he sit? Close? Far away? Just close enough? He felt like Goldilocks looking at the bears' chairs. *Just sit down.*

Zach sat on the couch and hoped Maisey didn't move away. All morning he'd had the feeling she didn't want to be near him. Maybe he was being paranoid, but she had withdrawn into an invisible shell.

He tapped the screen of his phone. "Let's make that call."

"Hello." Wyatt's voice came over the speaker, and Zach held the phone between Maisey and him.

"Hey, Wyatt. It's Zach Dawson."

"Maisey told me you'd be calling."

"Just to let you know, Maisey's on the call with me."

"Hi, Maisey. How's the trip?"

"It's amazing, but I can hardly wait to get to Florida and see you guys. It's pretty cold up here in Montana, so I'm ready for some warm Florida weather."

"Colder than Ohio?"

"Yes, way colder."

Wyatt chuckled. "Stay warm."

"I'll try. There's a nice fire going here, and it's warm. How are things in Florida?" Maisey asked.

"Nice and warm. Just waiting for you to arrive. Hope it holds for a couple more weeks. We don't want it to rain on our wedding."

"How's Caroline?" Zach asked.

"Busy teaching and getting ready for the wedding. I'm leaving all that stuff to her. She's closer to the venue where we're getting married, so she's taking care of all the last-minute details. Her parents are arriving in a few days." Wyatt's voice conveyed his happiness over the upcoming nuptials. "Caroline's brother, Nathan, tells me you're bringing our sweet Maisey to the wedding."

Zach nodded even though Wyatt couldn't see. "That arrangement has been made by numerous people. It will be nice to see you again. It's been over ten years since we were in high school together. I think you graduated a year ahead of me."

"That sounds about right. I was ready to leave high school behind when the time came," Wyatt said.

"Guess we have something in common besides high school. Accidents that ended our careers. But we both seem to have weathered those tragedies and moved on with our lives." Although Zach had moved on with his life, Wyatt had one thing Zach didn't have. A woman to love. Would his turn ever come, or had he burned all his bridges in the love department? He was afraid to try again because he'd made such a mess of his past relationships.

"Yeah, thanks to some great people in my life."

"Me, too." Zach could never thank Phil enough for the guidance he'd given. "Maisey said you'd be glad to talk to me about the adoption process."

"Absolutely. What would you like to know?"

"Whatever you want to tell me. We have an interview this afternoon with a family who adopted three siblings a year ago. The kids think today is a one-year celebration of their adoption, but they're going to learn they've won a puppy in the Twelve Dogs of Christmas Contest."

"Sounds cool."

"Yeah. It's great seeing how happy these kids are when they get their dog." The smiling faces of the other winners flashed through Zach's mind. "Before we present the winners with the dog, we always interview the family and talk about their circumstances. I need some ideas on what to say to them or what to ask them. What can you tell me?"

Wyatt spent the next twenty minutes telling Zach about adopting his little girl, Tasha, after her mother died much too young. Wyatt explained the process and mentioned that each state has its own laws for adoptions. He said that adopting Tasha was a super-special thing. Zach could hear the love for Tasha in Wyatt's words.

"Wyatt, thanks for sharing all this with me. I'm eager to meet Tasha."

Wyatt laughed. "She might talk your ear off and give you advice you haven't asked for."

"She's sounds like a lot of fun."

"With her there's never a dull moment." Wyatt

laughed again. "Caroline and I will have our hands full in the years to come."

Zach smiled at Maisey. He mouthed the word thanks as their gazes met. His heart tripped as she returned his smile. So much better than the strangely quiet woman who had sat at the table with him during breakfast.

"Thanks for talking to us, Wyatt. We'll see you in less than two weeks. Say hi to Caroline for us."

"I will. Be good to Maisey."

"You can count on it. Goodbye." The echo of Bryant's words set Zach on edge. Wyatt probably didn't mean it that way at all. It just seemed that way because Zach had Maisey's dad on his mind already.

Zach leaned back on the couch as he ended the call. He looked over at Maisey, who still sat on the edge of the couch, as if she was ready to jump up at any moment. "Now I feel better about our upcoming meeting."

"That's good." Maisey stood. "I'm going to pack and get ready to check out. Phil said we should leave here about eleven."

Zach glanced at his phone. Here she was again, the reticent woman from breakfast. "Any reason it's going to take you two hours to pack? We could hang out here by the fire and talk about our plans."

"There's really nothing to talk about." Her expression was dismissive. "I'll see you down here at eleven."

Zach stood. "Okay. I'm going to hang out here for a while if you change your mind."

"Okay. See you later." She gave a little wave as she headed for the elevators.

Zach returned to the couch and sat down. He placed his elbows on his thighs and put his head in his hands. Had he done something to offend Maisey? He tried to think back, but nothing came to mind. Maybe she just needed time to herself. After all, they'd been together a lot, not just the two of them but the whole group.

She might be one of those people who needed alone time to rejuvenate herself. He hadn't guessed she was that kind of person, but that would explain her sudden need to spend time by herself.

Or maybe she was homesick. She'd never been away from home for a long period of time. Adults could get homesick, not just kids. He'd been homesick his first year in college, but he'd had no home to go back to, with his parents in Germany.

His freshman year of college had been a tough year, but he'd found comfort with a family who had befriended him through a Christian athletic association. They had invited him to church and introduced him to their two high school boys. He'd forged a bond with the Overtons, but he'd let that all slip away after he'd started playing professional ball. Another regret.

Zach lifted his head and stared at the flames weaving and bobbing in the fireplace. A log snapped and sparks flew, just like the sparks that flew in his midsection every time he looked at Maisey's smile. Would she be another regret in his life, not because he'd hurt her but because he was afraid to go after her?

He thought again of the Overtons. He should've kept in touch. Why hadn't he? He knew the answer.

He'd abandoned his Christian faith that was all-important to them. He hadn't wanted to face their disappointment. Could he still get in touch with them? What would they think if he gave them a call out of the blue?

With those questions cluttering his thoughts, Zach scrolled through his contacts. Chuck Overton. The name jumped out at him. He sat there for a few moments and contemplated what he could say. Would Chuck even be able to talk midmorning on a Tuesday? He'd been a high school guidance counselor back then. Did he still have that job?

Zach clicked and brought up Chuck's number. Zach's finger sat poised above the icon to make the call. Even if Chuck didn't answer, Zach could leave a message. They could talk at a more convenient time. There had to be a reason he'd thought of this family today after not thinking of them for years.

God brought people to mind. Zach was seeing this happen over and over again. Like Maisey saying to call Wyatt, and Phil knowing to include Maisey in this project. Even if she was giving Zach a cold shoulder for the moment, she made him examine his past—which helped him make better choices for the future.

Zach punched the icon on the phone's screen. He listened to the ring until the call went to voicemail. "Hey, Chuck, you may be surprised to hear from me, but this is Zach Dawson. I was just thinking about you today and thought I'd give you a call. I'd like to hear from you and see how you and your family are doing. You can call me anytime at this number."

Zach ended the call and stared at the fire. Would Chuck get back to him? Zach hoped so. It would be good to connect with Chuck and his family again. He'd like to apologize for not staying in contact with them. It was never too late to set things right.

***

The church fellowship hall buzzed with activity as Maisey followed Phil and Zach into the room. The Petersons were celebrating the adoption of their kids with the folks in their church small group. Children scampered around the room as adults set up the buffet line along the counter between the fellowship hall and the kitchen.

Excitement filled Maisey's chest as she anticipated meeting this family. She recited the children's names to herself. Emilie, Toby, and Dillon. She watched the children playing and wondered which ones they were.

Zach stood next to her. "Do you know which children are the adoptees?"

Maisey looked at him. "Are you reading my mind? I was just thinking the same thing."

"No, can't read minds." He gave her a wry smile.

Maisey was certainly grateful for that. Things were a little better today, but thoughts from last night still pushed their way into her thoughts. She slammed the door on them, but they kept knocking. She wouldn't let them in. "Let's join Phil, and maybe we'll find out."

Maisey didn't wait for Zach as she made her way over to Phil, who was talking with the film crew about where they planned to set up their cameras and lights. She waited patiently until he had finished.

Phil turned and smiled at her. "What can I do for you?"

"I was hoping you'd introduce Zach and me to the family we're planning to talk to."

"Sure. They're right over here." Phil gestured toward the small stage at one end of the room.

Zach stood beside Maisey as Phil made the introductions. She gazed into the happy faces of the towheaded children who stood in stairstep fashion beside Jenna Peterson, a young woman of average height with light-brown hair and bright-blue eyes, and her husband, Kevin, with his close-cropped dark hair and dark eyes.

The older boy, Garret, gazed up at Zach. "Daddy says you're a really famous football player. Are you?"

Zach stifled a smile at the doubt in the child's question. "It all depends on what you consider famous."

"He says you played quarterback until you got hurt."

"That's true."

"My daddy was a quarterback, too, but I guess he isn't famous."

"All quarterbacks are famous." Zach smiled down at the little boy.

"Thanks." Kevin stepped forward and shook hands with Zach. "Nice to meet you, and thanks for making me famous."

"You're welcome. We quarterbacks have to stick together." Zach looked over at Maisey. "This lady makes me look good."

"You play football, too?" The smallest boy gave Maisey a puzzled look.

Maisey shook her head. "No, we just work together, and I make sure he doesn't go off script."

"What does that mean?" the child asked.

Maisey smiled. She was the one going off script now.

"She helps me ask the right questions," Zach explained.

"Yeah, that's what I do. Most of the time."

"Are you going to ask me a question?" Grant stared up at Maisey, expectation on his face.

"Would you like me to ask you a question?" Maisey hunkered down next to the boy.

Grant nodded.

"What should I ask?" Maisey said quietly.

The little boy leaned in closer. "Ask me what's my favorite thing in my family."

Straightening, Maisey reached into her purse and brought out her phone. "I'll type that question into my phone so I won't forget to ask you that when we talk to your family."

"Good." The child nodded. "I'm hungry."

The adults laughed at the quick change of subject. With that Phil called for quiet and gave thanks for the food and the gathering. He instructed the Petersons to go through the food line first. Then everyone else followed.

After Maisey filled her plate with fried chicken, salad, and sweet potato fries, she found a seat at one of the tables. Zach took a seat beside her. He started eating without saying anything. His proximity conjured up her thoughts from the night before. Why? She didn't want to think about them, but they plagued her mind like an invading army. She didn't want this.

They were ruining everything between them. They had a good working relationship, and she wouldn't let the devilish thoughts ruin that.

Go away, devil. Please, Lord, take hold of my thoughts and make them yours.

Zach was laughing with the kids and making funny faces. The scene brought to mind the times when he'd had her laughing when she'd been a little girl. He had Emilie looking at him with a worshipful gaze, just as Maisey had done all those years ago. Kids adored him, and so did she. Her mind settled on all the good things about him rather than her wayward thoughts.

Emilie scrunched up her face as she gazed at Zach. "Is she your wife?"

"You mean Maisey?"

Emilie nodded.

"No, we're just friends and work together."

"Do you have a wife?" Emilie asked.

"No."

"How come?"

An amused but serious expression crossed Zach's face. "That's a hard question to answer."

"I think you should get a wife." Emilie nodded. "Our daddy says our mom is the best wife, but she's taken. So you'll have to find someone else. I could help you."

Once again Zach stifled a smile. "Thanks for offering your help, but I won't be here long enough for you to find me a wife."

"Then Maisey should help you."

Zach turned to Maisey. "What do you think? Do you think you could find me a wife?"

Maisey's mind whirled. *Pick me. Pick me. Pick me.* The crazy mantra marched through her brain. "I don't think you really need my help."

"Seems to me I could use help since I'm still wifeless." Zach raised his eyebrows.

Maisey shook her head. "I'm not in the matchmaking business. Maybe you should hire a professional matchmaker."

"Those still actually exist?" Zach asked.

"I believe so. They're for very busy people who have no time to find their own dates."

"Guess those people have no friends or acquaintances who are all too willing to match you up with their friends or relatives."

"Are you speaking from experience?" Maisey took a sip of her lemonade.

A thoughtful expression crossed Zach's face. "That's how I wound up meeting all the women I've dated."

"Your friends must've been busy." Maisey ducked her head and took a bite of chicken. She'd probably said too much, reminding Zach of his many girlfriends. She was trying to remind herself that he was a man who had made the rounds with a lot of women. He couldn't possibly have an interest in her, so what did it matter?

"I suppose that's true."

"So you're not in the market for a matchmaker?"

Zach shook his head. "Not in the least. I've sworn off women for the time being, on Phil's advice."

"Phil wants to keep your attention on the task at hand?"

"Absolutely. Besides, the only people we're

meeting are families and dogs. No women to capture my attention."

"True." Maisey tried to smile. No women except her, and she obviously didn't count. She should be happy with that scenario, but the thought deflated her heart. She had really been in a dream world—one from her childhood. *Grow up, Maisey*.

Zach got up from the table, plate in hand. "May I take your plate?"

Maisey nodded. Always the gentleman. Why did he seem suddenly sad? Or maybe she was reading something into his expression that wasn't there.

When Phil made his way to the small stage, Maisey took a deep breath and headed to the stage as well. Phil invited the Petersons to join him, where chairs suited to every participant graced the area.

After everyone was settled, Phil acted as an MC as he opened the interview with another prayer. Then he handed the microphone to Zach, who talked to Kevin and Jenna about their decision to adopt a group of siblings and the process involved.

As Zach concluded his questions, Kevin stood and took the microphone. "I know this program will eventually go out to a larger audience than we have right here in this room, so I'm going to urge people to consider adoption. As Jenna and I mentioned, our involvement with a local crisis pregnancy center brought us to the point of adoption. Rather than just praying for the women who faced a crisis pregnancy, we decided to do something concrete. That led us to adopt these three precious children, who have enriched our lives beyond anything we could have imagined."

After Kevin finished, he handed the microphone back to Phil. "Now we're going to hear from the children."

Maisey took the microphone and talked to the kids, knowing Zach was off to the side holding their new puppy and waiting for his cue to come back to the stage. The boys talked about playing games with the family, and Emilie talked about learning to bake with her mom. Emilie, as the oldest, expressed her joy at being able to stay with her brothers, after their initial separation in the foster care system. The kids mentioned their parents reading Bible stories to them and having movies and popcorn on the weekends.

"I have one last question." Maisey stepped closer to where Grant sat. "Grant, what's your favorite thing about your family?"

Grant smiled as he jumped up from his chair and ran over and stood in front of Kevin and Jenna with his arms wide open. "Hugs. Lots and lots of hugs."

Tears welled in Maisey's eyes as Kevin and Jenna enveloped Grant in a hug. In a second Emilie and Garrett joined the family hug. Maisey hadn't expected that answer from Grant, but it was the perfect ending to the interview. She sniffed as she handed the microphone back to Phil.

"Ladies and gentlemen, that hug deserves a prize." Phil pulled a folded piece of paper from his pocket and unfolded it. He held it up for the camera. "I have a picture that Emilie drew and sent in for our Twelve Dogs of Christmas Contest."

A little squeal sounded from behind Phil, and he turned around and walked over to the little girl. "Do you know what that means, Emilie."

The child was all smiles. "We won a dog? The dog I wanted?"

Phil showed her the picture. "A dog like this?"

Emilie nodded, her expression full of expectation. "Yes."

"Come here, kids." Phil motioned for the children to gather around him. "I want you to meet your puppy."

Zach came on to the stage, a squirming brown-and-white puppy in his arms. The children jumped up and down and clapped. Still holding the pup, Zach hunkered down as the children gathered around him.

"Kids, let's sit in a circle on the floor, and I'll put the puppy in the middle." Zach joined the kids in the circle. "We don't want to scare him, so hold out your hand to let him sniff. That's how he gets to know you. Then you can gently pet him."

As Zach set the puppy on the floor, the kids held out their hands, and the pup greeted them all. The little dog wriggled from the top of his head to the tip of his tail with excitement as the kids petted him.

"What do you think you'd like to name him?" Zach glanced around the circle.

"We all decided if we won a puppy that we would name him Teddy," Emilie said.

"That sounds like a good name." Maisey joined the group.

Phil brought out his gift bag full of things for the new dog. "Here's a lot of things you'll need for your puppy. I expect to hear that you're taking very good care of him."

"We will." Emilie picked up the puppy and hugged him to her. "He'll get lots of hugs because we love to hug in our family."

As Zach, Maisey, and Phil watched the kids play, Kevin and Jenna came into the circle. Jenna carried a baby who looked to be about a year old.

Maisey stepped closer to Jenna. "What an adorable little girl."

Phil joined the two women. "Who is this little lady?"

Jenna whispered something to Phil, then he turned to the cameras. "Kevin and Jenna have a surprise of their own. I'll let them tell you about it."

Jenna shyly took the microphone as she looked over the gathering. "We've fostered kids for a number of years, including our little tribe here, before we decided to adopt. We've just been given the opportunity to take in another child. This beautiful little girl, Sophia. We're praying the Lord will lead us in our plan to adopt her as well."

Applause broke out in the room as Kevin hugged Jenna, and the kids—Emilie holding Teddy—jumped up to be included in the hug.

Kevin took the microphone. "This child is precious to us because we know her mother. She's a young woman who is struggling with the circumstances in her life. She can't take care of Sophia and wants a better life for her little girl. She was one of the women we prayed for at the crisis pregnancy center when she decided to keep her baby rather than have an abortion."

The Petersons and their concern for children made Maisey realize she hadn't done much in her life to help any women who struggled with the decision to keep a child when life looked so bleak. She vowed to look for opportunities to help. Doing this project with Phil was just a start.

Maisey looked over at Zach, who stood at the edge of the stage, his head bowed. More applause filled the room as Kevin and Jenna set the baby in the circle with the other children and the puppy. Zach joined in the applause, but a troubled expression crossed his face.

Phil said a final prayer, but the cameras continued to roll as the folks from the small group gathered on the stage to meet Sophia. Laughter and conversation filled the fellowship hall. Phil shook everyone's hand and praised the group for giving Kevin and Jenna support in their endeavor to give these children a forever home.

As the caterers cleaned up the kitchen and prepared to leave, Maisey looked around for Zach. She didn't see him anywhere.

Maisey talked more with the kids and helped them with the dog as she showed them everything in the gift bag. The kids tried the harness and leash on the puppy.

"You should try that out. Teddy will have to learn to walk on a leash, and this would be a good time to take him outside." Maisey looked at Emilie. "Let's carry Teddy outside and see if he needs to go."

Emilie nodded. "Yeah, we wouldn't want him to go inside, would we?"

In seconds the kids had donned their coats and headed for the door. As they stepped outside into the cold Montana air, their breaths created a cloud. The kids giggled as Maisey set Teddy on the grass and let Emilie hold the leash. He sniffed around.

"We have to stay out here until he goes?" Emilie looked at Maisey for confirmation.

Maisey nodded as she huddled in her coat. "Let's hope he doesn't take too long. It's cold out here."

The dog finally did his business, and the children cheered and loved on the pup. As they headed back to the building, Maisey spied Zach standing all alone at the edge of the parking lot adjacent to a snow-covered baseball field. He had his hands jammed into his pockets, and the troubled expression had morphed into a look of dejection.

Maisey ushered the children into the building, then went back outside. She watched Zach for a moment as he stood next to a dirty snow bank. He kicked at a chunk of ice that sat by the curb. Something was obviously bothering him, but Maisey had no clue what it could be. Everything had gone well with today's giveaway.

Maisey approached Zach, her breath forming little clouds in the air. "Hey, what are you doing out here in the cold?"

Zach turned. "Getting some fresh air and some time to myself."

"Is something wrong?"

"What could be wrong?" Zach hunched his shoulders.

"You tell me."

"There's nothing to tell."

"You say nothing's wrong, but this isn't your usual MO after one of our giveaways." Maisey narrowed her gaze. "You're usually right in the mix with all the participants. Yet today you're out here by yourself. Did I do something to offend you?"

Zach shook his head. "No. You've been everything you should be on this tour. But just like you the other day when you needed to go to your room instead of spending time with me, today I need to have this time to myself. No offense intended."

"Okay. Sorry to bother you."

"No bother. I'm glad you were concerned. We're good." Zach gestured toward the church building. "Go back inside before you get cold, and have fun with those kids and that puppy."

Nodding, Maisey didn't reply but headed toward the building, her boots crunching on the frozen gravel of the parking lot. No matter what Zach said, Maisey knew in her heart that things weren't right with him. Why wouldn't he talk to her? Why was he shutting her out? Was he getting back at her for going off to her room earlier today? Surely not. He wasn't that kind of person.

Maisey turned to look at Zach again. He appeared to be looking out across the nearby field. Then he pulled his phone from his pocket and tapped the screen. Someone had called him, and whoever it was made him smile—a smile she couldn't elicit from him. Was the call from an old girlfriend? That wasn't Maisey's business. What he did in his private life shouldn't concern her one bit, but it did. That was the problem.

CHAPTER TEN

"Hey, Chuck. Thanks for returning my call." Zach paced back and forth in the parking lot.

"It's good to hear from you, Zach." Chuck's voice still had that deep gravelly sound that Zach remembered. "I've been thinking about you, too. How are you doing since your injury?"

"Things are going well." Zach gave Chuck the rundown on his recovery and Phil's offer of work with his project. "We're in Billings, Montana. Can you believe that? I'm seeing parts of the country I've never seen before."

"Sounds like a great project. Where else are you headed?"

Zach gave Chuck the rest of their itinerary.

"You say you're going to be in the Fort Lauderdale area?"

"Yeah. We have a dog to give away in the vicinity, and I'm going to a wedding near there."

"Yours?"

Zach laughed. "Hardly. I've sworn off women."

Chuck laughed in return. "Don't give up on them altogether. They can be nice to have around."

"So far that hasn't been the case for me." Zach's mind filled with all the bad memories Chuck's statement had resurrected. They'd hit him especially hard when Kevin and Jenna had talked about adopting that little girl. His heart hurt just thinking about it.

"You just haven't found the right woman." Conviction sounded in Chuck's voice.

"Enough about me. How's your family?" Zach didn't want to talk about women, good or bad in his life.

"We've had our ups and downs." Worry came across in Chuck's tone. "Trey got married to a great little gal last spring, and they live in North Carolina. That was one of our ups. But Troy's been diagnosed with Hodgkin lymphoma and is undergoing treatment. Cindy and I are with him here in Houston, where he works. Cindy has been able to work remotely, and I'm able to teach my classes remotely as well. That's why I was asking about Fort Lauderdale. We live in the area."

Zach took in the information. "I would love to see you guys again. Any chance you'll be back in Fort Lauderdale in the next couple of weeks?"

"Yeah. Troy has his last treatment this week. So we'll be back through the Christmas holiday. Troy will stay with us through the end of the year."

Zach's heart sank at the thought of Troy having cancer. Zach remembered the lively teenage boys, twins. He'd played ball with them, and they'd spent hours playing video games and just hanging out while he'd been in college. "I'm so sorry to hear about Troy. How long has he been undergoing treatment?"

"He's on his second round of chemo, and he's doing well considering the circumstances."

"I'll certainly be praying for him." Zach wanted to do more. "Is there something I can do to help?"

"Your prayers will be enough."

Hardly enough. Zach wanted to find a way to help this family. Something he could work on to take his mind off today's terrible reminder of his past misdeeds. "I'm sorry I lost touch. You meant a lot to me during my college years, and I'll never forget your friendship."

"I'm so glad you reached out, and I look forward to hearing from you."

"Say hi to Cindy and the boys, especially Troy. Tell him I'm praying for him." Zach swallowed the large lump that had formed in his throat.

"I will. Thanks again for reaching out. Talk to you later."

"Sure will. Goodbye." Zach ended the call and stood there, unable to truly process what he'd just heard.

He'd known a couple of guys who played football who had beat cancer, so Troy had a chance to live a full life, but there were no guarantees. Why did bad things have to happen to good people? "Lord, be with Troy and heal him. Be with his family while they go through this tough time. Bless them with a good outcome. Amen."

The whispered prayer floated away on the cold breeze. Zach shivered, not from the cold but from the hurts that weighed heavy on his heart. For a moment the news about Troy had taken Zach's mind off Jayla, but that hurt tore into him again, as if someone had taken a knife and slit him open and his insides were falling out and he couldn't catch them. The pain was worse than the one he'd endured from the broken leg that had ended his football career.

Zach took a deep breath and tried to steady his

mind. After the full days of the last couple of months, he had started to feel good about what he was doing and how his life was going. Then today had hit him out of the blue, and all the bad stuff had crashed down around him. The peace he thought he'd found had evaporated in the happiness of a couple who were taking another child into their hearts.

Peace over the situation with Jayla wouldn't come. Today's events had triggered the bad memories of the grievous experience with her. They had bombarded his brain until it hurt, and his heart ached. He had to let it go, but he didn't know how. Confession? God already knew, but Zach had never told anyone else about the incident that tortured his soul.

The truth had been too painful to talk about. The secret would live and die with him.

Could he pray? He said he'd pray for Troy, but couldn't Zach pray for himself, too? He didn't know how or for what to pray. He closed his eyes as the cold seeped into his soul. For a moment he thought about Maisey. So sweet and so unruined by life. He shouldn't even think about her, but how could he not when she was his constant companion?

If he'd learned anything from today, he had learned he should keep his distance from Maisey. He had mistakenly thought he could somehow prove to her dad that he didn't have to worry about Zach hurting her. He'd made a shambles of every relationship he'd been in. Why did he think this time would be different?

His mind went around in circles, going from the decision to pursue her to ending that thought to wishing he could act on his attraction back to telling himself that would only lead to disaster. He was driving himself crazy with the waffling.

Wisdom told him to squash any thoughts of being with Maisey. But was that possible? This project pushed them together at every juncture. He had to make a determined effort to be friends with Maisey without letting any other emotions take charge. Somehow he would survive the task he'd given himself.

After the personal pep talk, Zach looked over at the building. He'd better get back inside before he turned into an icicle and people thought he was being unfriendly. Practicing his smile, he slogged across the parking lot. As he opened the door to the fellowship hall, he put on a smile and pretended everything was right with the world.

"Hey, Zach, we were wondering where you were." Phil approached him. "We want to take a photo of the whole group with the dog. You and Maisey included."

"And you." Zach nodded. "Sorry I disappeared, but I was talking to an old friend from my college days. I just learned his son is being treated for Hodgkin lymphoma."

"Tough news." Phil laid a hand on Zach's shoulder. "Is there anything we can do for them?"

"I asked, but he just said to pray. But I plan to see them when we're in Florida." Zach nodded. "I'm sure they can use help with medical bills."

"That's exactly what I was thinking." Phil's face lit up. "That can be our next project. Working with families of cancer patients. On our trip to Spokane, we can do a little brainstorming about future projects."

"Sounds good." But did it? For the most part

continuing to work with Phil made sense. Would the new project include Maisey, or would she go back to Kellersburg and resume her job and schooling? He was thinking too far ahead. Deal with the here and now, not some future project.

"Zach, you finally came in from the cold." Carrying the puppy, Maisey came over to him.

"Yeah, I got a call from an old friend." Zach didn't want to explain again about the sad news. "It was good to catch up with him."

"I'm glad you had a good conversation. Are you ready to get your picture taken? Teddy is." Maisey smiled down at the pup.

That smile took away some of the hurt, but he couldn't let himself rely on Maisey's smile to make him happy. She was everything he wasn't. Good, innocent, and loving. And cuteness personified. How would he ever succeed with the promise to himself when he continued to have thoughts like this?

"Sure." Zach pulled out his best smile as Maisey gave Teddy to Grant to hold while Emilie and Garrett placed their hands on the little dog.

Maisey waved Phil over. "Phil, you can stand next to me. If it weren't for you, none of us would be here."

With a reluctant smile, Phil nodded. The photographer moved several people so everyone's face could be seen in the photo. He put Maisey in between Phil and Zach, then told everyone to stand closer together.

"Maisey, you're a rose between two thorns." Phil chuckled.

Maisey laughed. "That's what my grandpa used to

say when I was little and sat between him and my dad. You guys aren't thorns. You're ambassadors of goodwill."

"Thanks. I'll remember that." Phil turned to look at the camera. "We'd better pay attention to the photographer's instructions, or he'll put us in timeout."

Phil and Maisey laughed and joked with each other. Zach wished he could joke, but the ache in his heart still lingered. He didn't feel like laughing.

When the photo session was finally over, Zach breathed a sigh of relief. He'd have to keep smiling and greeting people, but he only wanted to go to the hotel. Would today's events haunt him for the rest of the tour? If he planned to get through this project, he definitely needed some time on his knees in prayer.

"Looks like this is a wrap. After we say goodbye to everyone, we'll head to the hotel." Phil clasped his hands in a victory pose.

Zach nodded. "Ready to head out."

Maisey said goodbye to the kids and their parents and gave Teddy a pat on the head. "You guys take good care of that pup."

"We will," the kids said in unison as Maisey waved goodbye.

She settled in the van as the film crew stowed the last of their equipment in the back. "That was the best day yet. I'm looking forward to Spokane."

"We have another special dog to give away there. Our recipient is a young man who has type-one diabetes. The dog we are giving him is specially trained to alert a diabetic of a hyperglycemic episode when blood sugar is too high, or a hypoglycemic episode when blood sugar is too low. Some people with diabetes don't get the usual signs of shaking, sweating, or confusion that comes with a hypoglycemic episode. This condition, if undetected, can be life threatening. Having a diabetic service dog can mean the difference between life and death."

"Wow! I had no idea dogs could do that. This trip has been so educational." Maisey let out a long sigh. "The Petersons' story touched me so much today. It has got me to thinking about what I can do to help women who are in a crisis pregnancy. How wonderful it would be to save the life of an unborn child! I just kept thinking about how Jenna and Kevin saved that little baby, that precious life."

"Maisey, keep that in mind." Phil pointed a finger at Zach. "I mentioned to Zach that we'd be doing some brainstorming for future projects on our trip tomorrow. Your thoughts might be included."

"That would be amazing." Maisey looked Zach's way. "Wasn't today just the best?"

Zach nodded, fearing if he opened his mouth he'd say just the opposite. Today hurt in ways he couldn't begin to explain. He wanted to put today behind him. However, if Maisey was set on talking about crisis pregnancy centers, that was a futile wish.

During the rest of the ride to the hotel, Maisey gushed about everything they had accomplished on the trip so far. He should be happy that she was happy and excited, but her joyful chatter just made misery flood his heart. He could hardly wait until they got to the hotel.

From his front seat, Phil turned and looked at everyone. "Early morning start tomorrow. Meet at seven in the lobby. I'll have donuts and pastries to eat on the way. You're responsible for your own drinks."

"Got it," Maisey said.

Zach just nodded as the van pulled to a stop in front of the hotel. "See you all in the morning. I'm headed to my room. Got a headache."

As Zach jumped out of the van, Maisey followed close behind. "You're not going to eat dinner with us?"

Zach shook his head. "I'm going to order room service. I'd be miserable company if I joined you for dinner. See you in the morning."

Zach strode to the elevator and prayed Maisey nor anyone else would try to change his mind.

"Hey, I'm sorry you're not feeling so good." Maisey stepped into the elevator with him. "I thought you were out of sorts this afternoon. I hope you feel better in the morning."

"I'm sure I will." Zach could only hope, but he had an inkling that tomorrow's brainstorming session would do nothing to help him feel better.

The bell dinged, and the elevator doors opened. Zach let Maisey exit first and hoped she didn't want more conversation. They walked down the hallway together until they reached Zach's room.

Zach unlocked his room with the keycard. "Have a good night."

"You, too." A look of concern radiated from Maisey's blue, blue eyes. "Feel better."

"Thanks." Zach didn't turn back as he entered the room and let the door close behind him, shutting out Maisey and her cheery attitude. He didn't want cheer tonight.

Zach took off his coat and slung it onto the bed. Rubbing his temple's, he plopped onto the nearby chair. He kicked off his boots, stretched out his legs, and put his feet on the bed. He laced his fingers behind his head and stared into space. Like he'd been sacked a dozen times. That was how he felt.

Prayer was what he needed, but now that he was alone, he didn't know what to pray for. Maybe that was the problem. He was thinking too much of himself. He needed to look outward, not inward.

May these words of my mouth and this meditation of my heart be pleasing in your sight, Lord, my Rock and my Redeemer. The Scripture that he'd memorized from Psalms started Zach's prayer. *Lord, I pray this Scripture for the days ahead. Use me to make life better for others. Help me not to make it all about me. I pray again for Troy. Please heal him and make him whole. Help me to have Maisey's best interest at heart. Bring me Your peace. In the name of Jesus I pray. Amen.*

Zach sat in the chair. The pounding in his head had subsided. He opened his eyes and grabbed his phone. At Phil's urging, Zach had been reading through the Bible this year. He had let the business of the past few weeks keep him from his daily reading. He had some catching up to do. He poked at his Bible app and began to read the Scriptures assigned for two weeks ago.

In no time he was engrossed in the verses. He had discovered through the Bible reading this year that he hadn't forgotten everything he'd learned growing up in the church in Kellersburg. Almost every day he read a familiar Bible story from his time in Sunday school, or he came across a Scripture he had memorized in VBS or summer Bible camp. They were like renewing an acquaintance with old friends.

As Zach read 1 Peter 1, these words jumped out at him. *May grace and peace be yours in abundance.*

God wanted Zach to have an abundance of grace and peace. He had to grab on to that promise and not let go in the days to come. He would rely on God and not himself.

***

The arrival in Spokane was marked with cloudless blue skies, but cold weather. The snow that had fallen before their arrival still blanketed the city. The hotel near the Spokane River gave a view of the tumbling water and the park beyond. The banks glittered with the freshly fallen snow as the river looked like a silver ribbon trimmed in lace. Snow dusted the branches of the surrounding evergreen trees. The place sparkled.

God's creation. Maisey let out a contented sigh as she looked over at Zach. "Isn't it beautiful?"

Zach nodded but didn't say anything. He'd been very quiet while they were on the road, barely contributing to the brainstorming session. Phil had written down all her ideas, and Zach had only nodded his approval.

"After we take our luggage to our rooms, Phil said we can explore. He said we should definitely walk around Riverfront Park." Maisey gave Zach a questioning glance. "How about it?"

Zach shrugged. "Call me after you're settled, and I'll let you know."

"Oh, okay." Maisey headed for the elevator. She didn't want to explore by herself, but Zach didn't appear to have an interest in checking out the park. Did he not like the cold, or did he just not want to be with her? "I'll call you in a bit."

Zach made no move to join her in the elevator, so she pressed the button for her floor. Maybe he was trying to distance himself from her because he knew she had a monumental crush on him. He didn't want to encourage it. She didn't want to encourage it, but it wouldn't go away. She sighed as she let herself into her room.

Maybe this was a good time to give her parents a call. If Zach didn't go with her, she could talk to them while she walked. Then she wouldn't feel alone. She wouldn't bother him and make it so he'd have to turn her down.

Maisey bundled up with a stocking cap, puffy ski jacket, scarf, gloves, thick woolly socks, and her fur-lined boots, ready to brave the cold. She hoped her jeans would be warm enough as she headed into the crisp late-afternoon air.

As she crossed the footbridge over the river, the water sparkled in the low-lying sun, barely looking over the treetops. Darkness came early to this northern clime. She called her folks as she reached the other side of the bridge.

"Maisey, where are you today?" Annette asked.

"Mom, you have my itinerary."

"I know, but I forget. It's easier to ask you when you call than to look it up."

Maisey laughed. "We're in Spokane today and tomorrow. I'm exploring."

"With Zach?"

Maisey shook her head even though her mother couldn't see. "No, he didn't want to go today, so I'm on my own."

"Is it safe for you to be alone?" Concern sounded in her mother's voice.

"I'm walking through Riverfront Park, and there are lots of folks out enjoying the outdoors. The trees are twinkling with Christmas lights, and the big pavilion is all lit up. I'll take photos and send them to you. This park is a beautiful place. There are Christmas lights everywhere. On the trees, on the bridges, and overhead."

"Maisey, I want you to be careful." Her dad's voice sounded over the phone.

"I am, Dad." Maisey let out an exasperated sigh. They treated her like she was twelve. Everyone did, even Zach, and that was more disheartening than having her parents do that. "I'm walking on the trail that goes by the river. It's amazing."

"I wish we were there to see it with you," Bryant said.

"Listen to the roar of the river over the rocks." Maisey held her phone out.

"Sounds loud," Annette replied.

"It is. The water is tumbling over and around all these rocks that are dusted with snow. There's lots of snow on the ground here. They had a storm just before we came."

"At least you weren't driving in it," her dad said.

"Phil was very careful about making changes to avoid any bad weather. After we finish here, we're headed to Tucson. The weather there should be much warmer."

"You'll have to trade in your coat and boots for shorts and flip-flops." Her mom laughed.

"I don't think it'll be that warm." Maisey chuckled. "But warmer weather will be nice."

"I could use some," Annette said.

"Wish I could mail you some." Maisey walked on a trail that followed another branch of the river. "Oh wow!"

"What are you wowing about?" Annette asked.

"You should see this."

"See what?" Annette's voice filled with curiosity.

"There's this ice skating thing, like it snakes around. Cool." Maisey watched the skaters glide past her on the other side of the barrier. "I have to go skating."

"But you don't have your skates with you," her mother protested.

"I can rent a pair. I'll talk to you guys when I get back to the hotel. I'm going skating."

"Bye. Have fun," her parents chorused.

"I will." Maisey ended the call and headed to the entrance of the "skate ribbon." What a cool name. This was going to be so much fun.

In a matter of minutes, Maisey donned her rented skates and took to the ice. She hadn't been ice skating in a couple of years. Kellersburg's town officials had decided not to create the skating rink in the town square the last two years because the preceding winters had been warmer than normal, and the ice had been hard to maintain—besides, it was an expense the town couldn't afford.

She loved ice skating and had taken lessons. She

wondered if she could still do spins and jumps.

Maisey took a few laps around the ribbon, which had some surprising ups and downs that made the skate more challenging. She took in the lighted clock tower in the distance and the lights from the pavilion that could be seen from many vantage points in the park. She also noticed a pond area attached to the ribbon. That was where she could find out if she still could do a jump and land on her feet rather than her rear end.

After skating around the ribbon several times, her confidence grew. The old moves, like skating backward, came back to her with ease. She skated toward the pond. The area only had a few skaters, and that looked good for a few spins and jumps.

First she'd try a spin. She hoped it wouldn't make her dizzy, since she was out of practice using the techniques to overcome the dizziness. She went into the spin and focused like she'd been taught. She came out of the spin feeling a little dizzy, so she skated to the perimeter of the pond and meandered along the edge. She'd have the railing to hold on to if she felt like toppling over.

Success. She remained upright. Now for a jump. She'd never gotten too fancy with the jumps, but she'd been able to do a double axel with ease. Maybe she should start with a single and move up to a double. That made more sense.

As she did her warm-up moves, a wolf whistle sounded from outside the perimeter. She wasn't sure who it was intended for, but she ignored it and hoped they weren't whistling at her. She thought about her parents' concern about her going out alone. What if some stranger followed her when she left the skate ribbon?

Maisey shook the thought away. She could always call a ride-hailing service. If she was really desperate, she could call Zach to get her. She didn't want to do that. Besides, she was probably being paranoid anyway.

After she finished her warm-up, she glanced around to make sure she had plenty of room to do her jump. She didn't want to crash into someone and make a complete fool of herself. She took a deep breath and prepared for the jump. When she completed the single axel, loud clapping and whistling came from somewhere nearby. Did she dare look?

"Maisey. Are you ignoring me?" The sound of Zach's voice floated her way.

Relief mingled with annoyance and the crush-beating pace of her heart. She turned toward the sound. Zach leaned on the railing that surrounded the pond.

She skated toward him. "You scared me."

"You impressed me." He grinned. "How did I scare you?"

The spin she had performed might not have made her very dizzy, but looking at Zach's expression of admiration had her feeling lightheaded.

She blamed it on her parents. "So when I heard that whistle, my parents' warning about going out alone conjured up all kinds of bad things. I did think about calling you to get me."

"So you were thinking about me?"

"Only in case of emergency." Maisey didn't want Zach to have any inkling that she thought of him in any way other than business.

"So I'm good for an emergency."

"Yeah, I figured I could count on you to rescue me if I needed help."

"You can always count on me." Zach nodded. "Why didn't you invite me along? I thought you were going to call."

"You didn't sound like you were really interested in going, and I didn't want to put you on the spot." Maisey remembered his declaration at Thanksgiving about being there to rescue her, but could he rescue her from the crush she had on him? "How did you find me?"

"I wandered around the park and looked at the lights, and I stumbled upon this ice skating thing. So I stopped to watch the people skate." Zach smiled. "And who should I find ice skating? You."

"You should get some skates and skate with me."

Zach shook his head. "Not going to happen. I've already broken one leg. I don't want to break the other."

"So it's a good thing I did come by myself, because I would have found this place and not skated because you wouldn't put on a pair of skates and join me."

"I wouldn't have kept you from skating."

"I'm sure you wouldn't have done that, but I would've felt bad going without you."

"Do you feel bad now?" He gave her an inquisitive look.

"No, because I'm already here."

"When did you learn to skate so well?"

"When I was in high school, there was a lady

whose husband came to work at the plant for several years. While they lived in Kellersburg, she gave ice skating lessons until her husband got moved to another job, like your dad."

"She obviously taught you well." Zach motioned for Maisey to continue her skating. "Let me see you do some more of those spins and jumps."

Maisey produced her phone from the pocket of her coat and looked at it. "Okay. A few more. The rental time on my skates is almost up. I only took them for an hour."

"I'll settle right here and watch."

Maisey skated back toward the center of the ice. Knowing Zach was watching made Maisey nervous. She hoped she didn't fall and embarrass herself. She had done fine when she didn't know he was watching. So nothing should change just because she knew she had an audience.

Pretending no one was watching, Maisey skated around the pond and did a few jumps, then a spin.

Zach applauded, and she glided over to him.

"Good job." Zach smiled, admiration in his eyes.

"Thanks." The compliments made her heart spin, like her skates on the ice. "I'm going to skate around the ribbon one more time, then turn in my skates. You can meet me out front."

Zach saluted. "Will do."

Maisey walked out of the skate ribbon and found Zach leaning against the railing as he watched the skaters whiz by. Zach appeared to be in a much better mood. She was happy for that, but his attention made her longing for a romantic relationship with him even stronger. At least she wasn't thinking about a sexual relationship with him.

Until now. Oh great! Like reversing her course on the ice, she had to send her mind in another direction. She could do it. Ever since her wayward thoughts the other night, she had to beat them back with a mental stick.

"I'm ready," she said.

Zach nodded but didn't say anything as he headed down one of the trails.

"Do you know where you're going?"

"Back to the hotel."

Maisey shook her head. "This isn't the way I came."

"Then you'll see something new on the way back."

"Okay. I hope you know where you're going."

Zach gazed at her in the dim light. "Trust me. I know exactly where I'm going. I wouldn't steer you wrong."

"Okay." Maisey was sure Zach wouldn't steer her wrong, but she didn't trust herself. Why did he have to show up and make her heart do enough jumps and spins to win a skating competition? His accolades did nothing but generate a greater attraction to him.

"You don't sound too sure."

"I believe you. After all, you were the backup plan to rescue me from the bad guys."

"Only the backup?"

"Yeah. I was going to call a ride-hailing service first."

Zach pounded his chest with one hand. "That wounds me that I was only the backup."

Maisey chuckled. "I hardly think you're wounded,

but if you are, I'm sure you'll get over it very quickly."

"So callous. Here I'm hurting and you dismiss it as nothing."

Maisey let out a half laugh and half sigh. "You're really overdoing the sympathy card."

"Okay. I know where I stand. Second fiddle." He squinted as he looked at her. "I'm not used to being the backup, but I'll learn to live with that designation."

Maisey walked beside him. If only he knew that he wasn't the backup in her heart. He had first place there. What a mess she was! What would happen if she just blurted out that she loved him? That was the last thing she should do. Such a confession would ruin everything and make him feel more than uncomfortable.

As they walked together down the trail, Maisey had the temptation to reach over and take his hand. She stuck her hand in the pocket of her jacket to keep from doing just that.

"Do you see the building up ahead?"

Maisey nodded. "What's in the building?"

"A historic carousel." He grinned at her. "You want to ride it?"

"A merry-go-round?"

"This isn't just a merry-go-round. This is a one-of-a-kind carousel."

"How do you know?"

"Phil told me about it and said I should check it out when he sent me to look for you."

Maisey wasn't sure she liked that Phil sent Zach after her. Did everyone think she couldn't take care of herself? "Why would he do that?"

"He wanted to make sure you were back to go out to dinner. He's taking us to a very nice steakhouse." Zach glanced her way. "You wouldn't want to miss that."

"I suppose not."

"So are you game for a ride?"

"As long as you ride, too."

"Count me in." Zach grinned. "All I have to do is ride a wooden horse, not try to stand up on two skinny blades on a slippery surface."

"But you do have to get on the horse." Maisey gave him an impish smile.

"Are you trying to say I'm not very agile?"

Maisey feigned innocence. "Did I say anything like that?"

Zach gave her a wry smile. "You didn't have to. I read between the lines."

Maisey shrugged. "Believe what you'd like."

"I won't take offense, but I'll show you I can still swing this bum leg over a horse."

"I'll be watching." Maisey knew that was for sure. She loved to watch everything he did.

Zach bought the tickets for the ride over Maisey's protest that she could buy her own ticket, but when this trip was over, she could at least say Zach Dawson bought her a ride on a carousel. He had her going around in circles in her mind anyway. She might as well make it for real.

"Choose your horse."

"Wow! This is amazing. The horses are beautiful."

"You could ride the tiger."

Maisey shook her head. "Oh no, I have to ride a

white horse."

"Why a white horse?"

"Because the good guy always rides a white horse."

"I thought the good guy wore a white hat." Zach chuckled.

Maisey pretended to think. "Maybe both a white horse and a white hat."

"But you don't have a white hat."

Maisey wrinkled her nose as she patted the stocking cap on her head. "My stocking cap is off white. Does that count?"

"Okay. Just for today. Good guys can wear off-white hats."

Maisey laughed as she walked around looking for the perfect horse. "Here's mine. I love the blue saddle."

"So do you want me to ride in front of you, in back of you, or beside you?" Zach leaned on the horse next to the one Maisey had chosen.

"You might as well take that one. It suits you." Maisey put her foot in the stirrup and hoisted herself onto her wooden steed.

"You did that very well."

"Thank you. I chose a very-well-behaved horse." Maisey eyed Zach as she waited for him to get on. "Your turn."

"You think I'm going to fall off?"

Maisey grasped the brass pole. "I'm waiting to find out."

Zach laughed. "I may not be as graceful as you, but I can still get on a horse without falling off."

"I'm waiting. You're going to still be standing

there when the carousel starts."

Zach hopped onto his horse with ease, then sat there and grinned at her as the carousel started and the organ music sounded.

While the carousel made its circular journey, Maisey gazed out the floor-to-ceiling windows at the clock tower, the pavilion lights, and the Christmas lights twinkling from trees throughout the park. It was a true winter wonderland. Every once in a while she glanced over at Zach and found him staring at her.

He waved. "I'm still on my horse."

"I had no doubt you could stay on once you got up there."

Zach gave her a bemused smile. "Be kind to me. I'm a lot older than you."

"Respect my elders. Okay." Maisey didn't know whether it was good or bad that Zach mentioned their age difference. Did he still think she was a kid?

When the carousel came to a stop, Maisey's horse was very high and way off the floor. Could she get off without falling? Here she'd teased Zach about getting onto his horse, and she was having trouble getting off hers.

"Up in the air over there." Zach studied her as he dismounted. "If you're nice to me, I might consider giving you a hand."

Maisey put her foot in the stirrup. "Just like you got on, I can get off. I'm not twelve."

"I don't bite." Zach stepped closer and held out his hand for her to take. "I'm just here to give you an assist."

Her heart raced as she stared at him. She put her gloved hand in his and jumped off the horse.

"Thanks."

"You're welcome. And, Maisey, I don't think you're twelve. I think you're a grown woman who loves the Lord, loves people, and loves life. Don't change."

Maisey couldn't find her voice. She swallowed hard as she nodded and fell into step beside him as they left the carousel. While he'd been looking down at her, Maisey had resisted the urge to throw her arms around him. She'd pretend that what he'd said didn't matter. That it didn't make her love him more. He didn't see her that way, and she told herself that was for the best. When this was over and they went their separate ways, she would have fond memories and nothing more.

CHAPTER ELEVEN

The Tucson airport was relatively quiet on a late Friday morning. Zach stood next to Maisey as they waited for their luggage. To get a flight that didn't take them to places like Denver and Dallas for a connection and long layovers, they'd had to get up at three in order to catch a 5:00 a.m. flight.

Zach hadn't been able to sleep on the flight, but Maisey had. Her head had lolled off to one side and gently landed on his shoulder. His heart had hummed while she slept there, so peaceful, so beautiful, so incredible. When would he be brave enough to tell her how he felt about her?

He was a first-degree coward—afraid of her father, afraid of doing the wrong thing, afraid of his own feelings. What would it take for him to throw off his doubts and find a way to win Maisey's heart? He didn't have an answer. He only needed to get through these next two weeks, and then maybe he could work on that without having this project and the need to keep things on a business footing stand in his way.

Or would he find another excuse to keep from putting his heart on the line again?

"Sorry about falling asleep on you," she said as they approached the baggage carousel.

"You know my shoulder will never be the same." His heart would never be the same.

Maisey had a pained expression. "We just had to get up so early, and I couldn't keep my eyes open. I hope I didn't drool or snore."

Zach chuckled. "You did neither. You were a very peaceful and considerate sleeper. And you can quit apologizing. I was only kidding about my shoulder. You're welcome to sleep on it anytime."

Maisey took a deep breath and let out a heavy sigh. "Well, I hope that never happens again."

"It won't be the end of the world if it does." Zach would actually look forward to it, but what did it mean when she adamantly didn't want it to happen again?

"There's my bag." Maisey stepped up to the carousel.

"I got it." Zach swooped in and grabbed her bag. "Here you go."

"Thanks." Maisey smiled, but her eyes conveyed annoyance. "I hope you didn't hurt your shoulder doing that."

Zach laughed out loud. "Shoulder's good. I already managed to get Phil's bag before I got yours."

"There's your bag." Maisey pointed to the big black suitcase with the football sticker on the side.

Zach grabbed it, then turned toward the doors leading outside. "Phil and the film crew are already loading stuff into the van."

"Phil says he has a surprise for us this morning. Do you know what it is?"

"If I did, it wouldn't be a surprise." Zach wheeled the two suitcases toward the gray fifteen-passenger van parked a few feet away. "There's Phil."

After everyone was settled in the van, Phil turned

to the driver. "Take us to Tombstone."

"That's our surprise?" Maisey asked.

"That's it. I hope it's not a disappointment. I've always loved cowboy movies and the old west. I couldn't get this close to Tombstone and not go there." Phil raised his eyebrows as he looked at the occupants of the van. "I hope you'll indulge me."

"I think it's great!" Maisey grinned from ear to ear. "My dad will be jealous when he finds out I've been to Tombstone."

Zach took in the joy on Maisey's face. He wished that smile was for him, but seeing her joy warmed his heart anyway. He was thankful that whatever had bothered her in Billings had disappeared when they'd gotten to Spokane. Maybe the brainstorming or the skating had lightened her spirit. Seeing her joy took away his hurt, his remorse, his regret. She was good for him, but could he be good for her?

While they drove along I-10, Zach thought about yesterday's dog giveaway in Spokane. The boy and his parents had been overwhelmingly grateful for the gift of that dog. The boy would not only have a companion, but one that would keep him safe.

Tomorrow's dog would go to a multigeneration family. The kids, two girls and a boy, all in elementary school, had asked for a dog for their grandmother, who was hearing impaired. The drawing showed their "abuela" walking with the kids and a black-and-white dog. Phil hadn't said whether the dog trained to help the hearing impaired was black and white.

"You're awfully quiet. What's on your mind?" Maisey gave him a questioning glance.

You. "Just thinking about our dog for tomorrow and observing the scenery."

"The desert scenery is definitely interesting. Lots of barren landscape, weird-looking plants, and mountain ranges in the distance. And it's warm! But not enough for sandals. My mom thought I'd be wearing shorts and flip-flops."

"I think it's supposed to be in the low seventies or high sixties for the daytime highs while we're here, but it's going to be cool in the mornings." Zach showed her the weather app on his phone.

Maisey nodded. "I'll definitely be able to ditch the heavy coat, gloves, and hat."

"Phil has our wardrobe change all lined up. It'll be waiting at the hotel when we check in."

"My brother says that every other day I get a big package. I'm guessing that's our used clothes from each shoot."

Zach nodded. "Yep. You'll have a whole new wardrobe when you get back home."

"Amazing!" Maisey wrinkled her brow and let out a contented sigh. "I know I keep saying that, but this whole thing is beyond anything I've ever dreamed of."

Zach could relate to that. Being with Maisey was more than he'd ever dreamed of. Who would've thought that the little girl he used to babysit, with the teeth way too big for her sweet little face, would turn out to be such a beauty inside and out? Her inner beauty was what set her apart from all the other women he'd been with. That was what made it so hard to follow Phil's advice and forget about women for a while.

"You know what's so great about this job?" *You.* For the second time, Zach almost said it, but he clamped his mouth shut as he gazed at Maisey.

"What?"

"That I get paid to meet great people, visit new places, and learn." Zach realized he sounded like Maisey. Her goodness was rubbing off on him.

"What have you learned?"

That you are an amazing woman. Maisey was definitely rubbing off on him. Everything was amazing. "Too many things to name."

"That is not a good answer. There must be one thing you've learned."

Zach let out a heavy sigh. "You're not going to believe this, but I've learned that history isn't so bad."

Maisey's eyes opened wide. "Wow! Now that is amazing. Do I dare say I told you so?"

"If you want." Zach gave her a wry smile. "What about you? What have you learned?"

"Besides history, all about dogs. I keep being amazed at how many ways dogs can be trained. I never thought about having a dog to help people hear doorbells, phones, alarm clocks, or smoke alarms."

"What's so special about this giveaway is the kids thinking of their grandmother, their 'abuela,'" Zach said.

"That is one of the reasons we chose this winner." Phil turned from the front seat to look at Maisey and Zach. "You ready for lunch? We're going to eat at Big Nose Kate's."

"What's that?" Maisey asked.

"It's a historic saloon and restaurant," Phil replied.

"Cool! More history." Maisey grinned at Zach.

"I think the whole town is history." Zach nodded.

"Yeah, pretty much." Maisey pointed. "There's a sign for the town. Entering Tombstone, Elevation 4,539. Founded 1879. It's not really that old, is it?"

"Arizona didn't become a state until 1912. That's your history tip for the day." Zach looked over at Maisey with a know-it-all smile.

"I thought you didn't know anything about history."

Zach shook his head. "I never said that. I only said I don't like history. There's a difference."

"Okay. You got me there." Maisey gazed out the window. "This certainly looks like a dusty western town with all the old-time buildings lining the street."

The driver found a place to park, and they walked to Big Nose Kate's. The hostess seated Zach, Maisey, and Phil at a table on a platform near a window that looked out onto the main street, while the film crew sat at a table just below them. After the waitress took their order, Zach glanced around at the historic items covering the walls and the historic bar that ran the whole distance of the wall. He thought about the historic figures like Wyatt Earp and Doc Holliday, who had walked the streets of this town.

After their food was delivered to the table, Phil gave a prayer of thanks, then looked around. "When we're finished eating, we can go across the street and take in the reenactment of the shootout at the O.K. Corral. How does that sound?"

"I'm in." Maisey picked up the burger she had ordered and took a bite.

Zach loved Maisey's enthusiasm about everything they encountered. She made him look at so many things in a different light. History. His relationship with God. His future. There was no doubt that he wanted Maisey in his future. He could bide his time until the project was over, and then he would … he would what? He didn't know. He gave himself a mental shake. He'd better figure that out by the time they got back to Kellersburg on Christmas Eve.

"You're awfully quiet again. Thinking about history?" Maisey gave him a speculative look.

"No. The future. I've got plans. I just don't know how to execute them at this time."

"That's kind of like me. When I go back to Kellersburg, things will be really dull compared to this." Maisey waved her hand around in the air. "Work and school. Not very interesting."

Phil looked her way. "What would you think about joining another one of my projects?"

A surprised look crossed Maisey's face. "Really? I could do something like this again?"

Phil gestured toward Zach. "I want to keep this young man employed, and the two of you make a good team. So I'm thinking about something for you two in the future. We did a little brainstorming the other day, and you've given me some ideas to think about. I don't know what project will be next, but I plan to have one. I want you to be a part of it."

Maisey's eyes lit up. "That would be amazing." She cringed. "I have to come up with a new word."

Zach chuckled. "You can use that word as often as you like. It would be amazing to work with you again."

Maisey sat back in her chair. "But what does that do for my job and schooling back home?"

"You don't have to make any decisions now. It might be several months before another project is ready to go." Phil bobbed his head. "Just give it some thought."

Zach took in Phil's plans with conflicting emotions. If he had to work with Maisey on another project, he'd never be able to put his plans to win her heart into motion. He'd always have to treat her as a business partner, not a romantic one. He had to remind himself not to borrow trouble from the future. Besides, she never indicated any excitement about working with him again. She only talked about going back to Kellersburg to her not-so-exciting life.

When the waitress delivered the check, she looked at Maisey and Zach. "You two should get your picture taken in our costumes. We give you the stuff, and we take the pictures with your camera or your phone. No cost."

Phil nodded and motioned for them to go. "Sounds like fun. Go ahead while I pay."

Zach and Maisey followed the server to the back of the restaurant, where she showed them the costumes. Zach found a cowboy hat, a bandanna, and a long trench coat to put on, and their server handed him a rifle. She gave Maisey a red silky robe-like red dress, a matching feathered hat, and a boa. The lady in red. Then she handed Maisey a pistol and posed Zach and Maisey together, then took their phones to take the photos.

The waitress motioned with her hands. "Stand closer together. You can put your arm around her." After taking several photos, she gave them a sign that read Outlaw Gang. "Now lean over and act like you're whispering something in her ear."

Zach nodded. He hoped Maisey was enjoying this as much as he was. This was his excuse to hold her close, but maybe this wasn't such a good idea. He'd want to do this all the time, and that would not go well for either of them.

After the photo session, Zach gave the young woman a tip. "Thanks for suggesting this."

Maisey scrolled through the photos on her phone as they walked back to the table. "I'll have to send these to my parents. They'll get a kick out of this."

Zach wondered if her father would get a kick out of them. Surely he would. After all, this was all in fun. Maybe if he mixed a few selfies of Maisey and him with the town in the background, her dad would think nothing about the crazy photos in which Zach was holding Maisey just a little too close.

A couple of hours later, the group headed to the van. Zach thought about how much Maisey had enjoyed the reenactment of the shootout at the O.K. Corral. Afterward, she had gotten photos with some of the actors. More pictures to send her folks.

As the driver headed back to Tucson, Maisey went through her haul from the souvenir shops that had lined the main street of Tombstone.

"My mom's going to love this." Maisey held up a little green cactus Christmas ornament. "I never knew what kind of cactus this was until I asked the store clerk. I've always seen this cactus pictured in photos of the southwest, but I never knew it was a saguaro. I hope I said that correctly."

"You did." Phil nodded. "Too bad we couldn't visit here in the spring when the cacti are in bloom."

"Maybe someday I'll come back." Maisey's eyes filled with excitement. "This trip has certainly given me the travel bug."

"There are lots of wonderful places to see in this country. I've been blessed to see a lot, but there is so much more," Phil said.

As they approached Tucson on I-10, Zach took in the buildings of downtown. The skyline was small compared to the big cities he'd visited while playing football. He noticed the big A on the side of a mountain and recognized it as the A representing the University of Arizona. He'd had teammates who had played football for the U of A, as they called it. They'd mentioned "A" Mountain. Now he knew what they'd been talking about.

As they arrived at the hotel nestled close to a mountain range with saguaros marching up the slopes, Zach turned to Phil. "This is a beautiful place, but I thought we'd be staying closer to downtown and the airport."

"The folks we're giving the dog to live out this way." Phil motioned to the mountain range. "And you can't beat this for accommodations."

Maisey slid out of the van with a look of awe as she gazed upward. "Wow! I have to take more pictures."

"Go right ahead while I get us checked in." Phil headed to the hotel lobby.

Maisey held her phone out and looked at Zach. "Take a photo of me with the mountains, cacti, and palm trees in the background."

Howie from the film crew stepped forward. "You two get together, and I'll take the photo."

Not sure that was what Maisey wanted, Zach gave her a questioning glance. "Okay with you?"

"Absolutely. Wait till our folks see this." Maisey motioned for Zach to join her.

As he stepped up beside her, he wasn't sure how close to get. Howie solved that problem by staging the shot in the perfect spot as he put Zach's arm around Maisey and told them to smile. Zach didn't have any trouble smiling. He hoped when he looked at the photos he would find Maisey smiling, too. This was the second time in one day that someone had put them close for a photo. He wished for a dozen more days like this.

Zach cautioned himself not to wish for things that might bring him trouble. As he looked at the beauty surrounding them, he thought about God, creator of all this beauty. Zach had to make his wishes for Maisey a matter of prayer daily, not just here and there. Would God give Zach the answer he sought? How would he know?

Whatever God's plans were, they were best. Zach wished he didn't have to wait on an answer, but he had to learn patience. Love is patient. Isn't that what the Bible said? Zach had to work on that. Wow! He hadn't put his feelings for Maisey into words until now. Was he in love? He thought he'd been in love before, but those old relationships paled in comparison to what he felt for Maisey. And he'd never even kissed her, though he'd thought about it.

His feelings for Maisey were based on respect, admiration, and sharing a mutual faith. All those old relationships had been based too much on the physical. Regret inundated him. He gave himself a mental shake. He couldn't dwell on the past, because he couldn't undo what had been done. He had to look forward and do better with God's help. That was the key. God's help.

***

Five days later Maisey waited in the lobby as Phil checked his crew into the hotel where Caroline and Wyatt were having their wedding reception and all the guests were staying. Maisey gazed around at the intricate mosaics on the floors, walls, and ceilings. The past few days resembled the mosaics, full of a myriad of bright colors and storytelling. Every dog giveaway had had a story.

After Tucson, they had traveled to Dallas. They'd attended a huge church there that Sunday morning, where the singing was almost heavenly. Then, as a surprise, Zach had arranged for them to attend a Dallas Cowboys football game. The stadium was incredible, and being in person at a professional football game was something she would never forget. And being with Zach through the whole thing made it that much better.

The dog they had given away in Dallas went to a high school girl who'd wanted the dog for her elderly grandparents. They needed a companion, not a specially trained dog, but just a dog they could love. They had lost the dog they'd had had for nearly twenty years and had debated about getting another one. The granddaughter wanted to make sure they had a new dog. The gift was special, and Maisey had shed a few tears. The giveaways always seemed to produce those waterworks, and Zach always smiled.

In Johnson City, Tennessee, the dog had gone to a man who'd been injured while serving in the army. He used a wheelchair, and his young son had sent in the entry for a dog that could assist the man with his mobility. Every story touched Maisey's heart.

This morning they had given away their eighth dog in a small Florida town near Fort Lauderdale. This one went to a boy with autism. The specially trained dog would provide companionship and judgment-free support for the boy, who had a hard time connecting with other people. The dog would help regulate his emotions and improve his communication skills. Again a grateful and happy family received that dog.

After the whirlwind of dog giveaways, she could hardly contain her excitement about Caroline and Wyatt's wedding. Although she was part of the wedding party, the next couple of days would be a relaxing and fun time at the beach. She could hardly wait to get together with Caroline and tell her all about the trip. Did that include telling her about Zach? Maisey was pretty sure Caroline was someone she could confide in.

"Maisey, you're here!"

Maisey turned at the sound of Caroline's voice. Maisey quickly closed the distance between them and gave her friend a hug. "I'm so excited to be here, and this place is amazing." There was that word again.

"I know. Nathan and Melanie got married here, and I knew as soon as Wyatt and I decided to get married, we would get married here, too." Caroline leaned closer as she tilted her head toward the counter where Phil and Zach stood. "Zach Dawson?"

Maisey nodded.

"I remember him from high school, but this grown-up Zach Dawson is better looking now than he was then and definitely better looking in person than on TV." Caroline raised her eyebrows as she looked at Maisey. "Are you having a good time working with him?"

Maisey wasn't ready to confide in Caroline. Maisey had to work up to that. "It's been fun doing this project. Zach is wonderful to work with."

Caroline narrowed her gaze. "I was speculating about something more."

Maisey debated about telling Caroline anything. "Speculate away."

"Oh! So you're not telling."

"Really. There's nothing to tell." And that sadly was the truth, at least on Zach's end. Maisey dismissed the idea of telling Caroline about the childhood crush that was alive and well. No sense in letting her know the pathetic details.

"But you do have things to tell me about your trip so far."

"I do, but I'm sure you're busy."

"Yes, but I'm busy with you today." Caroline looked at her phone. "Tomorrow we have the rehearsal dinner. You can bring Zach, if you'd like."

"I'll think about it." Maisey shrugged. "No crazy bachelorette party?"

Caroline shook her head. "Wyatt isn't having a bachelor party either."

"That sounds sensible."

"For us." Caroline smiled. "After you get settled

in your room, get your swimsuit. We can go to the beach and chat. The weather's perfect. It's supposed to be in the low eighties."

"What about Wyatt?"

"He told me this was my day to relax, so he took Tasha, his grandparents, my parents, Melanie, Nathan, and their boys on some pirate-ship ride. Tasha was super excited about it, and so were Ryan and Andrew. Then after they get back, you, Melanie, and I are going to get mani-pedis.

"Wow! That sounds super." Maisey grabbed the handle to her suitcase. "I'll get my key from Phil and meet you down here in a few minutes, okay?"

"Sure." Caroline nodded.

As Maisey and Caroline talked, Phil came over and gave Maisey her room key. "Is this the lovely bride-to-be?"

Maisey nodded. "Caroline, this is Phil Waller. He's the head of our project and the owner of the Master's Dog Food Company, which is sponsoring the project. Phil, this is Caroline Keller, Nathan Keller's sister."

"Nice to meet you, Caroline." Phil shook her hand. "This is a lovely venue for a wedding."

"We think so," Caroline said. "You and your crew are welcome to attend, if you'd like."

Phil shook his head. "Thanks, but I wouldn't want to crash your wedding. I knew Maisey and Zach would be occupied with wedding stuff, so I've made arrangements for the film crew and I to meet some friends of mine in the area. We have plans for tonight and tomorrow night."

"That's good then. I'm glad you have friends you

can meet." Caroline turned to Zach, who stood nearby. "And this must be that famous football player who got his start at Kellersburg High."

Zach laughed. "Hello, Caroline. I didn't know if you'd remember me, being a year ahead of me in school."

"Remember you? I tell all my coworkers I went to school with you. They're in awe."

Shaking his head, Zach let out a halfhearted chuckle. "Are you sure you're not exaggerating a little?"

"No. They expect me to get a picture of you while you're here."

"We can do that right now." Zach motioned for Caroline and Maisey to join him in front of a giant potted plant in the lobby. "If you give me your phone, Caroline, we can do a selfie right now."

"Okay, great." Caroline handed Zach her phone.

Zach held the phone at arm's length as Caroline and Maisey stood on either side of him. "Smile for the camera."

"Thanks." Caroline retrieved her phone from Zach and put it into the pocket of her capris. "Now Maisey and I have a date with the beach and some mani-pedis."

"Have fun, ladies." Zach waved.

"Are you going with Phil?" Maisey asked.

"No. I'm meeting a friend who lives in the area."

"Okay. See you later." Even though Zach had told her he'd sworn off women, was he meeting one of his old girlfriends? One of the models he used to date was from somewhere in south Florida? Maisey gave herself a mental shake. Silly thoughts. Jealous thoughts. Wrong-headed thoughts. They had to go.

Maisey watched Zach saunter away, taking her hopeless heart with him. He had no idea how much she cared about him. He would probably never know.

"We need to talk."

Maisey turned to Caroline. "About what?"

"That look of longing on your face." Caroline's expression dared Maisey to deny it.

Maisey sighed. "I'll meet you here in half an hour to go to the beach."

"And we'll have that talk."

Maisey didn't say anything. She only nodded as she grabbed her suitcase and headed for the elevator. What would she tell Caroline? The truth would be a good place to start. Would she think Maisey was crazy for hanging on to this crush for years? Hadn't she thought about talking with Caroline? This was that opportunity.

Thirty minutes later, Maisey, dressed in her swimsuit and floral cover-up, walked into the lobby. She carried the bag filled with beach paraphernalia that Phil had had delivered to her room. The man was on top of everything.

Caroline waited near the front door. "Sun, sand, and a couple of beach chairs are waiting for us."

Maisey took a deep breath of salt air. "This is so nice. I don't know if I want to go back to the cold after this."

Caroline chuckled. "This time of year is super, but you have to put up with the hot, humid summers in order to enjoy the mild winters."

"I guess there's a tradeoff for everything." Maisey followed Caroline as they traversed the loose sand on the other side of the walkway that ran the length of the beach.

"Beach chairs straight ahead. Even an umbrella so we don't get a burn. I've been warned not to get sunburned. I wouldn't look good in my wedding dress with a sunburn." Caroline set her bag near a chair and sat down.

"I've got plenty of sunscreen, thanks to Phil. On this whole trip he has supplied clothes and accessories for every place we've been. I'll have a whole new wardrobe when I get home." Maisey held out her hands. "This is a dream job."

"And you have a dream coworker from the look of your face. Spill."

Maisey plunked a straw hat on her head as she smeared on the sunscreen. "I wish I knew what to tell you."

"Why don't you tell me about the places you've visited and about the dogs you've given away?" Caroline eyed Maisey. "We'll save Zach for last."

Maisey gave Caroline a rundown of the sights as well as the wonderful stories that went with the dogs that now had happy new owners. Maisey even sang the "Twelve Dogs of Christmas" song.

"That's the song that got you into this gig?" Caroline asked.

Maisey nodded. "Phil had me sing it and wanted me to join the project. The rest is history. I'm really looking forward to Baltimore and Boston. I've always wanted to visit those cities."

"Okay, you've stalled long enough. I want to know about Zach."

Maisey let out a harsh breath. "I don't know what

to tell you."

"You like him."

"Who wouldn't like him? He's fun. He's handsome. He's considerate." Maisey pressed her lips together, still trying to convince herself she should give Caroline the whole story.

"Then why is it so hard for you to admit you have a thing for him?"

Maisey placed her hands in a prayerful pose in front of her mouth as she stared out at the waves spilling onto the sand. A gentle breeze ruffled her hair around her shoulders. She grabbed her hair and held it behind her neck as she looked over at Caroline, who sat there with an expression of expectation. "I'm not sure how I feel about Zach."

"And why is that?"

"Because he's famous, and I don't know if I care about the Zach I've created in my mind or the Zach who's a well-known sports figure." Maisey sighed. "You see, I've had a crush on him since I was six and he was fourteen. You know our families used to hang out together all the time because my dad and Zach's dad worked together at the medical devices plant."

Caroline nodded. "So you're not sure that what you're feeling now is anything more than your old childhood case of puppy love."

"That's it. How do I figure that out, and why would he ever give me a second look? I'm not like any of the women he's dated. Like models and actresses, other famous people. I'm just plain Maisey Norberg from Kellersburg, Ohio."

Caroline smiled. "Maybe he's ready for something different. Ready for Maisey Norberg from

Kellersburg, Ohio."

"But I can't just go up to him and tell him how I feel, especially when I'm not sure myself." Maisey dug one foot down into the sand. "Besides, there's the business aspect I have to think about. It's not always good to get involved with a coworker."

"But you won't be coworkers forever."

Maisey dug her other foot into the sand. If she could just cover her worries like she covered her feet. "But we might be working together on another project, and if we're not, he'll be in Atlanta, and I'll be in Kellersburg."

"So I guess you'd better figure out what you want before this project ends."

"But I can't."

Caroline lifted her hands in a gesture of resignation. "Then I guess you just have to watch him walk away."

"But I don't want to do that."

"Then go after what you want."

"But what if he's not interested?"

"Sometimes you just have to be brave?"

Maisey narrowed her gaze. "Is that the way it worked with you and Wyatt?"

"Sort of. Wyatt was really brave from the beginning. He let me know he was interested, but I had some issues to work through. He was patient with me, and I finally had to be brave and let him know I loved him."

Maisey blinked rapidly and waved a hand in front of her face. "You're going to make me cry."

Caroline reached over and took Maisey's hand. "You have a tender heart, and something tells me

Zach needs someone with a tender heart."

"Why?"

"Because he's had a rough year recovering from that injury. It's kind of like Wyatt. You remember the way he was in the nursing home."

"And you gave him your tender heart?"

Caroline chuckled. "Not exactly. You know I told him to be kind."

"And he took your advice." Maisey wondered what she could say to Zach that would make a difference to him? "I don't know what I could tell Zach. Honestly, it seems to me he's got it all figured out."

"Maybe that's what he wants you to think. He doesn't want you to see his vulnerable side."

Maisey crossed her arms over her torso. "I wish I were brave, but I'm a chicken."

"Then you're the perfect candidate for the chicken dance at the reception."

Maisey shook her head. "I'm not vying for the bouquet. I'll leave that to all the other single women."

"Don't be surprised if that bouquet flies your way." Caroline gave Maisey a wry smile. "Or that some well-meaning person catches it and gives it to you."

Maisey let out a halfhearted laugh. "So there's a conspiracy brewing in the ranks of the wedding guests?"

"Could be?" Caroline settled back on her chair. "Just one last word of advice. Don't be afraid of your feelings. You don't want to let this opportunity with Zach slip through your fingers and regret it later."

"Okay." Maisey lay back on her chair.

Maisey didn't feel the confidence to go after Zach without a hint that he might share her interest. At least Caroline had known up front that Wyatt was interested in her. Maisey felt like she was flying without radar. This was probably where she should rely on God to guide her through this, but she wasn't sure God really cared about her love life or lack of it. He had bigger things to deal with.

CHAPTER TWELVE

Caroline and Wyatt danced alone on the small dance floor surrounded by numerous small tables covered with tablecloths in a rainbow of colors to match the mosaic tiles on the walls. Zach lounged against one of the pillars that held up the second-floor walkway looking down on the dance floor. He envied Wyatt. The man had found his true love. Did Zach dare think he might have found his in Maisey?

Too soon to tell.

Zach let his gaze linger on Maisey, who stood at the edge of the dance floor. The red dress that grazed her shoulders and flowed to the floor was made of some filmy material with sparkles all over it. The sparkles fit Maisey. Everything about her sparkled, from her sweet laugh to her bright-blue eyes. She looked as good as any of the models he'd dated. So pretty and so refreshingly unaware of her beauty.

Tonight he planned to wade into the treacherous waters of romance again. Maisey might shoot him down, but he had to quit being a coward. Her dad would just have to accept that his daughter had fallen for a less-than-perfect man. Was that a dream of monumental proportions? Maybe.

First Zach had to convince Maisey to take a chance on him. Then he had to convince her dad that her choice was a good one. A dream for sure.

"Mister, are you as famous as my daddy?"

Zach looked down at the pint-sized little girl with the dark hair and eyes. Her lacy white dress, which was a shorter version of Caroline's wedding dress, made her look like a little princess. "Are you Tasha, and is your daddy that man in the tan suit and the red tie dancing out there?"

The child nodded, surety written on her face. "That's My Wyatt. He's my daddy, and he's dancing with my new mommy. They love each other, and they love me."

"Love is a good thing."

Tasha gazed up at him, a question wrinkling her little brow. "You didn't answer my question."

Zach shook his head as he pretended to think. "You mean about being famous?"

The child nodded.

"That's a hard question to answer. Let's call it a draw."

"What's a draw?"

"A tie. We're both famous."

She continued to look at him, as if she wasn't quite sure his assessment was true. "I suppose."

"You made an excellent flower girl today."

She shook her head. "But I didn't do flowers. I did shells."

"Were you the shell girl then?"

Tasha giggled. "Yeah. I tossed the shells just like they showed me."

"I see you've met my daughter, Tasha."

Zach looked up to find Wyatt standing there. "I have. We've had quite a nice conversation. She wanted to know if I'm as famous as you."

"Leave it to my girl to make me the most famous guy in the room." Wyatt laughed as he gathered Tasha into his arms. "It's time for our dance, young lady."

"I enjoyed talking to you, Tasha." Zach waved while Wyatt carried his child to the dance floor, where Caroline joined them with her dad.

The terrible crushing feeling he'd had that day in Montana hit Zach again as he watched Wyatt twirl Tasha around the dance floor to the lively tune. Why was he having these episodes again? The injury, the surgeries, and hospitals had triggered that response early on after his breakup with Jayla. Since he'd started working with Phil, they hadn't affected him until Montana, now again today.

Maybe being near the place where he and Jayla had once vacationed had contributed to this episode. Zach wasn't sure what it was. Guilt? Unending remorse? Distress?

Could he escape? What would Maisey think if he abandoned her? Montana was different. He hadn't been her escort then. Tonight he was. He couldn't just walk out. He took a deep breath and hoped the sensation would subside. He would deal with it.

More dances ensued as Zach made his way toward Maisey, who talked with Melanie. They both wore that same red dress. Maisey, with her blond hair and blue eyes, stood in contrast to Melanie, with her dark hair and brown eyes. Maybe Maisey's presence would soothe his troubled soul. He manufactured a smile as he stepped up beside her.

"Hey, where did you go to?" Maisey grinned at him.

His heart did a little jig to the tune filling the air.

"I was waylaid by a beautiful girl."

"And what beautiful girl was that?"

Zach wondered if he detected a little jealousy in that question. Absurd. "Tasha wanted to know if I was as famous as her dad."

Maisey laughed. "What did you tell her?"

"It's a tie."

"I beg to differ." Maisey moved closer. "You're way more famous than Wyatt."

Zach couldn't help smiling. "You're good for the ego."

Maisey shook her head. "This has nothing to do with ego. This has to do with facts. You are more famous."

"Don't tell Tasha."

"I promise I won't."

Zach motioned to the dance floor. "When is it our turn?"

Maisey turned to him. "Turn for what?"

"To dance."

A hint of surprise crossed her face. "You want to dance?"

"I thought that was what one did when the music was playing."

"Yeah, but we have to wait for the father-daughter, et cetera, et cetera dances. Eventually, the disc jockey will give you your cue, and you can rush to the dance floor."

"Will you go with me?"

"You mean, you want to dance with me?" Maisey blinked, and those oh-so-kissable lips parted in an astonished expression.

"Does that surprise you?"

"Just a little."

"I am your escort."

"So you're required to dance with me."

Be brave, Zach. "I want to dance with you, not because I'm your escort, but because I think you're a special person, someone I care about."

Maisey's eyes sparkled, like her dress. "I'd very much like to dance with you."

Zach held out his hand, and she put her hand in his. He thought his heart might burst, this time from happiness, not old wounds. They didn't say anything to each other while they waited for their turn.

The disc jockey let the beginning of "Slow Dance" play, then said, "All dance."

"Our turn." Zach squeezed her hand and led her onto the dance floor. She fit perfectly in his arms. *God, please don't let me mess this up.*

Zach pulled Maisey close and hoped for this one chance at romance, like the song said. They didn't say anything as they swayed to the music. While he held her, all the stress of the evening washed away, like the waves on the beach. Could Maisey keep him centered? Could he be good enough to gain her love? Could he still be her hero, like he'd been when she was seven?

When the song ended, he didn't want to let her go, but he did anyway. "Thanks for that dance. I hope there'll be more."

Maisey smiled up at him. "I'm pretty sure I can be persuaded to dance with you again."

"Next slow dance is mine."

"What about the fast ones?"

Zach made a pained face. "I'm sure you don't

want to see that."

"Sure I do." Maisey snickered. "You have to do the chicken dance."

"Not going to happen."

"We'll see about that." Maisey gave him an impish smile.

Zach led her off the dance floor as an upbeat song began to play.

Maisey looked at him. "Listen. Are you sure you don't want to get out there and move to that beat?"

"I'm sure." Zach waved her toward the dance floor. "You have fun to the beat. I'll watch."

"Okay, if that's the way you want it. I'll have to find another partner." Maisey trotted off toward the other side of the dance floor and found another partner.

Ryan Keller was all arms and legs as he danced with Maisey. Then Ryan's younger brother, Andrew, had his turn. She danced with Wyatt, brave man, then his grandfather. Then with Caroline and a bunch of her cousins in a big circle, as they laughed and clapped to the music. Zach enjoyed watching her as much as he'd enjoyed dancing with her. She brought a joy to his heart that he couldn't begin to explain. Was that love?

Zach had to wait for his next chance to dance with Maisey, as the bride and groom cut the cake and the best man and matron of honor gave their toasts. As the next slow song started, Zach walked onto the dance floor and claimed Maisey.

"You think the disc jockey's got a theme going here with the slow dance songs?" Zach pulled Maisey close and breathed in the sweet floral scent of her hair.

His heart was mush. His bones were mush. His mind was mush.

"You mean the slow-dancing theme?"

Zach nodded and closed his eyes as he held Maisey tighter. He only wanted to think about how right she felt in his arms, but her dad's warning and Phil's advice to steer clear of women intruded into his thoughts. Did he listen to his heart or those men?

Life was made up of decisions—decisions that could determine the course of one's life. He'd made some bad ones, and now he was paying the price with his indecision about pursuing Maisey. He had talked with Chuck today about Maisey, and Chuck hadn't encouraged or discouraged Zach's interest in her. Chuck had encouraged Zach to pray. He'd expressed doubts about how to know the answer, but Chuck had assured Zach that the answer would be clear.

Zach felt as though this time romance was like walking across the hot sand on the beach. He had to go lightly. He couldn't charge into this like a rushing linebacker.

The song ended, and Maisey stepped out of his arms. He wanted to pull her back, but he held his arms to his sides. She smiled at him, and he thought his insides might float away. She had him completely entranced.

"Thanks again. Same song, second verse. I claim the next slow dance with you."

"Your claim is good, and I believe it's now." Maisey glanced at the disc jockey and back at Zach. "The song I requested is playing."

"When You Say Nothing At All" sounded over the speakers as couples throughout the room joined Zach and Maisey in the slow dance. Again Zach held Maisey close as he listened to the words of the song. Was she trying to tell him something by saying nothing at all, or was he wishing that was the case? Was his heart speaking to hers while they moved around in their little spot on the dance floor? If that was so, he hoped his heart was saying the right things.

The song ended. This time she didn't step out of his arms. She just looked up at him, her lips curved up. "Thanks."

"My pleasure." That was for sure. "Any time you need a partner, I'll be there."

Maisey glanced around the room. "I see what's coming. They're seating Caroline so Wyatt can take off the garter and toss it. Guess you'd better get in line with the other single men."

"Not me." Zach shook his head as he grabbed Maisey's hand. "I'm outta here. Go with me."

Maisey's eyes grew wide as she stared at him. Would she turn him down? He'd failed to follow his own advice about not rushing in.

"I don't know. I'm a bridesmaid. I can't just rush off." Maisey looked back to where Caroline had just taken a seat as the audience clapped in unison. "I'd better not. You can go if you want."

Zach wanted to kick himself. He could've handled that better. Way better. Maybe he was reading something into their dances that he shouldn't have. He was terrible at romance. He wouldn't go now, but he certainly didn't plan to join the other bachelors trying to grab the garter. "I'll stay for you."

Maisey didn't respond, just turned to watch as Wyatt knelt beside Caroline. The disc jockey played

"Pretty Woman" while Wyatt removed the garter. When Wyatt stood, the single guys gathered on the dance floor. Wyatt looked around, and Zach shrank back behind some of Caroline's older relatives and leaned against the wall. Then Wyatt turned his back on the crowd of guys and flung the garter into the air. Some guy that Zach didn't know snagged the garter and placed it on his arm. The other guys joked and laughed with him as they clapped him on the back.

Would Caroline toss her bouquet next? Maisey stood at the edge of the dance floor as Melanie handed Caroline the bouquet. Zach watched to see if Maisey would join the single women who had gathered on the dance floor. Melanie went over to Maisey and escorted her into the crowd. She didn't look pleased, but she didn't resist.

Zach had sympathy for Maisey's plight, but she was a bridesmaid. Single bridesmaids usually had to put up with the whole tradition. Caroline turned her back and tossed the bouquet high into the air. Her grandma Addie caught it and held it high. Laughter and hugs ensued as Addie left the dance floor and tracked down Maisey, who had already made her way toward the spot where Melanie stood. Addie tapped Maisey on the shoulder. She turned, and Addie thrust the bouquet at Maisey, who immediately tried to give it back.

Addie leaned closer and whispered something in Maisey's ear. Maisey stood there with a stunned expression. Caroline joined the little group and hugged Maisey, whose stunned expression turned to one of resignation. Maisey said something to Caroline and Addie, then the two laughed, and Caroline gave

Maisey another hug.

Was this Zach's opening? Determined not to let cowardice rule his heart, he strode to where Maisey stood, still holding the bouquet.

"Hi. Are congratulations in order?" Zach raised his eyebrows.

"No." Maisey didn't look amused. "This belongs to Addie. She just gave it to me for safekeeping. She said she's on a manhunt."

Zach laughed as he nodded. "Okay, if that's what you want me to believe. At least you're not after the guy who caught the garter."

"Ah. No." Maisey frowned. "You don't remember him from the rehearsal dinner? He's one of Wyatt's cowboy friends."

"You have something against cowboys?"

Maisey shook her head. "He's just not my type."

"Just what is your type?"

"Would you like to find out?"

Zach's heart skipped a beat. Was Maisey flirting with him? "I would. Do you want to get out of here? Plan our escape?"

"I have to talk to Caroline first. It wouldn't be good form to just disappear."

"Okay." Zach watched as Maisey glided away like a princess on a royal errand.

Zach held his breath. He couldn't tell by the two women's expressions what was going on. Finally Maisey hugged Caroline and turned to him with a smile. He had to stop himself from running across the dance floor to whisk her away.

"Ready to go?"

"I am. Let's take a walk on the beach."

"I have to be back by the time Caroline and Wyatt are getting ready to leave." Maisey held up her phone. "She's going to text me. So we shouldn't go too far away."

"We won't."

Zach resisted the urge to ask Maisey what Caroline had said. Was she warning Maisey to be careful with the philandering football player? That was a crazy thought. Maisey's dad was living inside Zach's mind, warning him not to do anything he might live to regret. He'd already done plenty of that.

"It might be chilly at the beach now that it's dark. Are you sure you'll be warm enough in that dress?"

"Maybe not. I have a pashmina in my room. I'll get it."

"Okay." Zach wished he hadn't opened his mouth as he watched her leave.

Maybe she would have second thoughts about a walk on the beach and leave him standing here wondering what had happened to her.

A couple of minutes later when she reappeared on the other side of the dance floor, he breathed a sigh of relief. His relief was short lived. Ryan and Andrew waylaid her, and in the next instant the frenetic notes of the chicken dance boomed over the speakers.

Looking Zach's way, Maisey madly waved for him to join her as Ryan and Andrew dragged her onto the floor. Zach knew he couldn't very well ruin the boys' fun, and if he did the chicken dance with her, maybe he would be her hero after all. He joined the group, and Maisey looked at him as if he'd hung the moon. He felt absolutely ridiculous, but if ridiculous won the heart of the girl, he would be ridiculous.

When the dance was over, Zach grabbed Maisey's hand and raced off the dance floor and out onto the portico in front of the hotel before anything else could stop them.

"Thanks … for … that." Maisey's words came out in between breaths. Then she placed the pashmina around her shoulders as she took another deep breath. "I must be out of shape. You, on the other hand, don't seem to be breathing hard at all."

Zach might not be breathing hard, but his heart was beating, or more like galloping, as fast as the beat of the chicken dance. "Any time you need a partner for the chicken dance, I'm your man."

"I'll remember that for the next time."

Zach hoped there would be a next time. Maybe at their own wedding. Wow! Where did that come from? He had no business jumping that far ahead. There was a lot of distance between a couple of dances and marriage.

Maybe his thinking was born from the fact that Maisey wasn't like any of the other women he'd dated. She was a keeper. She was the kind of woman who brought marriage to mind. But neither of them was ready for anything close to that. He still didn't know whether she actually liked him. The dances they had shared tonight gave him hope that she did.

Zach held out his hand. "Ready for that walk."

Maisey gazed up at him as she placed her hand in his. "Ready."

They didn't say anything as they walked down the pathway that led to the beach. When they reached the walkway that ran parallel to the water, they stopped. They stood there for a moment. The quiet night made the sound of the waves seem louder. The moonlight splashed onto the chairs and floral archway left from the wedding. The blackened sky sparkled with stars and reminded Zach of everything about Maisey that sparkled.

"It's so peaceful out here now. I love the sound of the waves," Maisey said.

"It is peaceful. Let's stroll down the pathway for a ways."

Maisey gazed up at him. "Okay."

Zach made sure to match his step to Maisey's shorter stride as they walked. He wanted to let her know of his interest in her, but he didn't know how to start. He'd never had trouble with this kind of thing with women before, but maybe more was riding on it this time. Or maybe he'd never had to take the initiative. The women had all come onto him, and he'd went along with their advances. Now he had to start the conversation with something. Anything.

"Just curious. How is it that Caroline Keller had you as one of her attendants? I didn't know you were close, since she's almost a decade older than you."

"I got the job by default."

Zach frowned. "By default?"

"Yeah. Melanie, Nathan's wife, was always going to be the matron of honor, but Caroline needed one more attendant to balance out the two groomsmen, Nathan and Wyatt's good friend Morgan. She doesn't have a sister, and she couldn't pick just one of her female cousins without hurting the others' feelings, so she picked me." Maisey shrugged. "She always says I reintroduced her to Wyatt when he was in the nursing home."

"How was that?"

Maisey let out a heavy sigh. "To tell the truth, Wyatt wasn't the easiest patient to deal with. In fact, he was very disagreeable. The day Caroline started her job at the nursing home, I begged her to take Wyatt his meal. She did, and the rest is history."

"So you're saying it was love at first sight?"

A little chuckle escaped as Maisey tapped the heel of her hand on her forehead. "Hardly. It took a while for them to realize they were made for each other. But that makes it all the sweeter."

Zach looked at her. "I think someone is a romantic."

"Caroline?"

Smiling wryly, Zach shook his head. "I believe you know I meant you."

"I do love a happy ending."

"We witnessed that tonight." Zach wished his happy ending would be with Maisey. Did he dare say that out loud? Not right now. He wasn't sure she was ready to hear that. And then there was the specter of Maisey's dad that haunted his thoughts every time he considered telling her how he felt. The chicken dance he was doing right now in his mind was as chaotic as the one he'd just done at the reception.

"I saw you talking to Tasha tonight. She's so precious and precocious. She tells you exactly what she's thinking." Maisey let out a contented sigh. "Tasha is such a wonderful part of Caroline and Wyatt's love story. She told Wyatt that Missy Caroline had to be her mom."

That awful sensation hit Zach right in the chest again. The feeling made him want to sit down on the sand and curl up in a ball. He ached. He stopped and hoped the sensation would go away.

"Zach, is something wrong?" Maisey grabbed his arm. "You don't look so good."

Zach looked at her through the maze of his hurt. Could he possibly tell her what was wrong. What would she think? He could ruin everything between them right out of the chute if he told her the horrific story. He couldn't tell her now. He had to win her heart before he could share this awful part of his past with her.

"You're right. I'm not feeling well." He tried to tamp down the terrible sensation that engulfed him. "Let's go back."

"Is it something you ate?" Concern painted Maisey's features.

Zach shook his head. "No. I'll be okay. I think I just need to lie down."

"I'm sorry you don't feel well."

"Thanks. I'm sorry I've ruined our walk." Lying down wouldn't actually help him. Maybe time alone with God would. He had to pray that God would heal this deep hurt. Would it ruin everything with Maisey? He'd pray it wouldn't.

Zach held Maisey's hand all the way back to the hotel as they walked in silence. He took a deep breath of the salt air and tried to let the sound of the waves ease the tension in the pit of his stomach. Was this God's answer? Forget Maisey?

Zach had to heal that wound before he could love Maisey the way she deserved. That was clear. Would that happen? With God's help, it could. Zach had to believe that.

***

The following afternoon the wheels of Maisey's suitcase went clickety clack as she traversed the paver sidewalk leading up to Zach's stucco and tan brick house in Atlanta. She tried not to let her mouth hang open. Although she knew Zach was a famous quarterback who had been paid millions to throw a ball, she had almost forgotten his celebrity status. In the days they had spent together, he had almost seemed like the kid who had grown up in a modest house in Kellersburg. This house said something altogether different.

Zach opened the door. "Welcome. My housekeeper has prepared food for us. I'll show you to your rooms, and then we can eat at the island in the kitchen. Dining room's too stuffy."

Maisey craned her neck to see the dining room through the doors on one side of the two-story entry that looked more like the lobby in a small hotel than the entry to a house. Zach was right. The dining room did look stuffy with its fancy wallpaper and wainscoting. The place hardly looked like a bachelor pad. It looked more like a family home, a very rich family home.

A round table adorned with a monstrous flower arrangement sat under the chandelier that glowed in the sunlight coming through the palladium window above the double doors. A formal living room filled with chairs and a surprisingly comfortable-looking tan sofa decorated with throw pillows was on the opposite side of the entry from the dining room. An Oriental rug that matched the sofa sat on the dark hardwood floors. Maisey liked this room. It invited you to sit down and visit.

Zach led them through the entry hall into another less formal living area with a deep-tan leather sofa and a matching love seat that formed a conversation pit in front of a large stone fireplace. A flat-screen TV sat on the wall above the fireplace. Maisey looked up and discovered a loft area that looked down on the room.

"Howie, Jess, and Shirl, follow me upstairs." Zach turned to Maisey. "You and Phil can relax here while I show them their rooms. Then I'll come back and take you to yours."

"Okay." Maisey plopped onto the nearby couch and looked at Phil. "Have you been here before?"

Phil nodded. "Several times."

"What does one person do in a house this size?" Maisey gazed around, her mind still in awe of her surroundings. When she looked back at Phil, she remembered he was a wealthy man as well. Maybe his house was even bigger.

"Enjoy it." Phil gestured around the room. "You haven't even begun to see it all."

"How did you get connected with Zach?"

"He did some dog food commercials for my company early on in his career. I took an interest in him and became a mentor of sorts, and we became friends as well as business associates."

"Why would Zach do dog food commercials when he doesn't have a dog? And I don't remember Zach doing any dog food commercials."

Phil shook his head. "You wouldn't have. The

commercials only ran in a few markets when my dog food company was just starting, maybe the second year Zach had been in the league. That same year Zach suddenly lost his dog, and he didn't want to do more commercials."

"How did he lose his dog?"

"The housekeeper let the dog out into the backyard, but she didn't know the yard people had accidentally left the gate open. The dog ran out and got hit by a car."

"How terrible!" Maisey put a hand over her heart. "Is the loss of his dog why he seems so sad sometimes?"

"I don't know." Phil gave Maisey a puzzled look. "I haven't seen that sadness, but I do know he didn't want to get another dog. He said he was gone too much and had to rely on other people to take care of it."

Maisey leaned back. The episode with Zach at the beach last night and that day in Montana bewildered Maisey. He was fine today, acting as if nothing had happened. They'd had a church service on the beach early this morning, with Wyatt's friend Morgan giving the sermon about using your God-given talents for His purpose. Was that what she was doing now? She hoped so.

Before she could answer her own question, the others returned. Howie, Jess, and Shirl made themselves comfortable on the sofas.

Howie looked around. "Zach, this is some place you've got here. Great accommodations."

"I try to please." Zach chuckled, then looked toward Maisey and Phil. "Follow me, and I'll show you to your rooms."

Zach led them down the stairs to a basement area, but it was like no basement Maisey had ever seen. It was like a whole other house with a living room, kitchen, and a rec room with a pool table and a small bar.

"Bedrooms are back here." Zach led the way down a short hallway. "Maisey, you can have this one, and Phil, you can have the one across the hall."

Maisey peered into the room with a bed, with a sky-blue canopy that matched the striped blue-and-white comforter, centered on the far wall. "This is lovely. Thanks."

"Go ahead and get settled while I show Phil his room." Zach made a sweeping gesture with one hand. "You have your own bathroom."

"Wow! This is amazing." Maisey couldn't believe how many times she'd said that word on this trip.

As Zach and Phil left, Maisey wheeled her suitcase into the room, then went and sat on the bed. She kicked off her shoes and swung her legs onto the bed and just lay there for a minute. The bed was every kind of comfortable. She better not lie here too long, or she might fall asleep and dream about Zach.

She still couldn't figure out what had happened on the beach. The dances they had shared made Maisey believe Zach actually considered her more than just someone he worked with. Maybe he was only being nice, but he'd said he cared about her. The caring might be nothing more than how he'd cared about her when she'd been seven years old. How was she supposed to figure that out?

A knock sounded on the door. "Maisey, are you

ready to go back upstairs?"

Maisey hopped off the bed and slipped her shoes back on. "Yeah. I was just testing out the bed. Very comfy."

"I've never slept in it, so I wouldn't know. Plenty of guests have, and I've never had any complaints."

The whole bed thing had Maisey's mind going where it shouldn't go again. Maybe that was another sign, a warning sign that she had to forget thinking of Zach in the context of romance. She raced up the stairs, leaving Phil and Zach behind and hopefully her wayward thoughts as well. Her mind was a mess!

"Hey, you that hungry?" Zach came up behind her.

Maisey's heart beat in double time. The race up the stairs must be the reason. "No, just doing what you said. Go upstairs."

"You know I don't run as fast as I used to. So slow down for me."

"Sorry. I didn't mean to outpace you."

Zach shook his head and let out a halfhearted laugh. "I was only kidding. You can move as fast as you want to. Follow me to the kitchen."

Maisey just shrugged as she joined the others in the kitchen just off the informal living area. Everyone stood around the huge kitchen island with high stools on three sides. Straight ahead was a professional stove surrounded by maple cabinetry. The island contained a sink that looked almost big enough to take a bath in. To the right was a wall of windows that looked out on the outdoor kitchen, eating area, and outdoor seating area filled with wicker furniture. Maisey tried not to let her mouth hang open as she took in all the amenities of this house.

Zach and his humongous house had her discombobulated. Why was she letting him make her crazy? Because she was in love with him and didn't know what to do about it. What did she do with these feelings? Stifle them? Pretend they didn't exist? Or shout them to the rooftops? That last one was a really bad idea. She would have to live with them and see where they took her. Somewhere good she hoped.

"Grab a seat, and I'll serve the food. Juanita, my housekeeper, has made some of her famous chili." Zach pointed to a slow cooker sitting on the counter next to the stove and the bowls of various items. "I've got toppings here. You can put whatever you'd like on your chili. Phil, will you say a prayer before we start?"

Phil said the prayer, then Zach ladled the chili into the stack of bowls sitting by the slow cooker. Gregarious conversation ensued as the group enjoyed the chili and the company. Maisey was happy to learn more about the film crew that she hadn't spent a lot of time with other than when they were filming.

The group shared what they had done during their longer time in Florida as they visited friends and family. When Maisey learned that Zach had met his friend Chuck, she realized how off kilter her thoughts about an old girlfriend were, especially after she learned about Chuck's son who was battling cancer. Maisey wondered whether that bad news was what had brought on Zach's strange behavior last night at the wedding.

Zach finished off his chili, then looked over the group. "I wish we had more time here so we could see some of the sights here in Atlanta, but Phil tells me we're giving away our dog tomorrow morning during a special ceremony at the boy's school. He's getting an allergy detection dog that will accompany him to school. So the school principal wants all the children at the school to be aware of what this dog means to our recipient, Ethan Holcomb, who suffers from celiac disease."

"I've heard of that, but I don't know what it is. Do you know?" Jess asked.

Zach nodded. "A person with celiac disease can't eat gluten. If they do, it damages the small intestine. It can't be cured, but it can be managed if a person doesn't eat any gluten. In some foods the gluten is obvious, but in others it isn't. That's where the allergy dog comes in. The dog can sense the allergen and alert the owner."

"Wow! This project has been an eye opener for me." Shirl raised her hand.

"And me," Howie and Jess said in unison.

"And me, even though I headed the project. I hope this documentary will let people know about service dogs as well as the issues that some people face." Phil nodded. "The best part of tomorrow's presentation is having the author of a children's book about an allergy service dog speak to the children. She will read the book, then we'll give Ethan his dog. To close out the program, Maisey will lead the children in singing the 'Twelve Dogs of Christmas.'"

Maisey let out a happy sigh. "That sounds like an amazing program. I'm glad I'm a part of it."

"Truly amazing." Zach smiled at her.

Maisey glanced toward the ceiling, then back at

Zach as she grimaced. "I know. I know. Amazing. Can you help me find a new adjective?"

"I think that adjective fits you. Don't lose it." Zach's expression was almost serious, but his eyes twinkled.

Maisey's heart thudded and her breath caught. Did anyone else in the room notice that he had an effect on her? She hoped not. Business was business. Romance was romance. And the two should not meet—but her heart wasn't getting the message.

CHAPTER THIRTEEN

Zach couldn't take his eyes off Maisey. He loved seeing her here in his house. He only wished they had more time to spend here. What would she say if he asked her to visit sometime? He needed to know where he stood with her before he could issue an invitation like that. Would she feel awkward? Would she even accept the invitation?

Phil stood, drawing Zach's attention away from thoughts of Maisey. "This is our itinerary for tomorrow. School assembly at nine. We'll be leaving here at eight o'clock. We do the program, which should take about an hour. As soon as the program is over, we head to the airport, where we'll eat lunch. We have a little extra time built in just in case the program lasts more than an hour, but still, our schedule is tight, with a one o'clock flight to Baltimore."

"A whirlwind day for sure." Shirl collected all the bowls and put them in the sink, then looked at Zach. "You want these to go in the dishwasher?"

"I'll take care of that." Zach walked around the island to the sink. "After I get that done, I'm going to watch the football game, if anyone wants to join me."

"That's sounds great," Howie said.

"I'll watch the first half, but I think this old guy will be heading to bed before it's over." Phil chuckled.

"I'm in." Jess nodded as he looked at Zach. "Do you miss playing?"

"Yeah, I miss it." Zach put the last dish in the dishwasher. "At first I couldn't stand to watch the games because I wasn't out there, but I decided that didn't make much sense. I love the game, and I like to watch as well as play."

Howie nodded. "I'm sure it was tough in the beginning to watch and know you'd be on the sidelines."

Nodding, Zach picked up the remote control from the end table and held it in front of him, and the TV screen came to life with a panel of people talking about the upcoming game. "For sure. Let's watch a little pregame show."

Shirl peered at Zach. "Sorry, Zach. I'm just not a football fan. I've got a good book to read, so I'm headed up to my room. You guys enjoy."

"No offense taken. We'll enjoy the game, and you'll enjoy your book." Zach waved. "See you in the morning."

Zach turned back to the others. He didn't want Maisey to leave, but he couldn't very well insist that she stay if she didn't like football. Zach wondered how he could convince her to stay. He remembered that guy Alex saying Maisey didn't care about football, so why would she join a bunch of guys to watch something she didn't like?

"What about you, Maisey? Football or no football?"

"I'll watch if that's okay."

"Okay? It's more than okay." Relief washed over

Zach.

Howie and Jess had already claimed the two sofas, as they'd stretched out full length on them.

Zach looked over at Maisey. "These guys know how to make themselves at home."

Jess looked over his shoulder. "I forgot Maisey needs a place to sit."

"You can sit on the other half of the love seat." Phil pointed to one side of the leather love seat, which looked something like the inside of a luxury car with two bucket seats with a console between them.

"You should take it, Phil. I can sit at the end of one of the sofas. There's a little room down here." Maisey looked at Jess. "Your feet don't stink, do they?"

Jess guffawed. "Take your chances."

Maisey plopped onto the sofa and pretended to sniff the air. "No bad odors, so I'll be fine here."

Phil stood by the love seat and looked at Zach. "Which side do you want me to take?"

"I get this side." Zach pointed to the left seat. "It's kind of molded to my body because that's where I sit when I'm watching TV. You're welcome to sit on the other side."

"Okay." Phil sat down.

"Let me show you how this works." Zach reached over and touched a button on the console. "An automatic recliner. You can adjust it to suit you with the touch of a button."

Phil pressed the button until the footrest rose, then stopped. "This is the perfect spot."

"Great." Zach sat in the other seat and adjusted his recliner. "If you guys want anything, there are drinks in the fridge and snacks in the pantry. Help yourselves."

"Thanks, but I'm still full from supper." Howie waved a hand in the air.

Jess echoed Howie's sentiment, and the group settled in to watch the game that turned into a defensive battle. The lack of scoring made Zach wish he were back on the field and could show them how it was done. He would've had his team up by two touchdowns by now. He couldn't help going over plays in his head and seeing the open receivers. Even though he liked to watch the game, he sometimes found it difficult to sit through a game and not be able to play.

When halftime rolled around, Phil stood. "You can let me know who won in the morning. As predicted, I'm ready to hit the sack. See you in the morning."

"Good night, Phil," the group chorused as he left the room.

After Phil left, Zach looked over at Maisey. "You're welcome to take Phil's place so you don't have to smell Jess's feet."

Everyone laughed, and Maisey made her way to the love seat. She pressed the button to see how the recliner worked. "Cool. Looks comfy."

"Sit down and find out." Zach reached across the console and patted the seat.

"Okay." Maisey sat down and adjusted the recliner to suit her small frame.

Zach watched her out of the corner of one eye. She looked uncomfortable. Was she wishing she hadn't agreed to watch the game? Foolish thinking. If she didn't want to be here, she could have easily left when Phil had.

He wished the console wasn't separating them. He'd love to sit and watch the game with an arm around her shoulders. Maybe he was imagining her discomfort. They had spent hours riding next to each other on airplanes and in cars.

He wished he could talk with her like he'd planned when they'd started their walk on the beach last night. Was that just last night? It seemed like ages ago. Would he ever be brave enough to tell her about the bad stuff in his life? Did she need to know? Something told him she did if he wanted more than friendship with her.

During halftime, the sportscasters gave highlights of the day's games. Then they gave an analysis about the current game and the teams. Zach gave his input.

"You make more sense than what they're saying," Howie said. "You ever think about becoming a sportscaster yourself?"

"Maybe if this gig with Phil comes to an end." Zach shrugged. "Phil has so many ideas he wants to run with, and he's got more energy than guys half his age. I hope I'm going as strong as that when I'm his age."

"You're right about Phil having a lot of energy." Maisey looked over at Zach. "But he did seem a little tired tonight, didn't you think?"

Zach gave a slight shake of his head. "I didn't see it."

"Maybe it was my imagination, but he did go to bed early."

"He knows when to slow down. I've worked with

him for several months, and he makes wise decisions." Zach's gaze held hers. "He chose you for this project."

Maisey's cheeks turned pink. "And you and these guys. He's put together a good crew, and we've worked together like a well-oiled machine, to quote an old cliché."

"We do work together well." Wishing he hadn't embarrassed her, Zach nodded, then motioned to the TV. "Game's about ready to start again."

The group watched the game with cheers and boos, mostly for the bad calls from the refs. By the middle of the fourth quarter the game had become a lopsided rout, and Jess and Howie decided to call it a night.

Maisey pushed the button and lowered the footrest. "Guess I'll head to my room."

Zach hoped he could convince Maisey to stay and watch the end of the game. He reached over and touched her arm. "Don't go yet."

"Okay." Surprised showed on her face as she returned the footrest to its former position.

"You seem to be enjoying the game."

A slight frown caused a pucker between her eyebrows. "Did you think I wouldn't?"

Zach hunched his shoulders. "I just remember your friend Alex seemed to think you didn't care for football, but tonight you sure seemed to know a lot about football for someone who doesn't like the sport."

Maisey shook her head. "Alex doesn't really know me. He thinks I'm like most other women. They don't like football, and he's put me in that box."

Zach gave her a wry smile. "So you're saying you do like football?"

Maisey nodded. "I learned to like it as a little girl when we used to go to the high school games in Kellersburg to watch you play. Then we watched you in college and in the pros. I learned a lot about football in those years."

"And here I thought you were just being polite when you decided to join the group to watch the game."

Zach thought about the history between his family and Maisey's. She had learned football watching him play. That touched him deep inside. He wanted to share more than football with her, but how did he approach that? This was new territory for him.

The broadcast of the game was background noise in his head as he thought through a half dozen scenarios of how he could talk to Maisey. How could he tell her what she meant to him? Blurt it out? Ease into it? Not tell her at all?

The two-minute warning stopped the game, and a commercial came across the screen. This was his chance. "Hey, Maisey."

She turned to look at him. "What?"

She looked so sweet. He just wanted to take her face between his hands and gently kiss her on the lips, but that bold move might torpedo the whole thing. She'd think he was a cad and wouldn't want anything to do with him.

When he didn't say anything, she frowned. "Yeah, is there something you want to say?"

Zach nodded. "I wish we had more time here."

"You said that earlier." Maisey nodded. "I know.

There are some cool things to see here in Atlanta. I wish we had more time, too."

"Yeah. This time of year there's Stone Mountain Christmas at Stone Mountain Park."

"That sounds cool," Maisey said.

"It is." This was not going where he wanted it to go. He couldn't believe he was having this much trouble telling a woman he cared about her.

The commercial break ended, and Maisey turned her attention to the TV. Zach knew where this was going. Nowhere. Her disinterest was obvious. She was nice to him because they worked together and their families used to hang out together. He might as well watch the end of the game and the postgame show and forget telling Maisey anything.

The game ended, and the sportscasters analyzed the game while Maisey sat there in the seat next to him and said nothing. She was a true football fan if she was listening to the postgame stuff. Maybe when that was over, he'd have a second chance to say what he should've said during the commercial break.

Zach's eyelids grew heavy. Maybe he should've hit the sack when the other guys had. He'd just close his eyes for a few seconds.

"Zach? Are you asleep?"

Zach blinked. Maisey's face came into focus. Leaning close to him, she looked so lovely with those kissable lips. He pulled her onto his lap and kissed her. She didn't resist, and her kiss was everything he'd dreamed about. Tender and sweet.

He suddenly realized what he was doing and pushed the button on the recliner, nearly spilling her onto the floor. He grabbed hold of her shoulders to keep her from falling. "Oh wow! I shouldn't have done that."

Maisey stared at him as she extricated herself from his hold and stood. Zach jumped up, and they stood there staring at each other. He rubbed the back of his neck, wondering if he should apologize. But the apology would be insincere. He wasn't going to say he was sorry that he'd kissed her, because he wasn't. But still, he shouldn't have. He wished she'd say something

Maisey held his gaze. "Please don't tell me you're sorry you did that."

"I won't because I'm not, but I hope it won't ruin our working relationship."

Maisey shook her head. "I won't let it."

"Good."

"I think I should be able to get even with you."

"Even?"

"Yeah." She stood on her tiptoes and put her arms around his neck. "I'm going to kiss you back."

Zach held her close as she kissed him. With her in his arms, the world seemed righter than right. Better than the best. Brighter than the noonday sun. She made him feel like he'd just thrown a touchdown pass to win the game, like he'd won the biggest prize of all.

When the kiss ended, she looked at him. "Maybe I shouldn't have done that, but I'm not going to say I'm sorry."

Zach laughed and hugged her tight. "Good to know that neither of us is sorry."

Maisey stepped out of his arms. He wanted to pull her back into them, but he recognized the temptation to do something that would hurt both of them. Bryant

Norberg's words flashed like a neon sign in Zach's brain. Don't do anything to hurt her. She's completely innocent when it comes to relationships with guys.

"Maisey, I want you to know that I care about you more than might be good for us right now. I want to work more on this relationship, but I think we have to cool it while we're working together." Zach held his breath as he waited for her response.

Maisey nodded. "I understand and agree."

Zach gently rubbed a thumb down her soft cheek. "Getting to know the grown-up Maisey has been ... I don't have words to describe it."

Maisey's expression brightened. "I'm so glad to hear you say that. I've been thinking you always saw me as that scrawny little girl with the skinned knees."

Zach smiled wryly as he shook his head. "Hardly. From the moment I saw you at church that Sunday before Thanksgiving, I knew you weren't a little girl anymore."

Maisey let out a contented sigh. "Confession time. I probably shouldn't tell you this, but I've had a crush on you since I was six years old. I just wasn't sure what I was feeling now was something real or the remnants of that long-ago crush."

Zach swallowed hard. His heart threatened to burst with happiness. "I hope you've decided your feelings have grown up and that I'm their recipient."

"You are." Maisey put her arms around him and snuggled against him.

"I'm a blessed man to have you in my life." Zach wondered if this was the time for his own confession. No. His confession could ruin the start of something good in his life. Someday, but not today.

Maisey stepped back and looked up at him, her blue eyes sparkling with tears. "I think I'm dreaming."

"You're not." Zach loved Maisey's honesty, but it made him wish he had the same honesty. He wasn't dishonest, just unwilling to tell her about the incident that haunted him.

"Where do we go from here?"

Zach wished he knew. Wished a happy ending was guaranteed, but it wasn't. He pushed a strand of Maisey's hair behind one of her ears. "Until we're done with this project, I think we have to keep things the same as they were."

"You mean pretend this never happened?"

"No, I'll know it happened. I just want to keep our working relationship the same, and that means no fraternization."

Maisey nodded. "I understand. Just five more days, and we'll be back in Kellersburg. I can wait that long."

Back in Kellersburg. Was he ready to face Maisey's father? "Good. Now we'd better get some sleep."

Maisey turned her face up to him. The longing in her eyes begged for one more kiss. Would he be able to stop at one more kiss? He had to stick with that. This relationship would be different than all the others he'd had. He wouldn't fall into the sack at the first opportunity. He wouldn't hurt her or break her heart. He had promised her dad. Besides Maisey's father, Zach wanted to please his heavenly Father.

Zach pulled her close. She went willingly into his arms. The kiss they shared had every promise for the future. He had to do the right things this time.

Zach held Maisey at arm's length when the kiss ended. "Good night. See you in the morning."

Maisey hugged him again, then trotted off to the basement. Zach watched her go, his heart in her hands. *Lord, give me the strength and the wisdom to treat Maisey the way she deserves to be treated. Help us to find our way in this new relationship. Thank You for giving me the opportunity to love this woman. Amen.*

***

Christmas lights beamed from every corner of each row house on this one block of Thirty-Fourth Street in Hamden, a section of Baltimore. Maisey gazed at the sight with awe. Phil had arranged for them to come here after checking into their hotel near the inner harbor in downtown Baltimore.

Maisey glanced over at Zach, and her stomach did one of those flip-flops that had happened almost every time she'd looked at him all day. Sometimes she still thought everything that had happened last night was a dream, but it wasn't. Zach Dawson liked her and wanted a relationship with her. Dreams did come true.

"Catching flies?" Zach leaned closer as they stood on the sidewalk.

Maisey gave him an annoyed look. "No. Just in awe of all these Christmas lights."

"I thought you'd save that expression for me," Zach whispered.

Maisey flashed him another annoyed look. "You're not making this easy, Mr. Dawson. People are going to guess what's going on between us."

Zach let out a harsh breath, and it formed a cloud in the cold night air. "I know, but I'm having a hard time keeping my own rules."

"Four more days." Maisey snuggled into her warm, fuzzy gray coat.

They were back in cold country, and she could think of nothing better than snuggling with Zach as they sat by a fire somewhere. That wouldn't happen until they got back to Kellersburg. She wondered what her parents would say about Zach and her. Would they approve? She didn't know why they would have any objection when they had known Zach since he was a kid.

As they walked along the street looking at the lights, Maisey had a hard time not reaching over and taking Zach's hand. He was right. It was hard to abide by the rules they had set for their working relationship.

Zach turned to Phil, who walked a few steps behind them. "I heard you talking to the author of that book today. Something about doing more books."

Phil nodded. "She had the kids so enthralled with that story. Then when we brought out the dog for Ethan, the kids knew why he needed the dog. It couldn't have gone better. I talked to her about doing more books like that about other kinds of service dogs."

"Are you getting into publishing now?" Zach asked.

"I just asked if she was planning more stories. I told her I'd give a big endorsement to her publisher if they gave her a contract for more books." Phil rubbed his chin. "If they don't, I might consider publishing them. There are lots of independent publishers these days, and I have a ready marketing tool for the books."

Zach chuckled as Phil went over to where the film crew was interviewing people who had come to look at the lights. "There he goes again with a new project. The man never quits."

"What happens for you after this project is over? Are you doing whatever Phil decides for the next one?"

"Good question. It depends on what the next project is."

Zach moved ahead without really answering her question, and Maisey worried that he was avoiding any discussion of the future. He didn't seem to share her countdown enthusiasm for when they would be free from the restraints of this job. She wondered where that left her. Why did she doubt his interest in her? Probably because she had dreamed of this for so long that it still didn't seem real that Zach Dawson wanted her to be his girl.

Phil had said something about her joining the next project. Like Zach, she had no clue what that might be or what it would entail. She shouldn't be borrowing worry from the future. She needed to do what there was to do now and not think about the weeks ahead, but she wanted Zach in her future. She didn't know what that would look like. How could they deepen their relationship if she was in Kellersburg and he was in Atlanta? She didn't want to ask or seem clingy.

Maisey gave herself a mental shake. Here she had just discovered that the man of her dreams liked her, and she was worried about what the future held. She needed to only think about today. What was that Scripture about worry?

The words popped into her brain. *Therefore do not worry about tomorrow, for tomorrow will worry about itself. Each day has enough trouble of its own.* The verse was somewhere in Matthew. She'd memorized it sometime when she was a kid. She had to put it into practice.

Besides, she shouldn't be thinking of herself or her love life. She should think about the young girl who would receive her dog tomorrow.

"Hey, you've gotten very quiet. What are you thinking about?" Zach raised his eyebrows as he looked at her.

"About our dog give away for tomorrow here in Baltimore. Did you know much about sickle cell disease before?"

"A little. One of my teammates had a cousin who suffered from it. I'm glad to hear there are new treatments for it."

"I didn't know anything about it." Maisey let out a huge sigh. "Every time I think I can't possibly learn another new thing, I do. Do I dare say this trip has opened up my world? It's been ..."

"Amazing." Zach finished her sentence, then leaned closer again. "And so are you."

"As are you." Maisey gave him an impish smile.

"Do you know what I discovered?"

"That I'm awesome."

"True. And you've found a new adjective on your own." Zach grinned. "But I've discovered something other than the fact that you're awesome. I found out there's a Christmas market here. We'll have to go."

"Do we have time?"

"We do. Phil told me our flight isn't until five o'clock."

"That does give us a little time for exploring, since our dog giveaway is in the morning."

"And Phil's taking us to eat at a restaurant that serves amazing crab cakes." Zach made air quotes with his fingers. "Or maybe I should say awesome."

Maisey giggled, but she wasn't sure she should admit she'd never had a crab cake. "Sounds awesome."

"We'll have an hour or so to roam through the market before we have to go to the airport. Boston's our last stop before we head back to Ohio and our last giveaway in Cincinnati, then on to Kellersburg."

"I can't believe this is almost over. It's gone so quickly." After spending every day with Zach for the past three weeks, Maisey couldn't imagine not seeing him for days or maybe weeks. Would he call? Why was she so insecure about this relationship? Because it was so new? Because she still couldn't believe it was true? Because he was famous, and she was a nobody from Podunk, USA?

"You look worried?" Zach peered at her in the glow of the Christmas lights.

"More like sad that this will be over soon."

Phil came up beside them. "Stop here for a minute. I've got news."

Maisey hoped it wasn't bad news. "What?"

Phil held up one finger. "I just received a text from Destiny, Zena's mom. She says the school assembly tomorrow has been canceled because there was a huge water leak today from the bathroom near the gymnasium, and they can't get it cleaned up in time for the assembly. So we can't do the giveaway there."

"Where will we give Zena her dog?" Maisey asked.

Phil sighed. "Destiny says we can use the church she attends, but that will have to be after school. It also means our attendance may be very small."

"That's too bad, but a small group might be just what Zena needs." Maisey looked from Zach to Phil.

Zach smiled. "I think you might just be right."

Phil nodded. "Leave it to Maisey to look on the bright side of things. You'll still sing your song even if the crowd is small. It was such a hit at the last school assembly."

"I know. The kids loved it."

"They loved you." Zach put an arm around her shoulders and gave them a squeeze. "The whole group will testify to that."

"Zach's right. You had their rapt attention as they sang along." Phil wagged a finger at her. "Best thing I ever did. Getting you to be part of this."

Maisey looked up at Zach as he kept his arm around her shoulders. Was he throwing caution to the wind and letting everyone know there was something between them? "You guys are going to give me a big head."

"You don't have a big head. You have a big heart." Phil grinned at her. "That's what makes you perfect for this project. And speaking of projects, my mind is going all over the place with ideas."

Zach chuckled. "I've noticed that. What are you thinking now?"

Maisey only half listened to Phil and Zach talk. Her mind was consumed with Zach's closeness as he still stood there with his arm around her shoulders.

"What do you think, Maisey?"

Phil's question made Maisey wish she'd been paying attention rather than thinking about Zach. She grimaced. "Sorry. I was gazing at the Christmas lights and wasn't paying attention."

Phil made a sweeping gesture in the air. "I know the lights are something to behold, but give me your attention for just a minute."

"Okay." Maisey felt like a schoolgirl reprimanded for not paying attention in class.

"I've decided I want to do this again next year. Not with the whole production, but I want to have a dog giveaway again. We had so many good entries. I'd like to keep doing this every year. What do you think?"

"I think it's a great idea," Maisey said.

"So you'll join me next year?"

"Wow! I don't know that I can make that decision right this moment." Maisey wondered what Zach thought about next year. He hadn't responded to Phil's plan.

Phil wagged a finger in the air again. "I understand, but I want you to know my future plans. I also intend to do another project besides the dogs. I haven't pinned that down yet, but I'd like you and Zach to be my partners in whatever I decide. Give it some thought."

"I will." Maisey looked up at Zach. "What do you think?"

"I think it's an amazing idea." Zach grinned at her

as he dropped his arm from her shoulders.

"You're stealing my adjective."

"I thought you had a new one. Awesome."

Maisey had to laugh. "They're both mine."

At that moment Howie, Jess, and Shirl joined the group.

"We've got a lot of good footage and some great comments about the lights." Howie patted his camera. "Some folks have been coming here for years. Some of them came when they were kids, and now they're bringing their own kids."

"That will add to our story. I hope we get things worked out for Zena." Phil nodded as he went on to tell the crew what had transpired. "We'll get it worked out and let everyone know in the morning at breakfast what the plan is. So let's head back to the hotel."

Maisey walked beside Zach as they made their way to the van they had rented. He seemed lost in thought. Was he thinking about Phil's proposals for next year? Did he wonder how that would impact their relationship? This was all so new. She'd never had a serious boyfriend, so she wasn't sure how to act, especially when they had agreed to keep it to themselves for now.

The secrecy of their relationship was only for a few more days, but Maisey wanted to shout it from the rooftops.

CHAPTER FOURTEEN

The red line running along the sidewalk in the Boston Common had Maisey on a mission to see all the historical sites along the way. Zach loved to watch her excitement about the history all around them. When he'd mentioned the Freedom Trail on their flight from Baltimore to Boston, she immediately expressed her interest in walking it. He had only agreed because he loved this sweet young woman more than he ever thought possible.

Everything from Maisey's love of history to her beautiful singing voice drew him to her. At this point, he could easily tell Phil about his feelings for Maisey without any repercussions, but Zach held back. Caution, fear, anxiety. The emotions held him captive to the secrecy surrounding their relationship. Then there was Maisey's dad. Zach still hadn't figured out how to jump that hurdle.

"This is amazing!"

Zach laughed at Maisey being amazing. He would never say or hear that word again without thinking of her. "I would have to agree. I've been to this area numerous times to play football, but I never took time to do the Freedom Trail."

"Aren't you glad I love history and can enrich your life with it?" Maisey snuggled under his arm.

"I am, but you know I wouldn't brave this cold

weather for just anyone."

"Do you like me enough to go ice skating?" Maisey gazed up at him. "I see the Frog Pond right over there, and it looks like everyone's having a super-good time."

Did he love Maisey enough to put on a pair of ice skates and make a fool of himself? "Let's see how long it takes us to walk the trail before we decide about ice skating."

Maisey's face brightened. "So if we walk this really fast, we can come back and skate before we have to meet Phil—is that what you're saying?"

Zach chuckled as he shook his head. "No promises."

Maisey sighed. "You're no fun."

"On the contrary, I think I'm lots of fun."

Maisey laughed. "You'd be more fun if you put on skates and joined me."

"You're not going to let this go."

"True."

"Like I said, no promises."

"Let's walk faster. That will help you keep warm." Maisey quickened her pace.

Zach hurried to keep up with her. He could think of better ways to keep warm, but he wouldn't dare mention them. This was a different kind of relationship than the ones from his past. He'd better put his thinking on a purer course.

Maisey used an app on her phone to describe all the things they saw along the Freedom Trail, like the Robert Shaw Gould Memorial about the African American regiment in the Civil War, the Park Street Church at one corner of the Boston Common, the

Granary Burial Ground, King's Chapel, the Old South Meeting House, the Old Corner Bookstore, Faneuil Hall, the Paul Revere House, the Paul Revere Statue, and the Old North Church.

Disappointment on her face, Maisey tapped her phone and looked at Zach. "We didn't walk fast enough. We don't even have time to see the USS Constitution or the Bunker Hill Monument. And I definitely won't get to skate."

"That works for me."

Maisey narrowed her gaze. "One of these days you'll skate with me."

Zach gave her a wry smile. "Not if I can help it."

"We're meeting Phil here in the North End at one of the Italian restaurants." Maisey held up her phone. "I've got directions right here. We should be there in less than ten minutes."

"I'll follow you."

"Except to the skating rink."

Zach laughed. "You're not going to let that go, are you?"

"Nope." Maisey lifted her chin as she looked at him. "Someday, Mr. Dawson, I'll get you on ice skates."

Someday, Ms. Norberg, I'll have to tell you I love you. But not today. An uneasy feeling settled in the pit of his stomach when he thought about talking to Maisey's dad. Surely the man would understand. But that wasn't the only thing that curdled Zach's stomach. How could he ever tell Maisey about one of the most devastating events in his life and still have her respect, much less her love?

The troubling thoughts accompanied Zach all the

way through lunch. He barely enjoyed his food. Phil kept talking about his plans for next year, and those tentative plans hit Zach right where he was most vulnerable. Too many things during this trip had brought to mind that terrible incident, and he feared he'd never rid himself of the dreadful memories.

Phil glanced around the table. "I've enjoyed working with you all. It's been better than I ever expected. After we do our giveaway in Cincinnati, I'll be catching a plane to Florida, where I plan to spend Christmas with my son and his family."

"How nice that you get to spend Christmas with them!" Maisey said.

"Thanks." Phil held up his glass. "I wanted to take this opportunity to let you know what a great job you've done. Let's toast to a successful trip and a project that'll change lives."

"Hear, hear." The group clanked glasses, then took a drink.

Zach muddled through the meal as the others talked with excitement about the eight-year-old boy who would receive his dog this afternoon. Every child who had received a dog had a story. In this story, Zach saw a miracle.

"I hope there are no more water leaks to ruin our assembly today." Maisey popped a piece of bread into her mouth.

"No water leaks." Phil gazed at Maisey. "Unless you count the ones coming from our eyes. I have a feeling this story is going to cause a few tears."

Maisey patted her chest. "I know. When I read Logan's story, I cried."

Zach touched her hand. "It doesn't take much to

make you cry."

She frowned at him. "I know, but how can you not shed tears of happiness over a little boy who had brain tumors three years ago, but now is tumor-free?"

Phil nodded as he waved a finger in the air. "We can always praise God that doctors have the wisdom to try something new when the old procedures don't work. Chemotherapy didn't work, but doctors, with the parents' permission, tried another cancer drug. Tumors gone!"

Maisey's eyes lit up. "I can hardly wait to see Logan get his rescue dog, a poodle mix. That dog is so cute."

"Maisey, we're going to have to get you a dog." Phil chuckled.

"Wes would be wheezing and sneezing if I got a dog." Maisey shrugged. "Someday when I quit sharing a house with him, I might get a dog."

Zach thought about someday. Could his relationship with Maisey turn into love that led to marriage? He'd thought about it before, but it was way too soon to tell. A lot had to happen before anything like that could occur. Was he brave enough to pursue that when it meant baring his soul?

***

The plane touched down in Cincinnati and taxied to the gate. Maisey couldn't believe the trip was over, or at least nearly over. One more dog to give away today. This time to a family with ten children, two of them their biological children and the rest adopted. What wonderful people to give a home to so many needy children who wanted a forever home.

This giveaway reminded Maisey of the Petersons in Montana, although they had fewer kids. She looked forward to meeting this family, the Bauers, and their little clan and the black puppy waiting in the wings. Phil had shown Maisey a picture of the fluffy pup the shelter was bringing to the church fellowship hall.

Again Zach was unusually quiet during the plane ride while he read a book and as they made their way to the baggage claim. Maisey didn't know what to make of these quiet episodes. Was he like that often? She'd witnessed it several times during the trip. They weren't just quiet times, but he seemed lost in himself, almost brooding. She wanted to ask, but she didn't want him to think she was nosy. Maybe this was part of getting to know him, know the real Zach Dawson and not the celebrity.

As they drew closer to the baggage claim, Maisey spied her parents. Her mother waved and ran toward Maisey. "Maisey, you're back."

Maisey was happy to see her parents, but they were hovering. Seeing her off on the trip. Now appearing at her arrival. She shouldn't be annoyed, but the feeling welled up inside, especially when she saw they had Alex with them. Why was he here?

Maisey embraced her mom, then her dad. "I'm surprised to see you. I thought I wouldn't see you until I got home later today."

"Hey, Maisey." Alex gave her a hug. "Your parents said I could tag along."

"Hi, Alex." Maisey forced a smile. What would Zach think? Maisey looked Zach's way and discovered his parents were here as well.

Zach hugged his parents, then stepped back and smiled. "This is quite a welcoming crew."

Zach's mom slipped her arm through Zach's. "When Bryant and Annette said they were coming to meet you, we decided to come, too."

"Are you joining the giveaway party?" Zach looked down at his mom.

Lara nodded. "Bryant said he'd talked to Phil, and he said we were welcome to come."

Zach turned to Phil. "You knew about this and didn't tell us?"

Phil nodded. "I thought it would be a nice surprise."

"It is." Maisey was happy about her parents being here, but Alex was another story. She wanted to tell him to … to what? If she just had the gumption to say "I'm with Zach," but she didn't. This is not how she had pictured her homecoming.

"While you're waiting for your bags, Ken and I will get the cars and drive around to pick you up." Bryant looked at Maisey. "You, Phil, and Alex can ride with us. Everyone else will go with Ken and Lara because they have their SUV with room for seven and any luggage we can't get in our car."

Maisey looked at Zach. He appeared to have no reaction. What was happening here? She had imagined coming home and telling everyone about her and Zach, but instead her parents had brought along a guy she had gone out with maybe two times. Talk about awkward. Hopefully it would all get straightened out once they got back to Kellersburg.

The luggage came, and in minutes people and luggage were loaded into the cars. Maisey sat between

Phil and Alex in the backseat of her parents' sedan. She wanted to be with Zach, but she told herself she was grown up enough to survive the well-meaning efforts of her parents in the matchmaking department. There would be plenty of time to be with Zach when they got back to Kellersburg.

"Is everyone ready for a Christmas party?" Phil asked as they crossed the Ohio River into Cincinnati.

"This will be a busy, busy Christmas Eve." Annette glanced into the backseat. "First here, then Christmas Eve service at church back in Kellersburg, then a get-together at our house. I'm sorry you won't get to join us, Phil, but I understand you wanting to be with your family for the Christmas celebration."

"I'd like to do this again next year, but I think we'll schedule it differently so we don't bump up against Christmas Eve," Phil said.

Annette looked at Maisey. "Are you going to do this again next year?"

Maisey shrugged. "Phil asked me, but I haven't decided yet."

"I've missed you so much while you've been gone, but I know it's a wonderful thing you're doing." Annette nodded as she looked between Maisey and Phil.

The mechanical voice on the GPS instructed Maisey's dad to exit the interstate.

Bryant took the exit and turned at the light. "We aren't far away now. Do I understand the children believe they are there for a party with the church youth? They don't know about the dog."

Phil nodded. "That's right. They're having lunch with Christmas cookies for dessert and a small gift exchange afterward. During the gift exchange, we'll present them with the dog."

Maisey rubbed her hands together. "I can hardly wait to see the joy. Mom, Dad, this has been the most wonderful trip ever. Phil has blessed these kids so much."

"Sounds like you might have made up your mind about going again next year." Annette turned and smiled at Maisey.

"Even though I loved this year, I'm still not decided about what I'm going to do. I have to pray about it."

"That sounds like my Maisey." Maisey's dad looked at her in the rearview mirror.

Maisey wished she knew what Zach planned to do, and she should pray about him, too. Everything had seemed so good until today's flight, when Zach had withdrawn, his nose in a book.

Her dad took the turn into the church parking lot. "We're here."

Carrying small wrapped gifts or gift bags, children and their parents were already making their way into the building. The Dawsons' SUV pulled up next to her parents' car, and the film crew scrambled to get their equipment.

Zach slid out of the passenger seat. He didn't look her way. Was he feeling awkward because of Alex? Maisey's stomach curdled. Why had her parents brought him? What a mess!

Surely Zach knew she had no interest in the other man. She had told him that Alex was just a friend. Maybe his appearance had made Zach doubt that statement. She couldn't deal with that now. They had a show to do, and the show must go on.

After everyone was inside, Phil introduced the group to the Bauers and their children. Maisey adored them all. The eight adopted children came from a wide variety of backgrounds. They were a true rainbow of God's children. The older ones helped the little ones, and the harmony impressed Maisey.

She stepped up beside Lindsay Bauer. "Your children are all so well behaved."

Lindsay laughed. "That's because they know well-behaved children can count on numerous gifts this time of year. Most of the time they are sweet, but no family is without its squabbles."

"I don't know how you do it." Maisey shook her head. "You guys are amazing."

"I heard that." Zach stepped up beside Maisey.

Maisey turned, her heart feeling lighter because he teased her. "Zach likes to tease me about my excessive use of the word amazing."

"You know what I think about when I think of amazing? Amazing grace. God's amazing grace. He adopted us into this family, and that's why Will and I decided we would adopt as many children as we could," Lindsay said.

"When we interview you, after we make our presentation, I'd like you to say that for the cameras," Maisey said. "That would be perfect."

"You might have to remind me. I might get nervous knowing I'm on camera." Lindsay bit her bottom lip.

"We'll make it like there are no cameras in the room. You'll just be telling your story." Maisey glanced around the room. "Looks like they're getting ready to serve the food."

The church pastor stepped to the microphone on the small stage and said a prayer of thanks. After the prayer, the children scrambled to get in line. Maisey got in line, her parents and Alex behind her. Zach, his parent, Phil, Jess, Howie, and Shirl followed.

Maisey took her plate and headed to a table. Before she could say anything, her dad sat next to her, and Alex sat on the other side. Alex was like a bad penny. He kept showing up. What could she expect? He'd come with her parents because he wanted to be with her. She couldn't fault him. He didn't know about Zach. She would just have to keep her cool until this was all over. Was there any way to let him down easy? She hated this situation.

They got through the meal and the dessert, with Alex asking her all about the trip. She just wanted to tell him about Zach, but this was not the time or place to dump that information on him, especially with Zach and his parents sitting across the table from them.

Alex gazed at her. "Maisey, your trip sounds fantastic. I wish I'd still been in Boston when you were there. I would've taken you to see the tree lighting, and we could've gone skating at the Frog Pond."

Maisey didn't want to look in Zach's direction. Then the pastor asked Maisey if she could play a few Christmas songs for the kids to sing and rescued her from Alex. She sat at the old upright piano and banged out the requested Christmas carols on the keys that sometimes stuck.

Finally, they announced the gift exchange. Kids took turns picking a present from under the little tree that sat on the table on the stage. They opened the packages and exclaimed over their gifts.

After the last gift was opened, Phil went to the stage and took the microphone. The kids all gathered in a group on the floor in front of the stage. Phil told them about God's gift to them when he'd sent Jesus as a baby. Then he told a story about his own childhood and how he got his first dog. Maisey's heart skipped a beat as she watched Zach standing in the doorway at the side of the stage. He held the black pup in his arms.

"Today we have a special surprise for the Bauer kids." Phil motioned to them. "Come up on the stage, kids."

The Bauer children trooped to the stage, and Phil instructed them to sit in a circle. Anticipation lit their faces as they looked at him.

"Zach, come on out and show the kids what they've won."

When Zach stepped onto the stage, a huge cheer went up from, not only the Bauer kids but the whole room. Zach held the puppy until the applause and cheers ended.

Zach knelt near the circle. "Okay, kids, we don't want to overwhelm our furry friend here. So I'll set him down in the circle and let him come and meet you. Stay still in your seat, and let him visit you. You can hold out your hand so he can sniff it and get to know you. Then you can pet him. No grabbing. Does everyone understand?"

The children nodded. The room grew quiet, as if the gathering was holding its collective breath while they waited for Zach to set the pup down in the circle.

Zach let the puppy go, and his tail wagged as he went from kid to kid. The joy on their faces touched Maisey's heart.

The puppy stopped in front of a curly-headed girl and wriggled under her hand. "I think I'm in love already."

A collective chuckle rolled through the fellowship hall at that sweet expression. Maisey laughed even as tears welled in her eyes. She searched for Zach, who had left the stage after he'd put the puppy in the circle. He stood off to one side, his arms crossed over his chest and a distressed expression on his face. Then he bowed his head, as if he was in pain. It reminded her of the way he'd looked that day in Montana as he'd stood out there in the cold all alone. What caused him this agony?

Maisey would like to talk to him, but the last time she'd tried to ask, he'd told her he wanted to be alone. His pain was her pain. She loved him, but everything felt like it was falling apart. Why?

Phil touched Maisey on the arm. "It's time for the 'Twelve Dogs of Christmas.'"

"Okay." Maisey took a deep breath and made her way to the piano. She would get through this song with a smile, even though her heart ached for Zach. Would he talk to her once they got back to Kellersburg? She could only pray that he would.

***

The church auditorium in Kellersburg glowed with candlelight as the congregation sang "Joy to the World." Zach didn't feel much joy this Christmas

Eve. His heart was heavy with regret, pain, and guilt. The Christmas spirit evaded him. Christmas was all about God's redemption. Why didn't he feel it? Instead he felt hopeless.

When Zach had said goodbye to Phil when he'd left for the airport, he had told Zach to call when he was ready to talk. Zach was pretty sure Phil meant the talk to be about more than business. The man had an uncanny way of knowing when Zach needed help.

Maisey sat at the other end of the pew with her parents and her friend Alex, who had ruined all thought of talking with her dad. In fact, Zach had gotten the distinct impression that Alex was there at Bryant's invitation. Maisey's dad was warning Zach off with this other guy. Had Maisey told her parents about her feelings for him?

To make matters worse, the guy was cozying up to Maisey by telling her he'd take her skating at the Frog Pond, almost as if he knew Zach hadn't indulged Maisey's desire to go skating while they'd been in Boston. How hard would it have been to go skating just for her? But he'd passed on the chance, and now he regretted it.

Surely Alex would be going home to spend Christmas Eve with his family. What if Bryant had invited Alex and his parents over for Christmas Eve? What difference did it make? Zach was getting the message. Her father made it clear that Zach wasn't welcome in Maisey's life. He was beginning to believe that was for the best anyway. He couldn't go forward with this relationship while an incident from his past plagued him, even made him ill. He had to deal with that before he could be the right man for

Maisey. Maybe Alex was better for her.

Zach's stomach soured at the thought of telling Maisey. He could just go back to Atlanta, pass on working with Phil again, and not have any contact with her, but that was the coward's way out. Zach couldn't do that to her. No matter how much it hurt, he had to look her in the eye and tell her they weren't meant to be together.

The Christmas Eve service ended, and folks greeted each other with hugs, handshakes, and Merry Christmas. Zach felt like he was on the outside looking in. He wanted to join in the happy well wishes, but his heavy heart wouldn't let him. He dreaded the evening with the Norbergs.

Zach's mom laid a hand on his arm. "Zach, we're going to head home and just walk over to the Norbergs'."

"Okay. I need to leave my suitcase at the house anyway." Zach remembered the gifts he'd bought for Maisey. Would giving them to her ease the breakup or would it make it worse? He could hardly call it a breakup when they'd barely gotten started. He'd just give her the gifts and that would be it.

Christmas lights festooned every inch of the Norbergs' house. He'd forgotten how much Bryant loved to decorate for Christmas. No wonder Maisey had enjoyed the Christmas lights in Baltimore so much. Zach punched the doorbell, and immediately Annette opened the door.

"Come in." Annette gave Zach a hug. "This is like old times."

"It is." Zach put on his happiest face, even though happiness evaded him. Despite the warmth of her greeting and warmth of the fire crackling in the fireplace, coldness surrounded his heart.

As Annette took their coats, Zach looked around for Maisey. She wasn't in sight. He wanted to see her, but he didn't want to see her. He'd spent the morning with her, but they might as well have been miles apart. How was he ever going to tell her goodbye?

He had a plan. He'd visit and enjoy the delicious foods on Annette's dining room table. He'd give Maisey her gifts in a private moment where he would tell her they couldn't be together. Just the thought of that made him sick at heart, but it had to be done. Then he'd make his excuses and go back to his parents' house. It was a plan, but it was a terrible one.

Maisey's laughter floated into the front hall where Zach stood. His heart skipped a beat. He would miss that sound after he left, but he couldn't let that dissuade him from doing what was best for her. He was all wrong for her, and he should have been stronger and resisted her appeal. This wasn't the time to wallow in his own misery. He had to look at this as doing the right thing for her.

With a plate full of food in his hand, Bryant approached Zach. "Zach, help yourself to the food."

"Thanks, I will."

Bryant followed Zach into the dining room. "I hear Phil is planning another project plus the dog giveaway for next year. Are you going to work with him again?"

Not if Maisey planned to be a part of it. Zach smiled instead of saying what was on his mind. "Haven't decided. I might consider sports broadcasting."

"That would be just your thing." Bryant took a sip of his drink, then eyed Zach. "How long do you plan to stay in town?"

"A couple more days." Zach wondered about the questions. "I need to get back to Atlanta after Christmas to wrap up end-of-the-year stuff."

Zach didn't want to be rude, but ever since Bryant's little talk about Maisey before they'd left on the trip, Zach felt uncomfortable around the man he'd grown up admiring as much as his own dad.

The doorbell rang. "That must be folks from church. There are several families dropping by for a few minutes here and there throughout the evening."

"That's nice. I'll let you greet your guests." Zach was happy to escape.

As Bryant went to the front door, Maisey, Wes, and Grams came into the dining room from the kitchen. Their laughter came with them, and Zach wished his heart was as joyful as theirs.

"Zach, I didn't know you were here." Wes came over and shook Zach's hand. "I see you survived working with my sister for nearly a month."

Despite the ache in his gut, Zach couldn't help chuckling. "It was hard, but I suffered through it."

Maisey came over and gave Zach a playful punch on the arm as she frowned at him. "Now tell him the truth."

"Okay, here's the truth." Zach looked at Wes rather than Maisey. "She made me learn history. She badgered me to go ice skating with her even though I have a bum leg. She dragged me through souvenir shops and made me stand out in the cold."

Maisey's eyes grew wide as she looked from Zach

to Wes. "He's exaggerating. He loved every minute of it."

Wes snickered. "Sounds just like Maisey. She likes to get her way and then makes you think it was your idea."

"Oh, and another thing. She constantly used the word amazing. Everything was amazing." Zach still couldn't bring himself to look at her.

"Zach Dawson, your truthfulness is anything but amazing."

Zach knew that for certain. He would be anything but truthful with Maisey when he told her later tonight that they couldn't be together. That their relationship could never work. One big amazing lie he would tell her. He would tell himself the same thing and try to believe it.

Wes clapped Zach on the back. "You're my hero. You managed to make it back in one piece after a road trip with Maisey the menace."

Zach gave Wes a wry smile, then finally looked at Maisey. "Maisey the menace?"

Maisey's frown deepened as she shook her head. "That was his nickname for me after I accidentally smashed his finger in the car door. That's all I did, and he keeps bringing it up as if it happened yesterday."

"But you forgot the time you gave me the black eye when we were playing tennis." Wes looked at Zach. "She hit me in the head with her racket."

"It was an accident. We both went for the ball at the same time." Maisey's face spelled annoyance. "He's bigger than I am. You'd think he'd be able to take care of himself."

"I didn't know you were so dangerous." Dangerous to his heart.

Grams puttered into the dining room. "Are my grandchildren arguing again? It's Christmas Eve. Let's have some Christmas joy."

"Hey, sis, I'm sorry I picked on you, but you're so fun to tease. Let's mingle." Wes put an arm around her shoulders and propelled her toward the living room.

Thankful that Wes had maneuvered Maisey into the other room, Zach hung back. The laughter and joyful conversation filtered around him, but none of it made him joyful. He made small talk with several folks from church who asked about the dog giveaway. He did his best to keep his distance from Maisey. Finally, to close out the evening, Bryant asked Maisey to play the piano so they could sing "Silent Night" before their guests headed home.

As folks left, Zach told his parents he had a gift to give to Maisey and then he'd be home. As Annette and Bryant bid good night to his parents, Zach followed Maisey out into the garage, where she dumped a bag of trash into the can in the corner. The garage was cold, and so was his heart as he looked at her.

"Maisey."

She turned at the sound of his voice and smiled. "Hey, I finally get to talk to you alone."

The smile nearly undid him, especially because this alone talk would break his heart and hers. He held up the red gift bag covered in candy canes. "I've got something for you."

Maisey scrunched up her face in a cute grimace.

"Yours hasn't come. I'll have to give it to you when it gets here."

Zach shook his head. "You shouldn't have gotten me anything."

"But I wanted to." She stepped closer and lifted her face to his, an invitation to kiss her.

He stepped back. "Maisey, open your gifts."

She dug into the bag, disappointment in her eyes. She found the Belgian chocolates first, and her disappointment disappeared for the moment. She pulled out the angel ornament, then the history book on Boston.

"Thank you. These are perfect." She reached out her arms to hug him.

Zach held her by her arms and stopped her attempted hug. "Maisey, I need to tell you something. I want you to listen and not say anything until I'm finished."

She looked at him, her eyes wide and her lips parted as she nodded.

It was all he could do to keep himself from kissing her and forgetting the whole reason why they couldn't be together. He took a deep breath. "I know we talked about furthering our relationship when we got back to Kellersburg, but you deserve someone better than me. I'm not the right guy for you. I have too many flaws, too many issues that keep me from being a good partner. I'm sorry I led you to believe otherwise. You made me think for a moment that it would be okay, but it won't be. I'm no good for you. I'm so sorry."

Tears welled in Maisey's eyes as she stared at him. She didn't say anything, just continued to look at him with disbelief. She took a shaky breath, and a little sob escaped. He forced himself not to gather her into his arms. She didn't deserve the hurt. He'd done what he'd promised her dad he wouldn't do.

"I'm going back to Atlanta the day after Christmas. I wish you the best. You're a charming and engaging young woman, and someday you'll find the right guy for you, but it just isn't me."

Maisey blinked rapidly as she tried to smile, her lips quivering. "Thanks for being honest with me. Thanks for the gifts, and have a Merry Christmas."

Zach wished she'd yell at him or throw his gifts back in his face. Then maybe he wouldn't feel so terrible. She did none of that. She held her head high as she walked by him back into the house. He hurried after her, but he didn't know why.

"Mom, see what Zach got for me?"

Annette joined Maisey in the kitchen. "Oh, chocolates. Those look so good."

"Have one." Maisey popped open the box.

"These are better than good." Annette looked at Zach. "You know how to buy gifts."

Zach wished Maisey would stop being so calm and sweet. He deserved her wrath, not her praise. "Thanks for the great evening. I'm headed home. Have a Merry Christmas."

"Merry Christmas to you, too."

Annette's words rang in Zach's years as he walked down the street, the cold seeping into his soul. How could he have a Merry Christmas when his heart was torn into a thousand pieces? He'd brought it all on himself for all the mistakes he'd made in the past. He hadn't counted on finding the perfect woman before he'd come to grips with those mistakes.

Maybe he needed to see a shrink. No. What he really needed was to get down on his knees and pray. Or he could pray right here in the middle of the sidewalk. Zach looked up into the cloudless sky where stars decorated the blackness. *Lord, I need Your guidance. Please point me in the right direction. Amen.*

CHAPTER FIFTEEN

"Did you know the town decided to do the skating rink after all?" Maisey plucked the last pan of cookies from the oven. "These smell so good."

"Yeah, I heard that someone paid the town to do it." Wes reached for a cookie as she scooped them onto the cooling rack. "I'll do a taste test to make sure they're edible."

Maisey shot her brother an annoyed look as she waved an index finger at him. "They're edible. That's just an excuse to get your grubby paws on my cookies. These are for the New Year's Eve party at church. You'd better only eat one."

"Why would you make them days ahead so they'll be sitting around tempting me?"

"Because I'm working this week. I'll hide them so you won't know where they are."

"You'd better." Wes waved a hand at her. "I don't know why you're working at the nursing home again. You made three times as much money working for less than a month on that tour than you make in a whole year at the nursing home."

"They expected me back, especially since one of the other CNAs is out on maternity leave. They need me." Maisey wished Wes would mind his own business. She had thrown herself back into work so she'd have less time to think about Zach.

Somebody needed her, but not Zach. She'd left the chocolates with her mom and put the angel ornament on her parents' Christmas tree way in the back where she couldn't see it. She'd chucked the book into the drawer of her nightstand. Someday when the hurt was over, she might be able to read it.

"You want to go skating when the rink's ready?"

"What a stupid question! I'll be first in line." Maisey chuckled, but even skating would remind her of Zach. How long before everything wouldn't remind her of him?

Maisey had run into Zach's mom at the grocery store after church today, and she'd pumped Maisey for information about Zach, who had left for Atlanta early this morning. Lara had asked Maisey if he seemed moody. Yes, but Maisey didn't say so. Lara speculated that he still had issues from his injury, but Maisey was almost positive something more troubled him. The conversation had been uncomfortable.

"Is Alex taking you to the New Year's Eve party at church?" Wes's question shook Maisey from her thoughts as he gave her a speculative look.

"He hasn't asked. I don't know that I'd go with him anyway. He's a nice guy, but I'm not interested. I don't want to lead him on." Like Zach had done to her.

Wes shook his head. "You're too picky. Alex probably figured that out. That's why he didn't ask you to go with him."

"I hope so." Maisey let out a halfhearted laugh. "And you should talk? I don't see you asking anyone to the party."

"That's because I want to be available, not tied down."

"What's good for you should be good enough for me."

"Fair point." Wes nodded as he shrugged into his ski jacket. "I'm off to help Dad. We're shoveling walks for a few elderly widow ladies in the church."

"Have fun." Maisey waved as Wes went out the back door to his pickup.

Maisey rummaged through a couple of drawers until she found cookie tins. She set them on the counter, then filled them with the cooled cookies. While she worked, she couldn't help thinking about Christmas Eve. She wished she'd at least argued with Zach and told him that he was wrong and that he was the right one for her. Instead, she'd just stood there and let him say they weren't right for each other.

His announcement had shell shocked her into silence. She'd wanted to take his chocolates and throw them on the floor and stomp on them and do the same with that ornament. The childish gestures would have only made her look foolish. At least she'd managed to keep her dignity.

Last night's snow had covered everything with a blanket of white. The pure beauty of the snow told Maisey she had a fresh start without Zach. She would be fine eventually. While she and Wes had shoveled the walks and driveway this morning, she'd relieved some of her anger by having a snowball fight with him. He was a big target and a good sport. He had no idea he represented Zach as she'd pummeled him with snowballs.

Maisey looked around as she tried to figure out a

good place to hide the cookies. Maybe the best thing was to bag them up, walk over to her parents' place, and leave them there. She bundled up in one of her new coats from the trip and her favorite pair of fur-lined boots and headed out.

She took in the beauty of the snow clinging to the tree branches, fence posts, and mailboxes. Most people had shoveled their sidewalks, and the snowplows had been out early to clear the roads. She wondered whether Zach had had any trouble getting to the airport. She looked heavenward.

His handsome face came unbidden to her mind. She let out a heavy sigh. He was probably sitting in front of his big fireplace, maybe with a new or old girlfriend, one that suited him better than her. Why did she have to think about it?

She'd already cried herself to sleep last night. She was glad Wes slept upstairs and couldn't hear her sobs. She didn't want to cry over Zach, but then his gift had arrived from the online retailer even on Sunday. She was tempted to throw the stuff in the trash, but just like stomping on the chocolates, that would be a childish act. She'd box the presents up and put them in the mail tomorrow.

Would that be like doing good to those who persecute you? Maisey shook her head. Zach wasn't persecuting her. He actually thought he was doing her a favor. Why hadn't she tried to dissuade him of that idea? Too timid? Too shocked? Too overwhelmed? All of those.

Just as Maisey reached her parents' block, the Dawsons' SUV pulled up beside her and the window rolled down. "Maisey, glad we saw you."

"Hi. I'm on my way over to see my folks. The snow is so pretty I decided to walk and bring them these." Maisey held up the bag. "Cookies. I'm hiding them at their house so Wes doesn't eat them before the New Year's Eve party."

Lara laughed as she held something out the window. "I found this while I was cleaning Zach's room. I believe he intended this for you. It must've fallen out of the bag he had with him on Christmas Eve. It has your name on it."

Maisey stepped closer to the car, and Lara handed Maisey the little box. "Thanks. Yeah, he gave me some stuff he picked up during our trip. I have some things I'm sending to him."

"That's sweet of you," Lara said.

"I want to make sure I have his correct address." Maisey scrolled through the contacts on her phone until she came to Zach's name. She read off his Atlanta address.

Lara nodded. "That's it. I'm sure he'll appreciate your gift. See you later."

Maisey waved as Lara's window went up. Maisey stood there wondering what was in the box. She hurried down the block. She would open it once she got inside. She wasn't even sure she wanted to open it and have another reminder of the man who had broken her heart.

Maisey opened the front door. "Mom, it's Maisey."

Her mom came into the front hall from the kitchen as she wiped her hands on a towel. "Hello. To what do I owe this visit?"

Maisey thrust the bag at her mother. "Cookies for

the New Year's Eve party. I'm hiding them from Wes."

Annette laughed. "I still remember the time he ate half the cookies I had made for the church Christmas cookie exchange. I was so angry with him, but he got his when he got that terrible stomachache."

Maisey joined the laughter. "I remember that. You were very angry, and I was so glad I hadn't eaten any."

"Me, too. I wouldn't have had any left if you'd joined him." Annette took the bag. "Come into the kitchen. I'm making chili. You want to stay for supper? I'll call your dad and tell him to have Wes come, too."

"Sure." The thought of hot chili on a cold night and her parents' love gave Maisey a sense of belonging. She didn't need Zach. She had her family. But even the chili reminded her of Zach.

"What's in the box?" Annette stirred the steaming pot on the stove.

"I don't know. I ran into Lara, and she told me it must've fallen out of the bag Zach gave me last night." Maisey wasn't sure she wanted to open it in front of her mom, but here it was.

"Let's see what's in it." Annette peered at Maisey.

Maisey set her gloves on the nearby chair and shrugged out of her coat, then proceeded to open the box. She let out a gasp as she looked at the ornament nestled in the tissue paper. She held it up. A graceful ceramic skater dressed in red dangled from a red braided cord. "It's lovely."

"It certainly is." Annette put her fingers under it. "Do you want to hang it on the tree?"

Maisey hesitated. She didn't, but how could she explain that to her mother without making her wonder why? "If it's okay with you, I'll take it home. It'll be a good reminder of our trip."

"You never did tell me whether you got Zach to skate?"

"I didn't. I think that's why he gave me the skater." Maisey wondered why he hadn't realized it wasn't in the gift bag that night.

"Did you hear about the ice rink?"

"I did. I'm so excited. It'll be ready for skating on New Year's Day. What a way to bring in the New Year!"

"Do you have your skates?"

Maisey laid a hand on her cheek. "I don't. Are they here somewhere?"

"I'm guessing they might be in the basement or the garage. You can look while I finish the chili."

"I'll look in the basement." Maisey didn't want to go into the garage and be reminded of the horrible scene with Zach. The garage would only be a last resort if she couldn't find the skates in the basement.

Maisey turned on the light and traipsed down the stairs. An old couch and chair sat in one corner accompanied by an equally old throw rug. A first-generation flat-screen TV sat on a pock-marked stand. This was her dad's version of a man cave. Maisey smiled as she glanced around.

In the opposite corner a gray four-drawer file cabinet sat against the wall. A couple of boxes graced the top. She pulled one down and pawed through it and found several photo albums.

She went to the couch and set the albums on her

lap as she opened the one on top. Faded photos stared back at her. Photos of sporting events. Photos of school plays and concerts when she thought she wanted to play the cello. She turned another page. Her heart jumped into her throat. Zach. A young Zach stared back at her. He stood next to Wes as the two boys held up the fish they'd caught at the lake.

Maisey slammed the photo album shut. She dumped them back into the box. She didn't need more reminders, but it was too late. The tears sprang to her eyes and rolled down her cheeks. What was that stupid saying? It's better to have loved and lost than never to have loved at all. It wasn't true.

Where were her skates? That was what she was down here for. No more photo albums. After searching in all the boxes, cabinets, and nooks and crannies, Maisey came up empty. Well, she could afford a new pair because her bank account was healthy.

Maisey tromped back upstairs. Her dad and Wes came through the garage door into the kitchen at the same time. They peeled off their coats, hats, and gloves.

Maisey's mom looked her way. "Didn't find your skates?"

"Nope."

"You'll have to look in the garage." Her dad hung his coat in the closet.

"Not today. Too cold now."

Maisey's mom got bowls out of the cupboard. "Now that you guys are here, let's eat."

They helped themselves to chili and sat at the kitchen table. Her dad gave thanks for the food. The cozy kitchen, the delicious food, and the warm conversation with her family wrapped Maisey in a cocoon of love. She didn't need Zach. Her childhood feelings for him had grown up in the harsh reality of his celebrity.

She wasn't sophisticated enough for him. They belonged in different worlds now. Even though she'd wanted to believe their shared history would keep them together, she'd been kidding herself. Zach had understood that and had done her a favor by ending things before they got serious, at least on his part.

The pain would subside. She would go on with her life, and Zach would be a distant memory. If only that were true.

***

The box had sat on Zach's kitchen counter for three days, but he couldn't bring himself to open it. He feared the contents would break his heart all over again. He'd spent the days since Christmas fasting, only eating an evening meal, praying, and reading his Bible. He hadn't shaved or changed out of his sweats. He'd slept in them, lived in them for four days. He was a mess. Thankfully, he'd given his housekeeper the week off between Christmas and New Year's, so she hadn't seen him in this condition.

Phil had called and said he was on his way to the house from the airport. Time to shower, shave, and throw the pizza boxes and takeout cartons into the trash. But first he had to open that box from Maisey. She'd told him she'd gotten him a present, but after their parting he'd doubted she would send it, but here it was, mocking him, making him feel rotten.

He took a deep breath and ripped off the end of the box. He dumped the contents onto the counter. Books. Bible study books. One on the fruit of the Spirit. Study books for the gospel of John, Romans, and James. A note fluttered to the floor, and Zach grabbed it. He opened it. Maisey's neat handwriting covered the inside of the notecard.

Dear Zach,

Since you mentioned wanting to study the Bible, and we never got around to doing that on our trip, I thought you might like these. I hope they help you with whatever is troubling you. Your mom gave me the skater, and strangely enough, I had bought one for you. To be honest, it was a little dig because you wouldn't go skating with me. So I'm sending them both your way, because I figured you really didn't intend for me to have the skater or you would've given it to me.

Despite our unhappy parting, I wish you the best in the future.

Happy New Year,

Maisey

Maisey's honesty touched his heart as much as it pained him. Zach closed his eyes until the pain subsided. He opened his eyes and stuck his hand down into the box and found the skaters at the bottom wrapped in tissue paper. He held them up. The female skater in red and a male hockey player in blue. The other gifts he'd given her were less personal than the little skater. Now here it was making him feel terrible.

With the books under one arm and the skaters dangling from one finger, he hurried to his room. He had to get ready for Phil's visit. The man was determined to get Zach to be part of his project next year, but Zach didn't know how he could deal with seeing adopted and foster kids day in and day out. It hurt his heart just to think about it.

A half hour later, Zach ushered Phil into the family room. "Phil, I'm going to state right up front that your project is a worthy one, but I can't see myself doing it."

Phil sat on the edge of the couch as he eyed Zach who sat on the opposite couch. "I'm not here to talk about the project. I'm here to talk about Maisey."

Zach swallowed hard. "What about her?"

"Why aren't you together?"

"Why should we be?"

"Because you're in love with her."

Zach started to shake his head but thought better of it. "I'm not the right guy for her."

"Wrong answer." Phil stood, crossed the room, and sat next to Zach. "You must've figured out that I was pushing you two together, and I thought it was working."

"You were wrong."

"No, you're wrong."

"We'll see about that."

Phil crossed his arms. "I have a date for New Year's Eve with a lovely widow in Kellersburg, and you're going with me. I've purchased your ticket. We fly out tomorrow afternoon."

Zach couldn't help smiling. "Carol Norberg?"

Phil nodded. "We've been corresponding through

text messages and phone calls ever since the visit to Kellersburg."

"I'm happy for you."

"And I'd be happy for you if you straightened things out with Maisey." Phil wagged a finger at Zach. "You're a fool if you let her go."

"I don't know if it's possible to straighten things out with her."

"What's holding you back?"

Zach had to tell Phil about Jayla and how that whole episode had colored Zach's life. Then he had to explain about Bryant's warning. Then he had to ask about the wisdom of telling Maisey about what troubled him. *Lord, I've been asking you for answers. Please give Phil the insight to help me make the right decisions about Maisey.*

Zach related the incident with Jayla and the conversation with Bryant to Phil. Zach and Phil prayed together. The conversation was a tough one, but Zach felt better for it.

After they prayed again, Zach looked at Phil. "What does Maisey need to know?"

"I think you should tell her." Phil nodded. "Your past isn't a secret. You were in the public eye. I know this particular incident isn't, but she's seen, like I have, that you are struggling with something. She needs to know why."

"I'm afraid it will change the way she sees me."

"It probably will, but that doesn't mean it will change her love for you."

"I hope you're right." Zach narrowed his gaze. "How do you know we love each other?"

Phil chuckled. "It was as clear as the nose on your

face, to quote an old expression. When you two looked at each other, I knew I'd made a wise decision to tap Maisey for the project. I had a feeling the moment I heard her sing that she would sing her way into your heart."

"If I go back to Kellersburg with you, I have to talk to Maisey's dad."

Phil nodded. "You do, and I have a feeling he'll give his blessing, especially after you tell him about the ice rink."

"That's the one good thing I've done lately."

Phil clapped Zach on the back. "You've done a lot of good lately, but that's one thing that will show Maisey how much you care about her."

"We have to have a plan."

"Yes." Phil got out his phone. "I'll talk to Bryant and arrange for him to meet you tomorrow evening in the church auditorium while the party is going on in the fellowship hall."

"What if he doesn't want to meet with me?"

Phil narrowed his gaze. "He'll meet with you. I can be very persuasive, especially if I get his mother in on the persuasion."

Zach smiled. "Then what?"

"You'll go to the skating rink, and I'll deliver Maisey."

"How are you going to get her to leave the party?"

"Did you forget I just told you how persuasive I am?"

Zach's heart was already lighter as he digested Phil's plan.

"One last detail." Phil held up his phone. "You're going to give Maisey this."

"A dog?" Zach frowned. "I thought she couldn't have one because Wes is allergic."

"This little gem, a Maltipoo, is hypoallergenic. Wes will be fine, and Maisey will love her, as well as you." Phil grinned. "I told her I would get her a dog. I'm just keeping my promise."

"I'll have to pray you can pull all this off."

"Prayer is in order for sure." Phil stood. "Now I've got to get some rest so I'll be ready for tomorrow. It's going to be a big day."

"You've got your regular room."

As Phil left, a good night on his lips, Zach sank into the couch and stretched out his legs. Excitement, trepidation, and anticipation filled his mind. Tomorrow was going to be a good, good day, God willing.

***

The anticipation was killing Zach as he drove around the town square for the tenth time. He'd already parked once, but he'd gotten cold, so he started the rental car and drove around again. Phil should've been here a half hour ago. Was Maisey refusing to come?

Zach's phone dinged, indicating a message. He parked and read the message. *Maisey insists on staying to bring in the New Year. We'll get there eventually.*

So much for Phil's power of persuasion. Zach looked over at his companion, a sweet fuzzy dog with golden fur. She lay curled up in the passenger seat, not a care in the world. He looked at the clock on the dash. Fifteen more minutes. Maisey was worth waiting for no matter how long she took.

The ice on the nearby empty skating rink glowed blue in the moonlight. The official opening was tomorrow, but he and Maisey would test the ice tonight. Two boxes of skates lay on the backseat. He might make a fool of himself on the ice, but for sure he didn't care about making himself a fool for love.

The clock turned to midnight, and Zach looked over at his furry friend. "Happy New Year, Angel. Soon you'll get to meet your new owner. I hope."

Ten minutes later the lights of another car shone through the back window as the car parked behind him. This was it. He got out of his car and approached the other car. Phil sat in the passenger seat, and Maisey sat behind the wheel. The driver's window slid down as he stood there.

Maisey stared at him. "Zach, why are you here?"

Because I love you. The words sat on the tip of his tongue as his pulse pounded, but he couldn't say them yet. He had to get this other stuff off his chest and know she could understand what caused him so much pain. "I have something for you. Come sit in my car."

Doubt filled Maisey's eyes. "I don't need anything from you."

"Just hear me out." What he had to tell her might make her think even less of him than she already did. "I was wrong about us. I should've listened to my heart instead of my fears. Will you come with me?"

Another car parked behind Maisey's. Phil got out of Maisey's car and gave Zach the A-Okay sign. He leaned over as he looked back into the car. "Maisey, you won't be sorry if you go with him."

Zach gave her a pleading expression. "Please let me tell you my story?"

"Okay. It appears that multiple people have orchestrated this event, including my father." She sighed and slid out of the car as Phil got into Bryant's car.

Bryant honked the horn as he drove away. Maisey turned to Zach. "So what do you have to give me?"

Her tone didn't give Zach much hope she would understand his foolhardiness, but maybe a cute pup would soften her heart. He opened the passenger door of his car and gathered Angel in his arms, then turned to her. "Maisey, meet Angel. She's yours."

Tears welled in her eyes as she shook her head. "I can't take her. You know Wes is allergic."

Zach held out the pup to Maisey. "Angel's a Maltipoo. She's hypoallergenic. She won't give Wes any problems."

Maisey let Zach place the puppy in her arms. "Are you sure?"

"I'm sure. Ask Phil. He's the one who picked her out." Zach smiled. "And Grams has been holding the dog for you."

"Grams?" Maisey let out a big sigh. "Can you believe her and Phil?"

Zach smiled. "Yeah. Love can blossom at any age."

Nodding, Maisey nuzzled the pup. "She's so cute. Thank you."

"You're welcome."

Maisey looked up at him. "Why did you do this?"

"Peace offering." Zach held her gaze. "I'm sorry. I was wrong to say we couldn't be together. I'd like a second chance, but first there are some things I need to tell you. Let's take the pup and sit in the car while I do that."

Maisey nodded as she carried Angel to the car and scooted in. Zach joined her as he slid behind the steering wheel. They sat there for a few seconds in silence.

"Happy New Year." The pup on her lap, Maisey smiled at him in the dim light coming through the windshield. "What do you want to tell me?"

"Happy New Year to you, too." Zach cleared his throat. "I haven't told this to anyone except Phil, and I told him because I needed his advice as to whether I should tell you."

"Just tell me."

"This is just between you and me."

Maisey nodded. "I understand."

"You know I dated Jayla Shaw, and we lived together for a couple of years."

Maisey nodded again, her face pinched.

"I know this wasn't pleasing to God, but I had abandoned my faith during those years. But I want you to understand I've left all that behind."

"I do." Maisey patted the pup's head.

"I'm not proud of those years, but Phil helped me get my life straight. I think my parents wanted to talk to me, but they were afraid of alienating me." Zach shook his head. "I probably wouldn't have listened to them. Phil was the one who gave me a wake-up call when I was injured."

"I'm glad for that. Is that all you wanted to tell me?"

Wishing it was, Zach took a deep breath. "No,

there's more. The part that makes me hurt inside."

"What's that?" Concern painted Maisey's face.

"One night I came home from a road trip and found Jayla passed out on the bathroom floor in a pool of blood."

"What was wrong?"

"Something went terribly wrong after she'd had an abortion." Zach shook his head. "I didn't know she was pregnant or that she planned to have an abortion. Only knew because she had the postoperative instructions lying on the counter in the bathroom."

Maisey's eyes grew wide, and she gasped. "What did you do?"

"I rushed her to the hospital. They saved her life." Zach swallowed hard as he placed a hand over his heart. "But there was no saving the life of my unborn child."

"I'm sorry. Is that why you always looked so pained when we were doing giveaways to foster and adopted kids?" The sorrow in Maisey's soft voice touched his heart.

Zach nodded, afraid his voice would crack if he spoke. He closed his eyes, and silence filled the car. Maisey touched his arm, and he opened his eyes. "I kept thinking of my child, the child I would never hold, the child I would never see grow up."

Tears welled in Maisey's eyes. "That must be a terrible memory."

"It is." He loved Maisey, and he had to tell her. "Maisey, I love you. I don't know how you feel about me now that you know all that. Is there a chance for me in your life?"

A tear trickled down her cheek as she nodded.

"Always. You know I love you. I've loved you since I was a little girl, and what you've told me doesn't change that. In fact, it makes me love you more because your heart is broken for the child you'll never hold."

"Maisey, you're amazing."

Maisey smiled. "Now who's overusing that adjective?"

"When it comes to you, there is no overuse of that word." Zach leaned over the console and brushed his lips against hers. "Now I have something else for you."

"More?" Maisey looked down at the pup that slept in her arms. "Isn't Angel enough?"

"No." Zach shook his head. "You deserve the world, and I want to give you what I can. Look in the backseat."

"Here. Hold Angel." Maisey handed the dog to Zach, then turned to look. "Ice skates?"

"Yeah. A pair for you and a pair for me."

An incredulous smile lit Maisey's face. "You're going to ice skate?"

"I am. I paid the town to make you an ice rink, so let's try it out."

"You're the one who commissioned the ice rink?"

Zach nodded. "Just for you. So put on your skates. While you're doing that, I'll give Angel a little walk."

When Zach returned, Maisey took Angel while he put his skates on. "I'm ready for my first skating lesson."

"What do we do with Angel?"

"She'll be okay in the car for a few minutes."

In the stillness of the midnight hour, Maisey and

Zach made their way to one of the benches surrounding the rink. They sat down and removed the blade guards from their skates.

Zach looked at her. "I don't know if I'm ready for this."

"You are." Maisey looked up at him. "I'll stand right here, and you put your hands on my shoulders until you feel balanced."

"If I fall down and break something, I'll still love you."

"That's good to know." Maisey stood facing him.

He put his hands on her shoulders. "This feels fine. Now for the music."

"Music?"

Zach nodded. "This is to commemorate our first dance together at Wyatt and Caroline's wedding and now our first skate together. I want this to be just the beginning of many firsts for us."

"I like the sound of that."

Zach took his phone and punched the screen. In seconds the beginning notes of "Slow Dance" filled the night air. Maisey guided Zach around the ice as the tune played. "I'll hold you up if you start to fall."

"We'll hold each other up."

"That's a good plan."

The song ended, and they stood arm in arm on the ice.

Maisey let out a contented sigh. "Thank you for everything."

"You're more than welcome." Zach tightened his hold on her. "I love you, and I want to work on forever. Will you come take that adventure with me?"

A frown puckered her brow. "How will we work

on forever if you're in Atlanta, and I'm here in Kellersburg?"

Zach kissed the tip of her nose. "Phil's moving his operation to Kellersburg so he can be close to Grams."

"Wow! I had no idea their relationship was so serious."

"When love strikes, it doesn't take long." Zach gazed into her eyes. "So I'm moving back to Kellersburg."

"What about your house in Atlanta?"

"It'll be there when I'm ready for it again." Zach held her at arm's length. "So what do you say, Maisey? Are you willing to see where this adventure takes us?"

The moonlight glowing around them, Maisey answered with a kiss, and Zach held her tight as they stood together on the ice. "I love you, and you'll always be my hero, and there's only one more thing I can say. Amazing."

Zach laughed and pulled her closer for another kiss. His life would always be amazing with Maisey in it. "You make my life amazing. I love you."

Dear Readers,

Thank you for reading *Hometown Hero*. I hope you enjoyed Zach and Maisey's story, the fifth book in my Kellersburg series. New beginnings and starting over are themes throughout the books in this series. This story shows how important it is to move beyond the past and past failures and heartaches and look to the future with God's help.

I would love for you to let other readers know what you think about *A Hometown Hero.* You can do so by posting an honest review wherever you purchased this book and also on Goodreads or Book Bub.

Please consider mentioning *Hometown Hero* on your social media sites, especially where you talk about reading! Word of mouth is the number one reason people pick up unfamiliar books. Every review and mention helps.

I've had so much fun writing these stories. If you haven't read the other books in the series, I hope you'll look for them. Although each book can be read without having read the others, I enjoy connecting the books through characters and settings. Please check out the other books in the Kellersburg series, *Hometown Promise*, *Hometown Proposal*, *Hometown Dad*, and *Hometown Cowboy*. If you would like to get information on my upcoming books, please sign up for my newsletter

Blessings,

Merrillee Whren

□ □ □ □ □

About the Author

Merrillee Whren is an award-winning and *USA Today* bestselling author who writes inspirational romance. She is the winner of the 2003 Golden Heart Award for best inspirational romance manuscript, presented by Romance Writers of America. She has also been the recipient of the RT Reviewers' Choice Award and the Inspirational Reader's Choice Award. She is married to her own personal hero, her husband of forty-plus years, and has two grown daughters. She has lived in Atlanta, Boston, Dallas, Chicago, and Florida but now makes her home in the Arizona desert. She spends her free time playing tennis or walking while she does the plotting for her novels.

OTHER BOOKS by
MERRILLEE WHREN

Dalton Brothers Series

Four Little Blessings
Country Blessings
Homecoming Blessings

Kellersburg Series

Hometown Promise
Hometown Proposal
Hometown Dad
Hometown Cowboy

Front Porch Promises Series

A Match to Call Ours
A Place to Call Home
A Love to Call Mine
A Family to Call Ours
A Song to Call Ours
A Baby to Call Ours
A Place to Find Love

Pinecrest

Second Chance Love
Second Chance Gift
Second Chance Forgiveness

Novellas

Puppy Love and Mistletoe
Puppy Love and Jingle Bells
Puppy Love and Christmas Cookies

Other Books
Miracle Baby
Second Chance Christmas

Village of Hope
Annie's Hope
Kirsten's Mission
Melanie's Resolve